THE SALVATION OF SAN MIGUEL

BY

A. R. ROBINSON

Copyright, 2017

DEDICATIONS:

To God: For giving me the inspiration, the concept, the sources, and the perseverance to research, write, and strength to follow this through to the conclusion.

To Elva: My wife, my editor, and my encouager. She had to endure countless ideas, thoughts and had to decipher my hieroglyphs of a hand-written manuscript for the job of typing this work.

To my students who wore the uniform of the United States Armed Forces. Many times I bounced ideas and scenes off them to see if I was close to reality. They shared their experiences from Iraq and Afghanistan and it brought us closer.

This is a work of fiction, and any resemblances to persons living or dead is coincidental.

Cover photo.
The door to the chapel at Mission Concepcion
in San Antonio, Texas
Photographer: A. R. Robinson

FOREWORD

One is either a native Texan, or one is not. I am, even though I was whisked from the state as a toddler and did not return until I was nearly forty.
The military brought my parents to San Antonio, and ushered us out, as the military will do. After a childhood and young adulthood spent in various states, my radio career brought me back in 1994.
This time, I ain't leaving.
In the quarter-century since my return, I have run across countless multi-generational. Texans who have spent their entire lives here. I envy them in a way, but my path enables me to have an appreciation of Texas that can only come from the comparisons drawn from living elsewhere. I decided in re-immersing myself in my native state that I would immerse myself in its history— not just through non-fiction historical texts, but in the literature that paints a picture of Texas not even the most learned scholar can match.
It is against that backdrop that I am pleased to recommend the storytelling of my friend Austin Robinson, whose talents I have known for a long time.
He has a teacher's heart for service, which he has shared

with countless students during his years as a college instructor. Now he offers an opportunity for all of us to consume a story that rings with Texas authenticity.

Austin's life in the classroom and his wife Elva's artistry inform the characters he brings, and the pages crackle with urgency across a Texas landscape filled with beauty but punctuated by violence.

Readers who embrace a crime yarn will enjoy it; readers who love a page-turner mystery will enjoy it; and people who love Texas are sure to enjoy it. I enjoy all three; but the thing I have enjoyed most is my friendship with the author. I am pleased to introduce him to you on what I hope is a long relationship between a writer and many readers.

Mark Davis
Talk Show Host, Salem Media Group
Columnist, Dallas Morning News, Townhall.co

THE SALVATION OF

SAN MIGUEL

Preface

Sheriff Juan Cordova joined his chief deputy Ester Long as he looked over the body. It had been stripped of all clothing, decapitated, genitals cut off, and burned.

"You think it's one of ours?" Ester asked his boss and brother-in-law.

"Probably not, but we couldn't tell if it was.No, probably just another Central American immigrant heading to the 'promised land', only to end up in Hell."

"Juan, we've got to do something to stop Caesar."

"I know, my brother, I know, but I've run out of resources."

The Medical Examiner from Del Rio arrived and within the hour was hauling the poor soul, or what was left of him, back to their facilities. Juan walked and paced for another half hour until he had an idea. It was a long shot because it had been twenty years since he had talked to him. It was a leap and a prayer, but as soon as he got back to City
Hall he'd make the call.

Two weeks later.

      A drug kingpin is dead, a small Texas town is saved, and an armedincursion by a Mexican drug cartel into U.S. territory has been stopped. I'm the one accused of killing the drug kingpin, but I didn't even fire the shot that killed him. Yes, I killed at least two Hezbollah terrorists, because it was either them or me. I'm shot, I'm bruised, and I hurt like hell. I'm in protective custody by DPS and the Texas Rangers to keep the U.S. government from taking me off to who knows where. My wife and her Texas Ranger bodyguard were nearly killed by Salvadorian gang. I may be fired from my job as a tenured college professor because I helped a former student protect his home. Hell, I'd never even heard of San Miguel until two weeks ago. I'm not feeling real good right now. To clear my name, I'm writing an account of what has happened in the last two weeks.

PART ONE

CHAPTER 1

The semester was over and I was glad. I had spent an inordinate amount of time during the semester researching the Mexican border and the cartels. Don't ask me why, but when something gets my attention, I can't seem to let it go. Now it was time to let it go. I was still relishing an email from a former student, a veteran, informing me that all my other student veterans were having a party in June, and I was invited. In fact, I was the guest of honor. I was elated by the invite.

One final look at my emails changed everything. I saw one unread.... How could I know that damn email would change my life forever? The name wasn't familiar, but I'm lousy with names. I can remember faces. The message was from Juan Cordova.

"Professor Reynolds, I don't know if you remember me. I was your student in the fall of '96. I am currently Sheriff of Vizaro County in south Texas and mayor of San Miguel. Please call me at the number listed below. I look forward to hearing from you.

Thank you,
Juan Cordova"

I tried to picture Juan, but in 20 years students change, this student was now a sheriff. I looked at my watch and realized I was going to be late getting home. I called my wife, Ellen, and told her about the email.

"I'll see you when I see you," she said in that way that a professor's wife has.

"Love ya."

With curiosity and a bit of trepidation, I made the call to Juan.

"Hello?" A tentative female voice answered.

"I may have a wrong number, but I'm trying to find Sheriff Cordova. My name is Jack Reynolds."

"Professor Reynolds," came a relieved response. "Juan has spoken quite well of you. I'm Tabitha Cordova. I didn't have you as a professor at the university, but some of my friends did."

"Let me guess. Some wanted me fired and others loved me."

She laughed. "A little of both, but I'm sure you get that a lot. It's Juan's impression of you that says the most to me. Let me get him."

"Dr. Reynolds, how are you?" Juan sounded cheerful, but guarded. "And your wife?"

"We're fine. She's an artist and has developed her own medium. She's got so many shows in the works that I just give support and transport. As for me I just finished my twenty-fifth year at the university."

Then I cut to the chase. "What's up?"

Juan's tone became even more guarded.

"Tabitha and I would love to have you and your wife come to San Miguel for a few days. An artist can always use a picturesque town for inspiration."

Something wasn't right. A long past former student contacts me, now a sheriff in south Texas, and invites us to visit. No explanation. No reason, at least none that Juan was telling. It was my turn to become guarded.

"You're not going to arrest me, are you?" I was attempting to sound lighthearted. He picked it up.

"Dr. Reynolds, I know this is out of the blue. There are things I want to talk to you about. I trust your counsel." He paused. "And I haven't seen you in years. The city of San Miguel will pick up your airline tickets and lodging. And no, I won't arrest you."

Now my mind was really reaching for clues. Juan was having troubles desperate enough to call in an old professor. And it was something that couldn't be emailed or spoken over the phone.

"When?"

"As soon as you all can leave." Juan sounded relieved.

"Don't buy the tickets yet. I've got to talk to Ellen and we both need to pray about it. Juan, you know me well enough to know that was going to be my answer."

"I would expect nothing less, Professor Reynolds, and if you can't make it, I enjoyed having you as an instructor." His statement was tinged with desperation and finality, but he wasn't going to push.

"Juan, trust me. I'll let you know in a couple of days. You've got my number. Don't hesitate to call."

After he hung up, I just sat there wondering what had happened. Too many questions. Too many cryptic messages. Still, there was a sincere plea for assistance. I called my wife, explained things the best I could, and asked her to start praying. I prayed on the way home. A verse from the Psalms stayed on my mind: "Be still and know that I am God."

Ellen met me at the door with a kiss and a concerned look. We knew what happened was far out of the realm of normal for us. A long past former student, now a sheriff, calls. In guarded tones he offers us a free trip to San Miguel, Texas, which we had to look up on a map, and God says, "I've got it covered."

There are always two ways to look at things, I tell my students:emotionally or intuitively. As a pastor friend of mine wisely said, that which you fear the most will come to control you. If we had based our decision on emotion, we would have said " no" immediately. We decided to go, not without some concerns. But those concerns would not be answered until we got to San Miguel. I called Juan to tell him we were coming. His excitement was barely contained.

"I've got you two round trip tickets on Southwest for Thursday at 11 a. m. from Love Field to San Antonio. I'll pick you up there and drive you to town. You'll be staying at our ranch. The house is big, and you'll have your own space. I'm glad you're coming." He sounded relieved.

I threw water on the fire.

"You said round-trip. When do we return?"

There was a pause.

"Juan? Our stay is not open-ended. Ellen has art shows coming up and I've got other commitments."

Another pause.

"Juan?'

"How about the following Thursday? A week."

I looked at Ellen. She shook her head.

"Juan, make it Wednesday noon and we'll come."

Another pause.

"You've got it, Professor." He sounded defeated.

Two days were not much time to get ready for a week long trip: have the mail stopped, call one of my students to ask if she'll house-sit, and find a ride from Fort Worth to Dallas. It would have been nice to say we were excited as we planned an all expense paid trip, but there was a strange methodological sameness to the process. Plan for hot weather, very few dressy clothes, straw cowboy hats, SPF- treated military camo hats, sunscreen, my Air Force survival knife, camera gear and meds.

I called Bill, our pastor, to see if he could give us a ride. He started to ask questions, excited for our good fortune. I just said I would bring him up to speed on the way to Love Field. I would also have a request.

As I hung up, I heard sobbing.

"Ellen, what is it?"

Through teary eyes, she said, "I believe somehow, some way, I'm coming back here without you."

I held her until the sobbing subsided. "I can cancel. That's no problem. We're really not obligated."

"Yes we are. God wants us to go."

Thursday morning was cool for May. Bill hit me with questions before we even got loaded. On the way to Dallas Ellen and I gave him the story, or as much as we knew, as well as our concerns. Bill was silent throughout the trip, taking it all in. As we headed into the airport, we asked Bill to pray for us. His expression changed from contemplative to deadly earnest.

Quietly but powerfully, he said, "Not only will I be praying, but I'll also get a prayer chain going 24/7 until your return." He then prayed a blessing over us, and we went to our gate. Southwest is always an experience to fly: fun people, singing flight attendants, and cattle-call boarding. The best thing is no charge for baggage.

For once, there was no cattle-call for us. Two seats had been reserved for us up front. As our plane took off, rising over the magnificent Dallas skyline, my thoughts were on what might await us in south Texas. Ellen read while I listened to jazz on my iPod. It settled my mind a bit. The flight was only an hour, just long enough for soft drinks and pretzels.

    As we deplaned, Ellen asked me what Juan looked like. I couldn't say. My only memory of him was a medium height Latino who did well on his classes. If we were worried about finding him, we shouldn't have been. As soon as we exited the airway, we were met by a handsome, physically fit Latino in his late-thirties, wearing a sheriff's badge, uniform, straw Stetson, Glock 45, and a big smile.

CHAPTER 2

"Professor, it's good to see you. And Mrs. Reynolds, it's good to finally meet you. Your husband has said wonderful things about you. I've viewed your art on-line. It's beautiful. Let's get your luggage." With Ellen suitably embarrassed, we headed for the luggage carousel.

"How did you get to the gate with that hardware you're wearing?" I just had to ask.

He smiled. "Being a county sheriff does have its perks."

We both smiled. Then I noticed someone I had first seen in Dallas. A man in starched jeans, white dress shirt, wearing a bolo, and leather jacket was following us at about a hundred feet. I felt nervous when I looked at him. I kept him in my peripheral vision as long as possible, but I lost him at the carousel. I put it down to paranoia.

We headed for the parking lot and a stunning white Dodge 2500 Lone Star Edition with the Vizaro county sheriff badge on the sides. Thankfully, the thing had step rails, or Ellen would have had to jump. With her in the back seat and me settled in the front, we headed out into

San Antonio, but not before I noticed our "stranger" get into a Chevy Suburban and head out after us.

"Since for the next week, Mexican food will be everywhere, let me take you to the best seafood place in San Antonio." Juan was energetic, but I did notice him looking in the rearview mirror.

The food was great. Ellen had baked tilapia and veggies, while I had fried catfish. Juan had fish tacos. Some things don't change. The Suburban had parked about a block away.

"Okay, what are you two hiding?" Ellen eyed us seriously. Juan looked at me and I looked at him.

"I never could hide anything from her."

We explained about the stranger and the tail. I didn't know what to expect. With a look I had seen only a few times (and thankfully I wasn't the one on the receiving end), she told us, "When we leave here, I want a full explanation of what the hell is going on."

I've never seen a sheriff shrink, but I could swear Juan did.

Once back in the truck we headed west on Highway 90. Juan glanced at me, and looked in the rearview mirror at my wife, sitting with her arms firmly crossed.

"Well?' I said.

For the next two hours, Juan told us the strange tale of San Miguel, a drug lord named Caesar Cortez, and the total disappearance of state and federal law enforcement from his county.

San Miguel is located nine miles north of the Rio Grande and just west of the Pecos river where it runs into the Rio Grande. History-wise, it's pretty dull. Settled in the 1870s, it was an alternate route for the cattle drives on their way from northern Mexico to San Antonio and the Chisholm Trail. Ranchers, farmers, and migrant workers made up the majority of the population, which kept the town small, around 1,000 at its largest. In the early 1900s the official count was 800, which may have been stretching the statistics.

The building of highway 90 along the river served to further isolate the town. Now its isolation provided an excellent route for human and drug smuggling which was slowly but surely killing the town. The Catholic Diocese of San Antonio no longer sent a circuit priest to the church's small congregation, saying that it was no longer financially feasible. Even the local Dairy Queen had closed. For a Texas town to lose its D. Q. was like a death sentence.

Thirty years ago, Juan explained, it had been a completely different place. The local farms and ranches had been productive. Workers came across the Rio Grande on a hand-pulled ferry. They worked, got paid, and went back across the border. It was such a common routine that the Border Patrol would come by, not to make arrests, but to make sure everyone was safe, had their green card, and got back home. It was a perfect synergy.

The situation started to sour as "coyotes" and drugs came into the valley. People began to leave, crops were destroyed, and cattle were butchered. It was an illegal movement the town couldn't handle. Into this mix came Caesar Cortez, head of the Santos Diablo cartel, evil personified.

Caesar Cortez, sometimes called "Little Caesar," seemed to have ome out of the womb evil. Born of peasants in the Mexican state of Chiapas, his birth name was Paco Gonzalez. He was a cute, bright child with a mischievous smile. As he grew, though, his cuteness masked a sadistic side. At age five he began mutilating cats, dogs, and even the family's beloved parrot. His father believed he was demonically possessed and wanted the priest to pray over him. His mother protected him constantly, justifying his actions by saying that he wanted to be a doctor.

At nine years of age his father finally got him to the local church and priest. It was nothing short of an assault on the chapel and anyone close by. The child wailed and cried as they entered the sanctuary. Then he broke loose. Grabbing a candle holder much bigger than himself, he swung and knocked out his father. The priest, taken aback by such fury, did not move quickly enough. Paco slammed him in the chest, and then rammed the stick through the terrified man. He grabbed the priest's crucifix and smashed it to pieces. For the next two hours, Paco went on a rampage for which desecration was too mild a word. An old woman coming in for prayer and confession came screaming out of the church, only to collapse and die from shock.

It took six of the village men to drag the boy out of the building. He was alternately screaming and laughing. Then and there, the village elders threw the boy out of the village and posted guards. Paco's mother ran after him and hugged him, accusing the men of scaring him. When one of the elders tried to describe the scene in the church, she shouted obscenities and curses, calling them liars.

There was a rumor in the village that Anna had been so desperate for a child that she had gone to a witch for help. All anyone knew for sure was that her only child was a full-blown sadistic psychopath.

In his teens he joined the Zapatista rebels, fighting against the Mexican army. Early on, he showed an understanding of tactical maneuvers. The Mexican army's worst defeat came at the hands of 22-year-old Caesar Cortez. Having discarded his childhood name, he had taken on names that well fit who he was: a psychopathic megalomaniacal narcissist with a messiah complex.

He took revenge on his home village when they would not show him and his men the respect he felt they deserved. The village ceased to exist. What word got out about what had happened reminded the hearers of Rwanda. By this time, even the rebels were wanting no part of Caesar. "Little Caesar" headed north for the drug trade, but not before dismembering his commanding officer.

Cortez became head of security for the Juarez Cartel. With the cartels in Matamoros and Juarez warring over the drug trade, he saw his chance. Caesar got the best in security from both, and declared the area from Del Rio to Presidio as his. No one argued.

"To say this guy is bad is an extremely gross understatement."

We drove for a few more minutes before Juan handed me a folder.
"You need to read the last page?"
"Why do you say that?"
"With your ministerial credentials, I thought it would interest you."
I looked at the report, wondering what macabre scene I'd read. What I read painted a strange and horrible picture of a monster worse than the worst Hollywood

slasher movie.

It seemed that Cortez kept a collection. Every statue of the Blessed Virgin hecame across, he decapitated, and kept the heads. He used them later for target practice. It appeared he saved his worst desecration for the statues in the small churches that dot the Mexican countryside. My hands were shaking as I closed the file.

"Stop at the next convenience store so I can wash my hands."

When we hit the road again, I took out my iPod and switched it to Christian music. I let the music flow through my mind and soul. Some things can only be washed away by that which is holy.

I don't know how long I slept, but I woke up as we turned off 90 onto San Miguel Road. The road was a typical Texas country road, paved with a 65 mile per hour speed limit. It was eight miles into town.

Like a lot of South Texas towns San Miguel was small. Most of the commerce was clustered around the town square. The town's population, 300 according to the 2000 census, had dwindled. The Dairy Queen stood closed and boarded up. The Catholic church stood just at the corner of the square.

Vizaro County is a lot of nothing in the southern part of a big state. Manhattan, Boston, and Baltimore could fit inside the county. The architecture of the town square reminded me of Mesilla in southern New Mexico. What was missing were the tourists. San Miguel had been beautiful and vibrant like Mesilla at one time.

The county courthouse and town hall were on the north side of the square. The building was not a traditional Texas courthouse. Instead, it was a two-story adobe with a red tiled roof that seemed almost too attractive for the town it overlooked. Then it hit me.

"Was this once a huge ranch?"

Juan smiled. "Yes sir!"

"And that was the original ranch house, " I offered.

"Very good, professor. The Rondon Ranch covered most of this part of the state. Therefore, the ranch became the focal point of the county. When the last of the Rondon family passed on in the 1920s, they gave this area to the county. The ranch house is big enough to house all the county offices, so it saved the county a bundle on building a new courthouse."

I tried to imagine what this rundown square looked like at an earlier time. Slowly I began to picture these adobe buildings for what they used to be. I noticed a few of the old iron hitching posts still standing. I could start to picture the square during a fiesta, after a holiday, a big cattle sale, or during harvest time. Cowboys, senoras and senoritas, a mariachi band and a barbeque pit, all running together in a celebration of life. And, of course, a bar fight or two off the square. I could tell Ellen was on the same wavelength as she pulled out her camera and started shooting. Juan left us for a few minutes, then motioned us into the courthouse.

At the front desk presided the county's Sergeant-at-Arms. Rosie Gomez was a bit matronly, but she oversaw county affairs like a governor. Nothing got past her, figuratively or literally. A widow for about ten years, the county was now her family. She smiled at us and offered her hand. She had a firm grip, and I felt she was holding back.

"Sheriff, there's no word from the state, as if you expected any." She smiled at Ellen and me. "So this was your professor. I wouldn't take him for one. He looks too commonsensical, and has too pretty a wife."

I tipped my Stetson. "You, my dear lady, are a good judge of character, and someone I would not want to cross."

"You are a wise man." She turned to Juan. "Sheriff, you'd better listen to him." Turning back to me, she smiled again. "Good to meet you, professor."

Turning serious, she spoke to Juan again. " Sheriff, you're not going to like this. Domingo went over."

Juan hung his head. "Damn, damn, damn that old man. He knows it's too dangerous."

Turning back to us, he apologized for his outburst, then explained.

"Domingo Garcia is an old man, 81 or so. He keeps to the old ways, and demands that his family go back to Mexico once a month. The family follows him like sheep. He says the Blessed Virgin will protect them. God help them. Follow me."

Juan led us back to a conference room. Around a table sat sevendeputies.

"Guys, this is Dr. Reynolds, the gentleman I told you about, and this is his wife Ellen. Jack, I've got seventeeen deputies for the entire county. Since we're also the police force for San Miguel, I keep at least four of them close to home. Let me introduce you to Ester Long, Mike Smith, Javier Galvan, Marta Sanchez, Chico Trevino, Marquis Lewis, and John Sexton.

All of them tipped their hats except, of course, Marta. Ester didn't look like any Ester I'd ever seen. He was African-American, easily 6' 6", and built like an NFL linebacker.

"Wasn't Long, Tabitha's maiden name?"

The big guy smiled and extended his hand. I thought he'd crush mine.

"Doc, you got that right. I'm her big brother."

"Let me guess. Middle linebacker."

"Right again. University of Houston, and three years with Cleveland."

I knew there had to be more of a story there, but that could wait. Juan motioned for everyone to have a seat. Rosie came in with Mexican breads and soft drinks.

Juan turned to Ellen. "Mrs. Reynolds, you're welcome to stay. It would be callous keep you out with your husband here."

Ellen looked thoughtful, then gave me a look that said, "I want to know everything."

"I'll do some photography."

Rosie placed a hand on her shoulder. "Come on. I'll give you a personal tour of my town. And don't worry. You and I will both know what happened here. Right, guys?"

The group responded with sheepish looks.

"Good. Ellen, let's go." There was no doubt who was in charge here.

What followed was an explanation of a town and a county in crisis. More drugs were being shipped across the border. Juan's crew had a number of cars, trucks, and one airplane in their impound area. The Texas Rangers had been making almost weekly visits to transport contraband to Austin. If Juan had been shady, he and his deputies could have been wealthy. It was a constant temptation.

Now there was a new twist. Illegals had almost disappeared. While that might sound good, there was something ominous about it. Word had gotten out that if anyone crossed into Texas and refused to be a "mule" for Cortez, when they returned, their various appendages would be fed to hogs. One illegal alien in custody thought he overheard the deputies planning to return him.

They weren't, but with that in mind, he beat his head against the cell wall so hard he had a massive concussion and a cerebral hemorrhage. He died within an hour. Terror of "Little Caesar" gripped the border.

For all that, the group around the table would back down to no one. This was their home, their town, and their county. What had recently been noticed was the gradual disappearance of the Border Patrol. Balloons, drones, and motorized patrols had once been common sights along the Rio Grande, but their numbers had been decreasing. Even DPS officers were not patrolling Highway 90 as much in the county. I inquired whether it was financially related. The response was unsettling.

Juan had called DPS, ICE, and the Border Patrol numerous times and had been met with silence. Even if there was a reply, it was cryptic. The overall impression was that a ten-mile stretch along the border was becoming a no-man's land. There was one problem with that. San Miguel was in that no-man's land.

It was as if their own country had abandoned them. With all eyes focused elsewhere, no news organization or paper seemed interested. I looked around the table. The faces reflected a myriad of emotions, and every one of them was focused on me.

I turned to Juan and said firmly, "Let's walk and talk."

CHAPTER 3

We grabbed a couple of soft drinks and exited the building. It wasn't until we were outside that I stopped.

"What the hell do you want from me?"

This former Army Ranger, now sheriff and attorney suddenly looked like the student I had years ago. With worry in his eyes, he tried to compose himself.

"I don't know what to do. We're alone. Hell, I'm alone. Jack, these people depend on me to have all the answers, and I don't have them. For all intents and purposes we've been abandoned with a wild dog at our doorstep. I took an oath to protect and defend this country, and the people of this town and county. I've usually had numerous resources to call on. Now, I have none.

When I had you as a professor, you first struck me as a know-it-all. But you made me work and I learned. I learned to think, to question, and to keep at it and do my best. Frankly, I was glad when class was over."

I hope I didn't look as puzzled as I felt.

"Then I saw the application of all you taught us. You really did want the best for us. Your faith, which is so dear to you, bothered me. How could anyone be so confident in their belief? I wasn't prepared for that. Then one day in class, someone asked you a religious question. Rather than sermonize, you gave as methodical and understandable an answer as I'd ever heard. Still, you were able to draw a line. You respected other faiths, but never compromised your own. You taught me to persuade and argue effectively. Believe me, your admonishment to know both sides of an issue helped me out of a lot of situations, both legal and military. Jack, I trust you. I have no one else to call on."

Now the Army Ranger was regaining control. "I didn't bring you here under false pretenses. I did want to see you, pick your brain, and ask for your prayers."

I was humbled. I've had thousands of students. Each was a gift of God. I had always encouraged them not to be strangers. Now one of those students had taken me up on that. As a professor, and as a minister, there was no way I could refuse this request.
My only thought was, "God, give me wisdom."

I gave Juan a hug and we walked toward the church of San Miguel. "I won't abandon you."

From the outside the church looked as worn as the rest of the community. The diocese had closed the church due to lack of funds. That was not to say there wasn't life there. An old woman, never married, of Hispanic and Mescalero Apache descent, had vowed to keep the church ready at all times. Maria was her name. It was fitting.

As we neared the church, I saw Rosie and Ellen walking in the same direction. The tear stains on their faces gave away that they had shared some of the same things as Juan had told me. I truly believed Rosie had become Juan's surrogate mother, though he would never admit it.

The church was unlocked as if we were expected. However drab this little church looked on the outside, the inside was the exact opposite. It was gorgeous. Beautiful paintings adorned the walls and part of the ceiling. Dusty windows outside gave way to stunning stained glass inside. All the woodwork was oiled and polished to a high sheen. Several candles were lit on the altar. You could feel the warmth of God's presence. Juan was crossing himself and genuflecting. Ellen and I were humbled, and Rosie's eyes lit up with a sparkle.

"Are you not Catholic?" I asked Rosie.

"No, I'm a Baptist, but the beauty of this place says welcome to anyone who loves God."

I couldn't have agreed more. Then I noticed an older woman with long ebony hair speckled with bits of silver coming toward us. Her Apache heritage gave her a height thatwas unusual among south Texas latinas, but her rich brown skin and eyes spoke of her Mexican heritage. Here was the keeper of the Church of San Miguel. Introductions were made.

"Juan, it's been a long time since you came to pray." Maria seemed to be part nun and part priest.

Juan blushed visibly. Maria raised a hand to calm him.

"You've been busy" was all she said.

"Rosie, it is always a joy to see you, my sister."

Rosie smiled. "The same, Maria."

She turned to us. "Doctor and Mrs. Reynolds, it is so good to have you here, even if it is a time of great need."

We sat and talked for an hour. Ellen and Maria hit it off well. I marveled at this church she kept in such pristine condition. It was almost a bit of Heaven on earth.

Maria, when asked why she kept the church in such great shape, answered humbly, "This is God's house and it should be honored as such. I'm not angry with the diocese. Disappointed, yes, but not angry." She paused. "But God kept saying there would be a new priest, and he is here."

She was looking straight at me. It was unnerving.

"Did Juan…?"

"No. When you and your wife came in, I knew the priest had returned especially for this time of need. The church will be open anytime you need a quiet place."

Thankfully, Juan's cell phone rang. It was Tabitha, wondering where we were. We excused ourselves to return to City Hall/Courthouse. Then we had a quiet ride to Juan and Tabitha's ranch house four miles north of town. The ranch house had to be at least 5,000 square feet. It was stoutly built, and probably around 80 years old, with an inviting atmosphere to it.

Events of the day had left us all tired. Tabitha had made a multi-cultural soul food dinner: black bean casserole and cheese enchiladas, rice, guacamole infused salad, roasted chicken, collard greens and cornbread. It was a visual and gastronomical masterpiece.

"Why collards?" I asked.

"Well, we've got to have some southern cooking. I like it and Ester likes it. It took a little bit of encouragement, but Juan and Mei have come to appreciate it."

Mei was Ester's wife. The Vietnamese daughter of a shrimp boat owner, (he had three vessels) she and Ester had met at University of Houston and married right after he was drafted by Cleveland. She was a physician and worked at the clinic in San Miguel.

I glanced at Ellen, not a fan of collards. She said, "There's plenty here that I like. It's no problem."

We finished dinner and moved to the family room, which was about a third the size of our house. Juan's two boys did the dishes. We sat sipping sangria and iced tea. The silence spoke of the elephant in the room.

"Jack, Ellen, please understand that I know you're not miracle workers. But we need a new set of eyes, ears, and brains. When you're in the middle of something, sometimes you can't see the full picture."

Tabitha, a clinical psychologist, provided the mental perspective. "It's like waiting on a big storm with rain by the buckets, lightning, hail, and tornadoes. You know it's coming, but you don't know when or how bad it will be. It's taken its toll on the people, and (she glanced at Juan and Ester) law enforcement." She placed a loving hand on Juan's shoulder.

Mei, looking thoughtfully at her giant of a husband, spoke. "We're seeing more stress-related illnesses at the clinic. The illnesses are real, but there's no definite physiological cause. It's because of fear these people have never known before." She pause. "Even Ester is not sleeping well."

The big man looked embarrassed. Then, as if to add to his discomfort, he yawned "Sorry."

We fell silent for a few moments. Then Ellen spoke. "You're faced with an enemy you know is evil, but you don't know his intentions. Your standard sources of help are nonexistent. And...I don't know you well enough to know where you are spiritually, but it seems as if God has abandoned you."

Everyone in the room was squirming. Tabitha flashed anger and Mei looked ashamed.

"There are times, when it appears that God is gone," I said. "You don't know why you've been brought to this.Tabitha, the anger I saw shows me your confusion. My guess is that you were raised in church."

She and Ester nodded.

"You didn't ask questions, because you just didn't ask questions of God."

The anger was visible again.

"Now, though your psychological background allows you to analyze, you still have no answers. It's okay to doubt. I say all that to say that God hasn't abandoned you. Now, how we'll get out of this mess, I don't know."

Ellen gave me a quzzical look when I said "we'll."

"I don't believe in coincidence. Juan, you were in my class, and now are Sheriff and Mayor. And you have military background. You also have a brother-in-law who could break people in half. The two of you have loving wives, both of them professsionals in fields that are helpful in this situation."

I continued. "I don't know how we'll come out of this. You've asked for our help. That shows me God has a sense of humor."

A longer look from Ellen this time.The phone rang, and Juan answered it. Ellen pulled me aside and said,

"We've got to talk. Now."

Back in our bedroom the looks became words. "What is this 'we' stuff and 'I' stuff? I'm scared for them, and for me."

Hugging my wife, my fears came also.

"We both knew something was going to transpire. I can't leave Juan right now. But I sure as hell don't want you here."

Now her anger grew. "You think you can tell me to leave? If you stay,

I stay. I'm not going back without you. Jack, I know you. Be sure this is God, and not you."

I held her tighter. "After today, and what we've seen, you know we've been brought here for a reason. I know you know as well as I that God's got a plan"

"I know, but I'm scared. I'd rather be scared here with you than back home without you."

There was a knock at the door. Juan stood there, and his expression had completely changed.

"Ellen, can I borrow Jack?"

"What's up?" I asked.

"Rosie just called and said there's something we need to see. Ester's already left."

I looked at Ellen. She hugged me and said, "Get going. I'm not leaving."

We headed back to town, and my mind was reeling. What is it that needs our attention? My silence caught Juan off guard.

"You're awfully quiet. I figured you must have at least ten questions by now."

"I'm curious", I said, coming out of my haze, "but my mind is on all that's occurred."

He was quiet for a moment. "Jack, this situation gets stranger by the minute. Deputy Marta Sanchez was patrolling up the San Miguel road close to the border of the next county. The road is a Ranch road and connects to I-10. She pulled over a semi, and they've got it in impound.

"What? Why?" I responded.

He raised his hand. "If Rosie says we need to see it, that's enough for me."

I had to agree. If that lady had told me the sky was falling, I'd listen.

Pulling into the impound lot, the situation took on even more urgency. The deputies were going over the truck with a fine tooth comb. Two bullet holes marked the driver's door, but it was when we saw the line of automatic weapons fire across Marta's big Dodge pickup that our curiosity turned to fear.

Juan slammed on the brakes and bolted out of the door. Rosie stopped him, reassuring him that Marta was okay, just pissed that her new Dodge looked like it had been in a gang fight. We both started asking questions, then we heard Ester yell from the trailer.

"Damn! We've got Fort Hood back here!"

It wasn't quite Fort Hood, but the trailer was filled to the top with military hardware.

"There's got to be sixty tons of stuff here. The truck was set for a one way trip."

The twenty extra tons were taking their toll on the frame and axles. We didn't know what to think. Rather, we did, but we didn't want to.

Juan spoke. "Ester, Marquis, catalog every piece in here. I need to debrief Marta. I want a tally as soon as possible."

Marta was sitting in the conference room, wincing as Rosie applied bandages to her arm. Her bloodied deputy shirt was off to one side and her sport top was soaked with sweat.

"It's a clean wound . She fared much better than the driver." Rosie looked at us. "She'll live, but be twice as ornery."

"That damn bastard messed up the truck and took out the air conditioner. And if one more guy walks past that door to peek, I'll remove any reason for him to want to look." She was pissed, but she was very much alive.

Juan closed the door and we sat down at the conference table. "Rosie, can you take notes?"

Having cleaned up the first aid kit, Rosie pulled out a legal pad and a micro recorder. Marta's breathing was coming slower and more easily now.

"We offered her some pain meds, but she refused to take them."

"I want to be clear about all that happened." Marta was relaxing as well as one could after being shot.

At Juan's prompting, she started from the beginning. "I was midway through my shift and had pulled on to a side branch near the county line. It was a full moon. The desert was pretty and peaceful."

"So your truck couldn't be seen from the ranch road?" Juan questioned.

"No sir. It was a good vantage point and place to eat."

"What happened next?"

"About 9, right after sundown, this semi came tearing down the road. No lights, using the moon to drive by. No markings whatsoever. I know we get trucks servicing oil wells around here, but this was more than strange." She stopped to calm herself.

"Go on."

She took a deep breath. "I pulled out behind him with my lights off, and followed for about three miles. As I said, with a full moon, everything was lit up. I was hoping his dust trail would mask me."

"Did you radio in?"

"Sure did. Jenny took it and alerted Mike. He was going to go north out of town."

"Go on."

"At that tight curve ten miles out, he made me, and he floored it. He was already going 50, and you know that road. He hit 70 in no time. I went to lights and siren. The guy definitely didn't know the route. The weaving of the rig caused him to hit a ditch. The tractor bounced and stalled. I saw Mike in the distance, but the driver seemed ready to bail, so I stopped and set up behind the truck door."

She paused. "Hell, sir. I was expecting some guy to run like a scalded dog. Instead, he hopped out and let loose with a semi-automatic rifle. His aim was wild, but mine wasn't."

"How many shots did you fire?"

"Six, sir. I hit him with three." She slouched. The adrenaline rush was subsiding.

"Rosie?" Juan asked. "What's the status of the driver?"

"Not good. Two were chest wounds and one in the throat. Mei stabilized him and we MedFlighted him to San Antonio. Chico flew in with him."

"Any I.D. or papers at all in the truck?"

Rosie shook her head.

"Wishful thinking on my part. Who's going to get Chico?"

"Justin left an hour ago." She motioned us to follow her out of the room. "You need to talk to Mike. There's more to the story."

The three of us left the room.

"What?" We both began to wonder about Marta's statement.

"Don't worry. Marta is correct in all she told you. Mike got there just as the gunfire ended. He called for aid, dressed Marta's wound, and got her to sit down. Then he checked the cab."

"And…"

"Talk to Mike." Rosie shivered as if pondering something more dreadful.

CHAPTER 4

Placing a hand on Rosie, Juan reassured her. "You've done well. We'll see Mike. Try to get Marta to go home, and you go too. Get Mei to give Marta something."

"I'll be okay." Rosie said. "As soon as I can get Marta bedded down, I'm heading in the same direction. Speaking of people needing to rest, you two look like hell. Have I made my point?"

"Yes, ma'am." We spoke at the same time.

We walked outside where the cataloging was going on. Mike, seeing us, came over.

"How's Marta?"

"She'll be fine, and twice as much trouble."

Mike's shoulders sagged. "Juan, that girl is damn lucky to be alive."

"Yea, she is, but she can handle herself."

"No!" he almost shouted. Calming himself, he focused on us. "Aside from all the explosives in that truck she could have hit, the jerk tossed a live hand grenade back in the cab as he broke for it."

We stood, stunned into silence.

I finally stammered, "A live grenade? But how? Why?"

Mike continued. "After getting Marta taken care of, I stabilized the driver, though there wasn't much I could do. Then I checked the cab. There, stuck between the passenger seat and the carpet was a grenade with the pin pulled. I nearly wet myself. Of all the things I saw in Baghdad, having a live grenade next to me was one I didn't experience."

"Why didn't it go off?"

"The lever had not come free. When he tossed it back in, he must have thrown it quickly. It landed just right to not go off." He teared up. "We could have lost her."

"Did you find the pin?"

"Uh," Mike paused, looking at his feet. "No."

"What the..?"

Mike raised his hand. "It's okay. I had some duct tape in the truck, so I wrapped that sucker up good, and gave it to Ester to catalog."

Juan gave the big Texan a smile and a hug. "You idiot. Go help Ester."

Juan and I went into his office and slumped in the chairs. I spoke first.
"You know where those supplies were going."

"Yes, and right through my town. I guess I'd better call Fort Hood Police and the FBI."

"I wouldn't do that quite yet," I offered.

"Why not?"

"You have a truck full of military hardware which you're still cataloging. A theft of this size should have caused a blip somewhere. And you have a driver willing to blow it up along with your deputy."

"Are you saying it's an inside job?"

"I'm not sure what I'm saying. I..." The phone rang.

"Juan here." His face clouded. "You're kidding. When? No, no, you had no choice. Come on home." Crestfallen, he hung up the phone.

"That was Justin. Chico arrived with the driver and they rushed him to surgery. Marta shot well. He died on the table." He paused. "San Antonio P.D. was there to assist. As soon as he was declared dead, the medical examiner was going to get the body and do the autopsy." He paused again.

"Well?'

"Justin, Chico, San Antonio P. D., and the medical examiner were waiting to get the body when ten guys in suits came in and showed a court order for the body from the Attorney General. The Feds took the body. There was no time to get a restraining order. Their orders were legitimate. They put the body in a van with government plates and left."

"The Attorney General of Texas?"

Juan's face flashed anger. "No! It was the damn Attorney General of the United States

Giving him a moment for his anger to subside, I suggested, "Juan, I'd call the Texas Rangers and the Governor. Somebody's playing with us and the state."

He picked up his phone. "Jenny, get me Harris at the Texas Rangers headquarters, then call Mark Alan, the governor's chief of staff. Tell him to call me because his life depends on it."

I got up and walked down to the snack area. I was tired. I was confused. I was beyond logic, but one thought occurred to me. Finding a vacant computer, I logged on to my email. Of course, Sam had emailed to keep me abreast of the party preparations. I wrote:

Dear Sam,
Something has come up totally out of the blue. I'm in San Miguel, Texas, with a former student, who, just like you, is a former Army Ranger. He's now Sheriff and mayor of this town. Things are really strange, and going from bad to worse. Be praying for us. It may be best to postpone the party. I'm tired and in over my head. To sum up:

    Situation: Critical.
    Supplies: Abundant.
    Manpower: Limited.
    Outcome: In God's hands.
Take care, and God Bless,

Jack C. Reynolds

After sending the email I put my head down on my hands.

When I woke up the next morning, the sun was bright and high in the sky. I rolled over and looked at the clock: 10:45 am.

"What?!"

It didn't surprise me that Ellen was up. She was normally an early riser. More than once she had said she would kill to sleep as soundly as did.

How and when did I get to the ranch? The last thing I remember was sending the email to Sam. I must have laid my head down after that and gone to sleep.

While showering I pondered. It was hard to believe it was barely twenty-four hours since we had flown out of Dallas. Whatever Tabitha was cooking smelled wonderful. A thought occurred to me that we'd need to explore. Juan probably wouldn't like it, and Tabitha might not either, but we needed all available resources.

Walking into the kitchen, I saw it was Juan who was cooking. There was a full meal of chorizo, potatoes, eggs, black beans, tortillas, sweet breads and fruit.

"Sorry I'm so late," I said apologetically.

"Don't worry about it. I didn't get up until 10 myself. The girls tookoff to Del Rio for the day."

"I'm going to bust my pants if you two keep cooking like this," I joked. Then I dug in.

Juan sat down. "This will give us the carbs, protein, and roughage we both need. Running on empty was an understatement for us this morning."

"Speaking of that," I asked between mouthfuls, "how did we get home? I don't remember much of anything."

Juan popped down a handful of grapes. "Combine the beans and fruit with the chorizo. That way you won't pay for it later in the day." Then he addressed my question. "We found you asleep at a computer, and after my phone calls they found me asleep at my desk. Surprisingly, we both staggered to the truck with help."

"You didn't drive, did you?" The thought of that gave new meaning to being impaired.

"Heck, no. My crew wouldn't let me. Once they got us here, Ellen put you to bed. She was worried you were pushing yourself..."

"Too hard." I finished the sentence for him.

He nodded.

"I might have been concerned also if I'd been coherent."

A concerned look crossed his face.

"Listen, sometimes after a heavy stress, my blood pressure will drop. I take medication for it. The doctors have never really found the source. I'll be fine. This meal is a good start. What are those papers?" Between bites he had been reading reports.

"Oh, this is the catalog of the semi. We've got enough firepower to start a war."

"Maybe that's the point."

You're probably right. We've got M16s, M4s with 40mm grenade launchers, and add to that P90s, M240 and M249 machine guns, M107 sniper rifle, Berettas, SIG pistols, M252 medium and M224 lightweight mortars. Hell, Jack, we've even got FIM9 Stinger missiles, not to mention thousands of rounds of ammo, many Teflon tipped. Toss in 200 pounds of C-4, several cases of "frag" grenades, 65 land mines, both anti-personnel and anti-vehicle, radios, night vision goggles, automated movement sensors, body armor, and we're better equipped than some small countries: sixty tons."

I stopped eating and took the list from him. "You think this guy planned to run directly through town?"

"I shiver at that thought, but yes. But how did he expect to cross the Rio Grande? The little ferry would sink. The river's no more than seven feet, but it's rising from recent rains, and trying to pull that stuff out of a wrecked truck is not just hard. It's crazy dangerous." He shook his head.

"Maybe he was expecting to use something else."

Juan's eyes widened. "An assault bridge! But where…" He caught himself. "Jack, we've got to get more intel, but all my usual sources are dried up."

"What about your calls to your friend in the Governor's office and the Rangers? How do you know these people, aside from law enforcement?"

"Mark Alan and I were law school classmates. He cheated off me, so I've got something on him." He smiled. "Don't get me wrong. We're good friends, but if I ever needed a special favor and he didn't do it, let's just say his past might start nibbling on him." Juan shook his head. "Mark got back to me early. He said the Governor knows something is transpiring, but for right now his hands are tied. I mentioned your thoughts on the…"

I interrupted. "I wish you hadn't mentioned me."

"Why?"

"It might seem awkward, listening to a civilian."

"Nonsense! Your advice was wise. Mark said so, and the governor agreed. Listen, we all know more is going on here than we see. We don't have all the pieces."

"What about the Rangers?"

"Harris is an old family friend. He was a pallbearer at my father's funeral." He paused. "He listened quite intently, and said he'd call the Justice Department. He didn't mention the arms cache we intercepted, but he expressly brought up the taking of the body."

"And…?"

"The DOJ guy told him to kiss off, it was none of his damn business. Then he hung up."

Juan took a deep breath. "The twerp basically told the head of the Department of Public Safety to kiss off and hung up on him. To say Harris was mad would be a gross understatement. I won't go into detail as to what Harris said he'd do to the guy. He'll back us as he can, but it all goes back to the governor."

"Juan."

"Yes."

"You said we need intel. I'll make a couple of calls, but we need to use another asset: your wife."

"Why Tabitha?"

"She's a clinical psychologist, and it could be helpful if she reviewed Cortez's file."

Juan looked as if I'd just added seventy pounds to his backpack. He put his head in his hands.

"I can't argue with your line of thinking. I'd rather not have her get into this monster's mind. She's carrying enough as it is."

"I know how you feel, but our wives have skills, too. Ellen can pick up on the spiritual condition of people or places better than I can. I need that insight. Tabitha wants to help. Just ask her. If it's her decision to do it, fine. If not, we'll wing it."

Juan looked at the clock. It was 12:15 p.m.

"We gotta go. I have a squad meeting at one. By the way, can you ride a horse?"

Feeling uneasy, I replied, "Yes, but not well. Why?"

"You, Ester, and I are doing some recon tonight. Horses are better and give us more flexibility."

"Where are we going?"

Juan smiled. "To the belly of the beast."

CHAPTER 5

While we got dressed and Juan packed food to nibble on, I put in a phone call. This was going to be awkward. A good friend, but one I didn't talk to often, was in a position to help us with intelligence we needed.

"Hello."

"Bruce, it's Jack. How are you?"

"Jack, long time no hear. How's Ellen?"

"She's fine. That boy of yours is growing like a weed. Thanks for the emails and pictures. Listen, I know you're frustrated at me for not getting out there. I'm sorry."

"Jack, whatever frustrations I had are long gone. By the way, Mom's seen Ellen's work, and says it's gorgeous. But hey, what's up? Where are you?"

"A south Texas town called San Miguel."

"Whoa! Did you say San Miguel?"

"Yes."

"I'll call you right back."

He hung up. I was at a loss to understand what just happened. Just then my cell phone rang.

"Bruce?"

"Yes. Listen, and listen good. Something is transpiring in that area and you and Ellen need to leave, now!"

"We can't."

"Why?"

I explained the whole situation and the desperate need for satellite photos of Cortez's camp across the Rio Grande.

"You're asking an awful lot of me. That little phone tag I played was so I could get on a secure line. Give me the email at the Sheriff's department. If, and I do mean if, I can get you what you need, better it go to a law enforcement address." He paused. "Jack, we're monitoring the situation, but it's essentially hands off. As you know, government agencies don't like others playing hide and seek. Someone is doing that to us, DEA, Border Patrol, and your people. If you can get Ellen out, do it. But please be careful." He laughed. "And as you know, this phone call never occurred."

"Thanks, Bruce. Uh…what phone call?"

In the truck, Juan asked about the call. Without giving away too much, I told him I was trying to get us some better information.

"You'd be a lousy poker player, professor. I know you're holding a bit more in that hand, but I'm not about to call you on it." He sighed. "I've fought in Iraq and Afghanistan, but the 'uglies' keep getting closer.

I patted Juan on the shoulder. "It's hard to fight evil. Evil has no moral guide or rules of engagement. Whether it's Cortez, Bin Laden, or the Taliban, ISIS, you're fighting evil. These are dogs and pigs that will devour anything. They have no scruples. It's greed. In

Iraq and Afghanistan it's greed over 'their' interpretation of the Quran. If you don't agree, they kill you, man, woman, or child. Cortez is the same. Greed, lust for power, and a psychopath means that all is to be devoured and destroyed. You're dealing with pure evil. Don't try to understand it. You can't. We just fight it with everything at our disposal."

Juan smiled. "You always could put things into perspective."

We didn't talk for the rest of the short trip. It was 1 p.m. when we arrived, and six deputies were waiting. Rosie met us and let us know the girls had gotten back from Del Rio. Juan motioned us on and took Tabitha aside. I gave Ellen a good long hug.

"How was it?"

"Good. I got a lot of great pictures. Lunch was true Mexican." She paused. "But Del Rio is edgy."

"How?'

"Fear, primarily of the unknown. They know something is going down, but not what, or how it will affect them."

"Police presence?"

"High visibility. A lot of Border Patrol also."

"Did you and Tabitha talk much?'

"Yes." She glanced over toward Rosie. "I'll tell you later. You're wanted.

I turned toward Rosie. She pointed at the computer. "We just got an email with a huge PDF file addressed to Deputy Jack Reynolds."

"Bless you, Bruce," I thought.

"Rosie, just download it and give it to me. Trust me, it's a gift from heaven."

As we gathered, she brought the stack of pages to me. "You weren't kidding about a gift from heaven. You must have friends in high places."

Everyone had begun to get back on a regular footing. The initial part of the meeting was a review of where we were. Juan let it be known that he, Ester, and I would ride down to the river. We wouldn't take the road. We would branch east to Eagle Nest Creek and follow Mile Canyon. The twelve hundred foot bluffs would give us a good view. The Rio Grande makes a big bend, basically forming a finger three times as long as it is across. It peaks between Mile Canyon on the east to Pump Canyon on the west. Juan eyed my stack of papers. Without telling how I got them, I laid out a group of precision satellite photos, including infrared. They were a variety of scales, and quite thorough. Maybe too good.

"These are targeting scans. How did you…?" Mike blurted out.

Everyone was riveted by the detail.

Trying to ease the tension, I told Mike, "If I told you, I'd have to kill you." It didn't work.

The photos showed a massive staging area. There were command structures, barracks, three helipads, and lots of vehicles.

Deputy John Sexton, a veteran of the Vietnam war, was transfixed. "I count fifty Humvees, many with 7.62 mm machine guns. Narco tanks but there's no striker vehicles or APCs. That's good." He stopped and looked closer. "Oh Lord! Please tell me this isn't what I think it is."

Juan took the photo and let out a low moan. "Gentlemen, for those of you who haven't been in the military, these two small helos are Hughes Defenders. They are fast and well armed, but that's the least of our problems." He turned back to the deputy. "John?"

He pointed to the bigger helicopter. "This, friends, is one bad-ass machine. This is a Russian Hind-

D attack copter. Whereas our Apaches use speed, agility, and stealth, this is a flying tank. It's heavily armored, carries a Minigun on a chin mounting, a variety of missiles, and six of your meanest friends in the back. In the hands of a capable pilot, it's one tough bird to kill, but it can do a ton of killing." The air had just gone out of the meeting. Marquis broke the silence.

"Man, I could've controlled the whole south side of Chicago with that ride. No wonder the other drug lords don't go after Caesar. How did he get it?'

Juan spoke. "Probably from the late Hugo Chavez. A gift to keep the cartel in our backsides."

"The Humvees?" another deputy asked.

John answered this time. "Probably Chavez also. Or stolen from the Mexican army."

"With all this," Deputy Barton asked, "are you still going down to the river?"

Juan answered, "Yes. We still need human intelligence. These are great. Jack, thank you to whoever you called." He raised his hand. "Don't tell me." Changing back to the immediate subject, he said, "We'll keep in radio contact every half hour. I'm also concerned about Domingo, the old fart. Maybe we'll run into him.

We'll come back by the roads. Have everyone who's doing their rounds in the southern sector pull close to the road, in case we need backup. Start looking over the weapons we've got. We may need them. Both John and I have used Stingers before. We'll teach you how. If that bird comes after us, we'll need them."

Down the hall, Rosie's voice rang out. "Oh, crap. The bitch is back."

Given that Rosie wasn't prone to profanity, I wondered what female could bring this out. Javier was looking out the window.

"Hide all the men. Selena is back."

"Who's Selena?" I asked.

Marquis leaned close. "A cobra. Very beautiful and very deadly."

A fully tricked out Escalade LXT pulled into a parking spot. The woman who got out was drop-dead gorgeous. She was about 5' 10", a tall Latina, with full brown hair surrounding a face you might find on a statue. The jeans and button shirt were just tight enough to make a man want to see more. The shirt was unbuttoned two buttons down to reveal enough cleavage to disorient any male she was interviewing. She walked with the slow but determined stride of someone who expected servitude, not just respect. She carried a shoulder bag that, besides her purse and recorder, I had a feeling held a weapon. On her hip she brazenly wore a 10" Bowie knife. I was beginning to understand what Marquis meant.

Turning to Juan, whose frustration at her arrival was readily apparent, I asked for her story.

Selena Isabella Guerrero had been a university journalism professor in Mexico City. Her strong nationalistic fervor led her to rant often against the U. S. and its "occupied lands," as in land still belonging to Mexico. That was not out of the ordinary in her circles. She had called for armed insurrection by Latinos living in the U. S. What cost her position was her demand for the President of Mexico to join Mexican armed forces with the drug lords to flood the U. S. with cheap drugs, then launch a military invasion from Juarez, splitting the Southwest. Her plan was to take New Mexico and Arizona, then move east through the Rio Grande valley, setting up a provisional government in San Antonio. All

U. S. military installations would become possessions of Mexico. Negotiations would then ensue for the repatriation of California and other occupied lands. Selena pictured herself leading the "negotiations."

That got her fired, but now she was the leading reporter for a nationalistic-leaning newspaper. The drug lords became her obsession. She saw them as the new conquering champions. She had become blind to the brutality because of her passion, Caesar was her passion.

"Buenos dias, vieja," Selena tossed at Rosie.

She looked toward Juan. "Sheriff."

"Selena." Dry ice would have been warmer. Juan motioned to the deputies to get on with work.

Selena spoke with a voice of pure honey. "What is it? Afraid I'll corrupt the troops?" She breathed in, lifting her chest for full effect. "Sheriff, you really need to know a true Latina rather than a half-breed mongrel." Her knives were quick and deep. Going for Juan's wife, she was wanting him to react, to get him off guard. Juan wasn't buying it.

"What do you want, Selena?"

She changed her tactics. "Oh, I just want to see what changes I would make when this becomes my hacienda. It will when Caesar comes and Mexico reclaims what is hers by birthright. I might even let you keep your drab little ranch house. Of course, all your lands will revert to the previous owners." She put special emphasis on previous.

Juan responded in low, measured tones. "Selena, if you had as much intelligence as you have arrogance, you might be smart."

Zing! Fire came to her eyes.

He continued. Rosie was stifling a laugh.

"This is land that has been in my family's hands

for nearly 200 years. I had relatives that fought at both Goliad and the Alamo. You'll get this land over my dead body."

Her eyes narrowed. "So may it be, *traidor*."

"*Prostituta*," he replied.

Faster than flash, she had the Bowie knife out and aimed at Juan's throat six inches away. Juan didn't flinch or blink.

"Sheath it, little girl, or I'll blow your pretty hair and face all over *your* hacienda."

It was Rosie who spoke. She had a Glock pointed right at the base of Selena's skull.

A moment of confusion flashed in Selena's eyes, and just as quickly she formed another plan. In the guise of sheathing her knife, she began to rotate it to a downward thrust toward Rosie. Before she could attack Rosie, Juan had his pistol out.

"Selena, two fingers. I will not hesitate to kill you."

Silence hung in the air for a few seconds.

Shaking her head as if nothing had happened, she sheathed the knife.

"I can see we got off on the wrong foot." She eyed me. "Especially in front of guests." She extended her now empty hand. Before Juan could speak, I broke in.

"I'm Reverend Jackson Reynolds, a friend of Juan's." I shook her hand firmly, and noticed that hers was shaking. Selena's eyes registered fear and confusion briefly. Then the cobra returned.

"A Padre. Well, you've got your work cut out for you. They need your prayers."

Her obvious condescension implied she had no need of prayer I saw my opening.

"Oh yes, I pray for them everyday, but I believe you are more in need of prayer."

Once again, her eyes flashed.

"Selena, you are so filled with hate that you don't know what love is. On top of that, your narcissism covers a life full of hurt. You loathe those around you as a projection of your own pain."

Her eyes narrowed like a serpent ready to strike, yet I caught a glimpse of fear.

"Let me guess," I continued, "physically and sexually abused by your father?" No movement. "Your brothers?" Almost imperceptibly, she started to shake.

I kept on. "I'm sorry your brothers did that to you, but what hurt you more was that your father did nothing to stop it, except maybe encourage you to fight. You want fatherly love, but you believe you must fight for it. That's what draws you to the drug lords, Caesar in particular. Selena, he will cast you aside when you have served his purpose."

She drew close, about six inches from my face. Rosie and Juan each put a hand on their guns.

"Padre, you might want to say some prayers for yourself. You talk too much."

I shrugged. "Maybe so, but I will pray for you. By the way, for someone who hates Texans so much, it's funny that you wear a knife named after a hero of the Alamo."

Selena screamed something unintelligible, whirled, and stormed out of City Hall, almost taking the door off the hinges as she left. As she stormed across the plaza, the three of us finally relaxed.

Rosie turned to me. "You do like to live dangerously. How long have you had these suicidal tendencies?"

"All the signs were there, Rosie. Signs of abuse, with no protection. What at one time was probably a cute little mouse had to become a street rat to survive. What she can't see, or doesn't want to see, is that Cortez likely knows that. He'll use her, then kill her when he's done with her."

Juan started talking. "You know she could have had that knife in you before we could get a shot off." He paused. "I'm curious. Why did you introduce yourself the way you did?"

"You forget that I am an ordained Baptist minister. To introduce myself as a university professor would have tapped into old hurts. Instead, my introduction threw her off balance. If I'm dealing with a cobra, I want to be a damn good mongoose. As to your previous point, a former pastor once told me that if it's not on God's timetable, I'm invincible."

I paused, thinking. "I can guess that right now Selena is Googling my name on her laptop. She doesn't like to be outmaneuvered. She'll know more about me next time we meet, and I won't have the advantage of surprise."

They nodded silently.

CHAPTER 6

At seven that evening, dressed in dark colors and camo, we headed due east out of town. I had been nervous about what horse I was to ride. Juan assured me I would be fine. My mount was a fine Peruvian Paso, a breed known as the Cadillac of horses. With a broad back and a mild temperament, he was a blessing to ride.

We had enough light to ride the canyon rim safely, and hopefully, unobserved. As we rode, Ester was trying to find out from me what kind of student Juan had been. I responded, "I don't teach and tell."

The former pro linebacker cut an imposing figure on his black stallion. The sight him caused me to think about the Buffalo soldiers of 140 years ago, troops who bore the brunt of the Indian fighting in Texas. Why did this man leave a promising career to go into law enforcement? His story was simple, and as many simple things are, profound.

Ester loved football and his community. Coming from a family of faith, the "Good Samaritan" attitude was part of his nature. It was during his third season in the

NFL that things changed. It was midseason. Another game, another loss, but the Cleveland ans still loved their team. Long after the crowds had left, Ester and

some of the other players were headed out to eat. A lone black teen was waiting for them. He looked out of place in that part of town, where gangs ruled. He'd stayed around, hoping to get an autograph or two. Admiring his diligence, several of the guys willingly signed his book. The young man, after thanking them with a big smile, turned and headed the three blocks to the bus stop. The guys piled into Ester's SUV. He was the designated driver since he didn't drink. They'd gone two blocks when they saw a group beating the autograph seeker. Ester started to gun his SUV toward the one-sided fight. He had a black belt in Aikido and was ready to use his skill. Just then, a big hand reached over and turned the vehicle down another street. Ester was insistent that they had to help. The kid was helpless. The words from his teammate were like a knife in his heart.

"Let it go. You can't get involved. The kid was in the wrong part of town. It's his own fault. If you get involved, you might get hurt. Worse, you could hurt one of those kids trying to be brave. Then the kid's parents sue you and the team, and your career is crap. Hey, I'm sorry for the kid, but he knew the risk."

Ester did find out the boy's name and address. The young man had been the only child of a mother desperately trying to get out of poverty. Ester quietly paid for the funeral, casket, burial plot, and headstone. He left Cleveland at the end of the season when his contract expired.

Returning to Houston, where Mei was finishing her residency, he needed direction. He couldn't sit by, having made good money, while people all around faced situations where they needed help. He wasn't sure why, but a bachelor's degree in criminal justice appealed to him. Friends and family said he'd make a great attorney, but that didn't seem like a fit. He and Mei visited Juan and Tabitha after Juan became Sheriff, then mayor. At some point, the discussion turned to the local healthcare situation. The town's doctor had retired and everyone had to travel to Del Rio, sixty miles away. Mei's heart went out to the town. They needed a doctor, preferably one that didn't expect to be paid. Ester had invested well, so Mei had no medical school debts. Juan also mentioned the need for more deputies and a plan began to crystallize.

    Ester's dad was a prominent attorney in Houston, and when he heard their plans, ideas began to grow. With a little encouragement, the African American Attorneys Council of Houston set up a fund to underwrite a clinic in San Miguel. It was set up as a non-profit, and donations were tax deductible. Mei got paid from the fund, the people of San Miguel got a very good clinic, and the AAACH could crow about their work in South Texas, strengthening ties with the Hispanic community. Not to be outdone, the Latino Attorneys Union sent money for the training of new deputies.

    We left our horses north of Highway 90 and hiked the last mile to the 1700 foot bluff at the end of Mile Canyon. It gave us an excellent view of the compound. Cortez wasn't trying to hide anything. Juan handed out nightvision goggles and rangefinder binoculars.

    "Did you get these off the truck?"

"No, eBay." Juan smiled. "You can find just about anything."

After a good laugh, we settled down to business. The compouound was brightly lit, and men were gathering around a central area. Ester had a digital camera with a 400mm lens propped on a tripod. Juan's orders were to take pictures of everything. Around 9:30, Ceasar walked out to the middle of the open area. He spoke in English. He boasted that no one stood in their way, and they struck fear in both the other cartels and the Mexican government, but that he was most feared by the "Americanos." His megalomania was on full display. He appeared to be putting on a show, but for whom?

Turning to look at Juan, I could tell he was having similar thoughts. Caesar knew we were watching. But how? And why the show. Ester, apparently not having caught on to our thoughts, whispered,

"He is not getting to all the troops. Look at that group off to the right side and to the rear. They ain't from these parts."

Juan and I focused to where Ester pointed. He was right. There was a group of six soldiers there, definitely not Latino in origin. Three of them wore caps. The tall blond, probably their leader, wore a beret of some sort. They weren't enjoying the show.

Juan spoke, muffling his anger. "Oh hell, this just keeps getting better. They're Russian."

Ester and I both looked at Juan.

"Not only are they Russian, they're Spetsnaz. Russian Special Forces."

For a while we were all speechless. It was like we came for a knife fight and our opponent had a machine gun. A roar from the compound drew our attention back.

"Oh my God!" was all Ester uttered. There in the

middle before Caesar, bound, were Domingo Garcia, his son, daughter-in-law, granddaughter, and grandson. Caesar stepped forward and shouted at the old man, laughing in his face. He grabbed the daughter-in-law as her husband begged for mercy. Caesar's face was demonic as he laughed, then had Domingo's son gagged.

Turning to six other men, he said something then stepped away. The next two hours made the word depravity seem kind. The six men methodically and sadistically raped, sodomized, and then dismembered the daughter-in-law, the granddaughter, and Domingo's son. Caesar then brought out the grandson, Miguel. Domingo was on his knees weeping, pleading, and praying for Caesar to stop. This seemed to inflame him more..

Suddenly, the blond Russian stood between the boy and Caesar, and an argument ensued. Caesar backed down and had the boy taken away. Whoever that Russian was, he was one person Caesar apparently feared, at least a little.

As we headed back to the horses, we all knew that spectacle had been put on for us. How he knew we were there had finally dawned on us: Selena. She must have seen us ride out. It wouldn't take a rocket scientist to guess where we were headed. She had called him, and he'd guessed about when we would be in place. Had we caused the death of Domingo's family? No, they probably would have been killed anyway, and just as brutally. This way Caesar's ego had an audience.

Anger radiated off Juan and Ester. I was more concerned about Ester. The big man, at that moment, could have torn a grizzly bear to pieces. Part way into the debauched spectacle, he had started to go back to the horse to get his rifle. He had to stop
this, but Juan stopped him. It was Cleveland all over again, except in this case, they knew the victims. Ester

was determined to kill the "monster son of a bitch." Juan ordered him to stop. As the brothers-in-law stared at each other, Juan tried to explain why Ester couldn't do what Juan himself wanted badly to do.

At a distance of 200 to 300 yards, Ester might have gotten off a kill shot. Then again, he might not have. Ester was better at close range fighting, but that was not the point. A shot from the American side across the border at a Mexican national, even if he was worse than a rabid dog, would be an international incident. Whether Ester killed or wounded anyone, Cortez won. Ester would be the criminal, and Juan would have to arrest him. It would be a media spectacle with Caesar portrayed by a friendly media as a victim of American aggression.

I tried to help Juan get this across in a way that didn't make us the enemy. Selena would be the beneficiary of Ester's actions, granting her the mythical status as taking on the treacherous "gringos" who handicapped and abused Mexico. It was a no-win situation.

"Well then, let's just get the hell out of here," growled the big man.

We rode back just north of Highway 90 to San Gabriel road and turned north. We met Chico and Javier about a mile north. None of us spoke for the twenty minute ride. Juan took Chico's truck and told him to bring the horses with Javier. Juan got in on the driver's side and Ester sat in the bed of the truck. I got in back, thinking I'd give Juan some space. As I swung a leg over the side, Ester hit me with a stare that needed no explanation. I changed my mind and rode up front. I just made myself as small as I could.

We rolled into the impound lot at 1:30 am and it seemed no one had gone to sleep.

We were met by everyone who didn't have anything official to do. Ellen ran up and hugged me like she knew something bad had happened. Tabitha hugged Juan. He mumbled something back, then led her by the arm to his office. Ester just bulled right past Mei, leaving her in tears. I went to her and placed my hand on her shoulder. Confusion and hurt showed through the tears.

"Give him a little time." I hung my head.

Ellen had me by the arm. "What happened?"

I looked up to see expectant faces looking at me. After opening the tailgate on the truck for a seat, I told the story. Shock, disbelief, anger, hatred and fear came from this close-knit group. Domingo, no matter how much of an old fart, was still one of them. Some asked questions. Others simply burned with rage. Marquis walked over to a fifty gallon drum, and with a strength born of intense anger, picked it up and heaved it thirty feet into a pile of trash. All this time, he said nothing.

Ellen and I got into the truck to head for the ranch. My pain and agony was soul-consuming. About halfway to the ranch, Ellen told me to pull over. In shock, my actions were robotic as I stopped the SUV at the side of the road.

"Tell me what's going on inside. I know you've seen something no one should ever witness, but please talk to me."

Ellen's eyes were soft, caring, and anxious. I turned off the motor. How could I put the feelings, conflicts and worries in my heart into words? But I knew I needed to try.

"I'm lost." Tears burned my eyes. "I never asked for this. Why are we even here? Helpless is too small a word. Why did God bring us here? Why did he let that… spectacle happen?" The dam gave way on my emotions.

"I'm scared. Scared for you, for us. I feel totally helpless to do anything to help Juan or anybody."

I continued sobbing, for how long I don't know. Then an arm took my arm and a hand took my hand, and a soft kiss caressed my cheek.

"Jack, we're doing what God told us to do. How or why may not be answerable at this moment." Her soft voice was comforting. "I've been asking the same questions that you have since we left Fort Worth. You and I have a role in it. What you saw tonight no one should see, but God saw it too. Caesar will be held accountable, whether now or later. I know you know this, but the three of you were not responsible for what happened to Domingo and his family. Don't accept that condemnation."

"I'm just scared, especially for you. If that monster comes here…" Her hand touched my mouth.

"Didn't God tell you a long time ago to fear no one but Him?"

"Yes."

"Didn't He also tell you not to be a mother hen over me?"

"Yes, but…"

"No buts! You're carrying everybody's load. You can't. We can't." Tears started in her eyes.

"I love you because you love God first and me second. I don't know how all of this will play out. You've got to give all you're carrying right now to God and seek His wisdom. Of course," she continued with a small smile, "we're in over our heads. "

We both chuckled through the tears and fear, then she continued. "Jesus brought us here to help and minister, but in His strength. Now you've got to let go. You're no good to Juan or to me if you try to carry this thing."

With a faith born of years of walking with God, Ellen summed it up.

. "We may never get home again, but if that happens, we both know where we'llbe. This won't even be a dream. Now we need to sit down and write a will. After that, we just let God continue to lead."

With that, she gave me a hug and a kiss. Once we arrived at the ranch, we put together a quick but complete will. For all the tragedy that night, the love was good, and led to a peaceful sleep.

CHAPTER 7

As usual, I was the last to get up, and everyone was eating breakfast. It was nine o'clock. We were all still ragged from the night before. Juan and Tabitha had made it home about three. He had called the Governor, DPS, and the Rangers, but expected no return until late in the day. Juan and Tabitha decided to send their sons to Galveston and Mei's family. They had shared just enough information with her parents to keep them apprised, but not enough to worry the boys.

Juan arose and got dressed to head into town. Tabitha held his hand a little tighter and longer. Rather than pull away, he bent down and gave her a kiss on the forehead. He asked if I was coming, and I told him I'd be along a little later. As I went to get dressed
and have my devotions, Ellen went around and hugged Tabitha as both women shed tears.

Ellen stayed with Tabitha that day. Everyone at City Hall looked like crap. There
was no fear in their eyes, just a steely anger backed by a resolve to keep on. Walking by Mei's clinic, I saw a

sleeping giant. Somehow Ester had crawled through his temporary hell and now could rest. Mei caught my look, came out, and gave me a hug.

Juan and every deputy were huddled in the conference room like a council of war. Frustration and anger filled the room. Their hands were tied in response to Domingo's family's murder. They had weapons, but had no clue as to when and if Caesar would cross the river, and there was still no help forthcoming from the state or federal sources. If the room full of deputies had been cats, and Caesar a pit bull in the middle of the room, he would have been shredded meat. As it was, they were declawed, neutered, and helpless.

As I walked across the square, praying, wishing, and hoping, something like a cool breeze caressed my face and my mind. Then I was shaken from my tranquility by the sight of four Suburbans and two vans driving into the square. It looked like a church group that had gotten lost. It turned out that this was no church group and they were definitely not lost.

The first man out waved and yelled, "Dr. Reynolds, you pick the strangest places to vacation." Forty-two more familiar faces bailed out of the vehicles. As I hugged Sam Lawrence, I cried like a baby. I couldn't stop the tears. That cool breeze of refreshing had just become a March wind of hope. These were all my former students, veterans of the United States military, representing every branch. Sam, a sergeant major and ArmyRanger, had served in Bosnia and Iraq. He was a reservist. It had been his idea for the party we were to have had. Brad, Army intelligence from the Gulf War, was there. Mike, Ron, Casey, Jean and Tod were my Marine Corps contingent. Sarah was an Army sniper. Jonas drove Abrams tanks like sports cars, at least that's what he claimed. Penny was an Army sargeant and a master with any kind of weapon . Jerry, Marsha, and Carlos were all Air Force officers. Their expertise covered intelligence, planning, and flying. Carlos had led Air Force search and rescue in both Iraq and Afghanistan. Lieutenant Fernando Trevino was a Navy Seals instructor. Slight of build as a student, he had grown up big and fast. Dominique Lewis was a Major and attorney out of the JAG (Judge Advocate General) office. Tina was a lieutenant in the Army, and pregnant with twins. Mike Nguyen was a sergeant with Special Forces background. He was good at destruction, somewhat like a couple of his assignments in my class.

    A voice boomed out, and a big man grabbed me in a bear hug. It was Zack Nichols, Army Sergeant, two-time student of mine. Financial problems had cut short our first semester together. He was a jack of all trades, master of none, and a little bit xenophobic. There they all were, all smiles, and wondering why their professor was crying like a baby.

    I finally spoke. "Don't get me wrong, but why are you here in San Miguel?" I truly was puzzled.

    Sam was the one who spoke. "Professor, when I got your email, it was short, not sweet, and downright scary. So when I thought about what to tell the group, I just mailed them your message. It was unanimous that we'd better check on you."

    Sarah spoke next. "Jack, you've helped us out at different times to get through things. You sounded like you needed some help."

    I was at a loss for words, a rare condition. These warriors I still saw them as my students in class.

    Zack blurted out, "Hell, we weren't gonna let you cancel class, I mean a party, this time."

    Juan came walking across the square. "Jack, who are all…Carlos!"

"Juan, *mi amigo*!" They grabbed each other in a hug. Carlos turned to the group. "Hey guys, we were in class together. I cheated off him."Realizing what he had said, he turned to me, red-faced. "Oops. Sorry, Dr. Reynolds."

Everyone was quiet for a moment. I stared at him for a full thirty seconds before I burst out laughing. "You've been shot at in two countries, and I can still get to you."

Carlos introduced Juan to everyone then Rob Mateo, a captain in the Air Force, spoke up. "Jack, you always respected us for what we did and respected the uniform. Now could you tell us what the heck is going on?"

My elation at their arrival was tempered a bit. They had every right to know what they had driven into. Juan and I decided that Sunne's Café would be the best place to talk. Sunne barely kept it open for breakfast and lunch. As we walked in, she met us at the door, smiling.

"Juan, who are all these people?"

"Sunne, these are all friends of mine." I then meekly asked, "Do you think you can feed them all?" From the look she gave me, I thought she would kill me.

She feigned hurt. "How dare you think I can't. I may clean out my stock, but that just means I need to get more. It's good."

She then called in two additional cooks besides her husband, Byron. Some of the group helped bus the tables. Everyone was laughing and joking. About halfway through, Chico came in to get Juan. His attention was briefly diverted when he saw Sarah. She returned the look. Something flickered between them.

In a town as small as San Miguel, the arrival of a large group doesn't go unnoticed. Soon a few adults were walking by, glancing in. The children were more matter-of-fact, stopping and staring in the windows. One beautiful little girl waved at Sarah, and the redhead couldn't resist going over and picking her up. Sarah could speak Spanish, and the child was talking. Turning away to tell Sam something, Juan came back in the café. When I looked back at Sarah, the little girl was gone. Sarah was seated her face in her hands, with everyone else at her table talking in low tones. When she looked up, there was an intense anger behind the tears. What had the little girl told her?

  With everyone finishing, it was time to let them in on what was happening. Juan gave a full account of what had transpired over the past few months, leading up to our experience the night before. Everyone was silent, their faces pondering what they'd heard. Sarah got up.

  "Guys," she said as the tears started again, "a little girl just came in and asked me, 'Will you not let me die?' Jack, she said her papa was killed by those creeps across the border."

  All eyes turned to me. "She's probably right. Many of the residents here are undocumented. They fled the cartels. You've read about immigrants from Central America and students in Mexico killed. Well, when illegals are caught in Arizona, they're brought to Presidio, Texas to be sent back Why, because if they were sent back across in Arizona, they would be murdered." I paused to let it sink in. Then I continued. "The cartels come across the border also. At Fort Stockton, like here, many families have fled. Now the cartels, in groups of two or four, show up at high school basketball games, and follow school buses. They're sending a message that says we know where you are and we can get you at any time. These people are in a state of fear. Juan told you about the intercepted weapons. They're having to plan for the cartel invading this country right here. This is what you guys drove into. I care for you guys too much to draw you into this."

Again it was silent. Then Sam got up. "If there are no objections, ladies and gentlemen, let's do our jobs. Sheriff, if you'll show us where everything is, we'll set up a joint command and planning."

"Who made you CO?" blurted Zack.

Sam looked innocent. "I guess since I was coordinating the party, I just assumed. Does anyone else want the job?"

Everyone looked at Zack, some frowning. He backed down. "Okay, Sam, it's official. It's your show." He looked around. "Well, you heard the man. Let's go."

As everyone left, Sam put his hand over his face and shook his head. I leaned over and said, "Now you know what I put up with in class. And I had him twice."

The prevailing silence was broken by a siren and horns blowing. A Sheriff's truck came barreling into the square. Everyone hurried out to see what was wrong, as Deputy Justin Chambers brought the Ford F250 to a grinding halt.

"Get the doctor, quick! I've got Domingo."

Everyone was shocked into inactivity.

"Damn it, get Mei! Domingo's in a bad way."

Devon Akers, my student who was a trauma specialist, raced over to assist. Justin and Ramone laid the old man on the ground. Domingo was babbling incoherently. Devon and Mei got to him about the same time. No introductions were needed. The doctors spoke an unwritten language.

Devon sized him up. "He's in deep shock and severely dehydrated."

Mei added, "His pulse is through the roof. Juan we can stabilize him, but we've got to get him into an

ICU. He's probably got organ shut down. Tell Louisa to get an IV bag going." She looked at Devon. "Doctor, do you wish to assist?"

"Of course. The more the merrier. But what are those marks on his neck?" Then he looked at Domingo's hand. "Those SOB's".

Four deputies carried the old man to the clinic. Justin was leaning against the truck, cursing everyone just across the river.

Sam looked at me. "Are those marks what I think they are?'

"Yes," was all I said.

Juan was now standing in front of Justin, calming the young deputy. A peculiar scent started to emanate from the bed of the truck. Jenny, who had come out from her dispatch position, smelled it and promptly threw up.

"Justin, focus for me and tell me everything."

Ester handed Justin a bottle of water.

"I'd just turned off 90 to head toward town." He took a big gulp of water. "About a mile in front, this thing, I mean Domingo… I…"

Juan spoke again. "Focus, Justin. Walk us through it."

Justin took another drink. "It was Domingo walking, almost bent double."

Everyone who could stand the stench craned to hear.

"They'd tied his hands and put a chain collar on him, and then they'd attached four chains to the collar. He was dragging four boxes." He stopped to take another gulp. "I got him. Thankfully, I had the bolt cutters in the truck. They'd pad locked that collar on him. The collar and the boxes are in the truck bed. He was incoherent, babbling, but worse, much worse. I think he was saying, 'My fault, my fault.' I'm sorry I didn't radio in, but I just got him some water, got him in the truck, and got here as fast as I could."

The young deputy appeared bordering on shock.

"Mike, get him inside and laying down. Ester and I will take it from here."

Juan watched the deputy walk into the building. There was anger in his eyes like I'd never seen before. It was like unstable dynamite just waiting for a bump. Slowly the two men lifted the chains. Then, almost reverently, they removed the four boxes. I moved in closer. Juan looked at me.

"Are you sure you want to see what's in here?"

I looked him straight in the eyes. "It's not a matter of want, it's a matter of need." I looked back at the group of former students. "For their sakes."

Juan started to say something, but left it hanging. I was already breathing through my mouth to control the gag reflex when they opened the first box. It was Domingo's son, or his putrefying, bloated head. Flies swirled everywhere. Someone behind me lost it. Gently they closed the lid and moved on to the next one. It was Domingo's daughter-in-law. The third was his granddaughter. What evil could have done this to this beautiful child? Only a special place in hell was suitable for him.

After gently closing the third box, they came to the fourth. Why four? There were only three people. Juan checked it over for signs of a booby trap. He found none, so they opened the box. It was filled with selected body parts. The men were filled with rage, and God help anyone who became the focus of that rage. I looked up and cringed. Selena came prancing across the square,

"Hey, who are all these visitors, and what's the surprise?" Her voice was filled with attitude. It was the trigger.

Juan leaped up and started toward her like a bull charging an unwary matador. I started to move to intervene, but a hand caught me by the shoulder. It was Marquis.

. "He's got to do this," he said.

As Juan stormed toward Selena, Ester quickly moved in behind her. It was too late when she realized she was in trouble. Juan grabbed her by the arm while Ester quickly removed and tossed away her knife.

"What are you doing?" About that time the stench hit her. She struggled to get free. Juan pulled her over to the first box and looked her in the face.

"I'm going to show you what your boyfriend likes to do to innocent people."

Before she could scream, Juan grabbed her hair, while Ester pinned her arms to her sides. Then he shoved her face into the open box yelling,

"This, Selena, is what your boyfriend does." Selena had closed her eyes and was trying to hold her breath. Juan shook her head. "See it! Smell it! Taste it!"

They moved to the second box and then to the third. At the third one, she gasped, and got the full force of the stench, and a flies. She was choking and gagging by the fourth box. Juan let go and Ester released her. She struggled about twenty feet, then fell, the perfect hair a tangled mess, the makeup all but gone, and the clothes covered in her own vomit. Juan tossed a her a bottle of water.

"That's more than they gave Domingo."

He turned and went in the building, Ester by his side. Selena grabbed the bottle and took a big drink, as if to remove the filth. All it resulted in was another round of wracking coughs and dry heaves. The wreck of a woman looked up and croaked out,

"I'll kill you. I'll kill you all."

I turned and looked at my students. There was not a shocked face in the group. They then turned and headed for the impound lot. All I wanted to do was shower for hours. The olfactory sense is the strongest, and that smell would always haunt me. I was headed to the SUV when Rosie caught me.

"Jack, they need you in there."

I shook my head.

"No, now more than ever they need what you have. They need a friend they can trust to hear them and talk to them," she insisted.

I gave in. "Okay, Rosie, but my students need places to stay, if any will."

She smiled and hugged me. "I'll take care of them, and yes, they'll stay. Thank you."

As I reached Juan's closed door, I hesitated. I decided to push past the doubts I had. I knocked.

"Rosie, I said to hold everything!" shouted a frustrated voice.

I stuck my head in. "I'm not Rosie. I'm nowhere near as good looking."

Juan looked up. Dejected, he invited me in. He sat behind his desk, head in hands. His badge and gun were on the desk. His and Ester's Stetsons were tossed thoughtlessly on the table. The big black man sat in a chair with his legs stretched out, his eyes gazing at something a million miles away. Both men were broken. Their jobs required them to keep a rein on their emotions. They took their oath seriously, and in their eyes, they had savaged it. Juan had even removed his law school diploma from the wall, and it now sat in the waste can.

I just sat down and prayed silently, "God, give me the words."

I had left the door open slightly, and a big brown tabby known as Pancho Villa took in the view, walked over to me, and launched into my lap. As he settled in, he started a loud purr that sounded like a diesel.

"Damn!" It was Ester. "All the time I've been here and that cat has never let me touch him. How do you get the lovey-purry treatment?"

"Thank you, God." was my thought. The cat had broken the tension in the room. I kept petting the big cat, waiting for someone else to speak.

"Well, we really screwed up that one." Juan was mentally and emotionally beating himself to death. "All these years and all we've been through, and to throw it all away like that. Damn, I'm such an idiot."

Ester just kept looking at the cat.

"There's no rationale for my actions."

"Our actions," corrected Ester.

"I bet by tomorrow it will be all over the pages and television around the world." Ester's head sank down on his chest.

Pancho Villa looked at me as if to say, "Now it's your turn."

So I spoke. "Well, if you two are anywhere near the end of your self-pity celebration, let's analyze this rationally."

A spark of hurt and anger flashed from both of them. Good.

"Did you screw up? Yes. Were your tactics excessive? Yes. Should you have used a little restraint? Yes."

Ester stared at me. "Are you trying to turn the knife harder?"

Juan started to speak. I held up my hand.

"Rowr!" Pancho added his own emphasis.

Now I was in my element: analysis, personal emotions, and communication.

"Be quiet and listen! Did you screw up? Yes. But your friend had been tortured and his family butchered. The anger you showed was actually restrained compared to what you could have done to Selena. The head into the box was an effective way to make a point. Excessive, yes, but you couldn't help that she swallowed a boatload of flies. Had she been choking with the possibility of dying, you'd have helped...I think. Selena needed a dose of reality, very hard reality. But like with an addict, sometimes even the truth doesn't help.

You two have ruined her perfect world of denial, blindness, and arrogance. When she saw the face of the child, she saw her own face, what she is on the inside. She hates you for that. Then again, you could have killed her. Yes, you screwed up, but it could have been a lot worse. Now get off your pity couches. There's too much work to do."

Juan was still wanting to give in. "What about her reporting this?"

I sat, not having an answer.

"I don't think she'll be contacting anyone without these." I turned to see Marquis standing in the door with Selena's cell phone and laptop.

"My God, Marquis," said an exasperated Juan. "Now we can add breaking and entering to everything else."

Ester looked at the smaller brother with a look that said, "Are you really that stupid?"

Marquis feigned hurt. "You hurt me real bad, Sheriff. Do you think I would stoop to petty crime?"

"Yes."

Marquis just smiled. "Yea, you're right, but not in this case. Because Selena hadn't moved her truck from the square, it fit the criteria for being abandoned on public property. We towed it to the impound lot. The doors were unlocked, and when I saw these in plain view, I felt they needed to be put in a secure location."

"Sounds good enough for me," I said, as Pancho purred in agreement. "Even the cat agrees."

Before anything else could be said, Mei came in and gave us a report on Domingo. He was in critical condition, and an ambulance was taking him to Del Rio. The prospects weren't good. Javier was riding with him since he was family, a cousin. Rosie came in and announced that DPS was coming with their forensics team. Juan started to protest, but she quieted him with a reminder that San Miguel didn't have the resources for a thorough analysis, and everyone here was too close to the case. Juan could only nod in agreement.

Mei had been standing there, watching her husband carefully. She could see he was starting to withdraw. She walked over to him, curled up in his lap, and gave him a long kiss. Pancho Villa perked up at this. Ester started to say something. Mei just put her hand over his mouth and said in Vietnamese,

"Be quiet and strong, my big grumpy panda."

CHAPTER 8

Tabitha and Ellen arrived shortly thereafter, having been apprised of the situation by Rosie. Along with spousal hugs and kisses, they each brought a gym bag with a change of clothes and toiletries. I was still wavering between depression and giddiness at the arrival of my students. All of them were trained military. Many had seen combat up close and personal. They were a God-sent asset. Ellen went out to renew contacts and hug a few while I took a shower; a very long shower.

"Hey, don't use all the water," Juan said as he got into the stall next to me.

"You doing better, mi amigo?" I listened as much for the tone of voice as the words.

"Yeah, I am. Between your tough love and Tab's loving psychoanalysis, I"ll make it. I still hate that I lost it, though."

"Don't beat yourself up, my friend. We all have our moments, As I said, if you had really lost it, Selena would be dead, you and Ester would be in jail, and Marquis would be Sheriff."

"God forbid!" laughed Juan. Yes, he was relaxing.

"Speaking of God, Juan, you might want to take time to pray for God's help and wisdom. You need to forgive yourself, and Selena. That will be hard, I know. Also pray for wisdom on how to use the assets we have."

Juan was quiet for a minute before he spoke. "How many do you think will stay around? Heck, we don't even know if and when Caesar will cross the river."

I thought before speaking. "You know Carlos won't leave, and I'm sure Sam will stay as long as he can. The rest? I can't ask them to stay. And in answer to your other question, the question is not if, but when. God bless you, mi amigo." I dried off and changed into my clean clothes.

The crew did what trained military do. They saw what they had and started to analyze the best way to use it. In the conference room, Sam had set up headquarters. My Air Force crew was analyzing satellite imagery and topo maps of the area, and our opponents. Rangers and Seals were discussing strong points, defensive positions, and booby traps, using our limited number of mines, augmented by about 200 pounds of C-4. The C-4 had been found under all the other stuff in the truck.

Tina, God bless her, carrying twins, waddled herself into her logistics role, assessing our supplies and determining how best to use them. Everybody seemed right at home. I only picked up on two negatives. The lack of real human intelligence from across the border tied our hands. There was also the problem of what to do if the Hind attack copter got loose. We had four Stinger missiles. Two were fine, one was questionable, and the last was good only as a high explosive paperweight.

The impound lot was a fire ant mound of activity. Deputy Smith, Mike, was looking over the far eastern end of the lot. Hands on hips, he had the bemused look of a parent. I wandered over and saw what had his paternal attention. A large oil field truck was sitting there abandoned. It was sun-beaten, five of its eight tires were flat on their wheels, and it looked as if it hadn't moved in ten years. Yet three of my students were climbing all over it as if it held hidden treasure. To them, it did hold something. What it had was yet to be seen.

Jonas, a former Abrams tank driver, was nosing through the cab and underneath the front chassis. Barach Hassan, a Palestinian, and former lieutenant in the French army, was a mechanical whiz. A good day was taking an engine apart, cleaning it, and putting it back together. The bigger the engine, the more he loved it. He was my only Muslim veteran, albeit not of the U.S. armed forces. We had a special bond since I'd had him as a student. His transition to American culture had been rough, but he had really come to appreciate the United States. Our mutual respect overcame our religious differences. He was also a good weapons man and survival instructor.

Penny Jones, a sergeant, was all fire. She was as good a mechanic as they came. Some of her improvisations on Hummers and strike vehicles had later become standard equipment, saving lives and helping in quick turnaround, should the vehicle be disabled. She may have topped out at 5'4", causing some men to literally look down on her. If they did, they paid a heavy price in extra labor and bruised body parts. Her singular love, though, was automatic weapons. Like any vehicle, machine guns were mechanical, and when cared for correctly, gave you much love back in destructive force. She was all over the back of the truck, paying special attention to the location where a small crane had been. She looked toward us.

"Do you have a portable welding torch?"

Mike replied, "Over in the garage. There are two. Take your pick."

"A quarter for your thoughts," I asked.

"You know, when we got out here, everyone went to work. These three were fixed on that oil field truck. They just asked if they could use it. That Middle Eastern guy…"

"Barach."

"Yea. He just said it will work. But you know what else they took? A Minigun and 2,000 rounds of ammo."

I patted Mike on the back. "Don't try to figure it out. Whatever it is they come up with will be impressive."

Juan had come out next to us and was marveling at the sight. Rosie broke our contemplation.

"We have a visitor."

"Who else?" Juan wondered.

"It's official. Both of you need to come in." Rosie looked concerned as she led the way. When we entered the front door, Juan and I stopped and stared. It was the guy who had shadowed us in San Antonio. Rosie did the introductions. At the same time, Ellen joined us.

"Sheriff, Jack, this is David Matthews of the Texas Rangers."

Ranger Matthews stood there in jeans, white button shirt, bolo tie, ostrich quill boots, and a Stetson. If it wasn't for the Beretta and the badge, I might have laughed. He was a walking stereotype.

"Sheriff, Professor Reynolds, Mrs. Reynolds." He nodded to each of us in acknowledgment.

I took the lead. "Why didn't you introduce yourself in San Antonio? We would have gotten off on a better footing/"

"Sorry for the cloak and dagger stuff. I hate it. We've been keeping an eye on this situation, and your introduction, Professor, took us by surprise."

Juan was perplexed. "Why didn't Harris say anything to me when I called?"

"The Commander told me to apologize for keeping you in the dark." Matthews looked at his feet. "He was as angry as any of us had seen him after he called the Justice Department. We're still somewhat hindered, but Harris wanted you to know we've been trying to cover your back."

"I guess that's the best we can hope for. So what brings you here? I'm sure it wasn't just to deliver a message."

Ranger Matthews looked straight at me. "I'm here to get Dr. Reynolds."

"Whoa!" Juan, Rosie, and Ellen instinctively closed ranks around me.

"Why? It better be good, Ranger." said Juan.

"Sheriff, I'm not here to take him into custody. Someone needs to talk with him. I promise I'll have him back to you in three hours." He looked at all of us. "As a Texas Ranger, I stake my badge on it."

Ellen moved in front of me. "He's not going anywhere unless I go with him. Is that clear?" She planted her feet, arms crossed and dared the Ranger to try. He actually wilted a little.

He looked at me, and I gave him the "Hey, I can't do anything" look.

He gave in.

"Okay. Well, shall we go?"

Juan grabbed my arm and put a radio in my hand. "If I don't hear from you in three hours..."

"I'll be back," I said, doing my best Terminator imitation.

We headed north of town up San Miguel road. It was a pretty straight shot for forty miles to I-10. That we went north was a surprise. To my knowledge, there was nothing but range land in this part of the county. I was wrong.

After about twenty-five miles, the Ranger turned the Ford Expedition on to a side road. Ellen had been holding my hand, and now her grip tightened. We made a couple of turns and then arrived at our destination, a mile-long landing strip.

The strip was reinforced concrete, made to accommodate medium sized aircraft. I later found out it was used by DPS, DEA, and the military. Off to the side, flanked by a DPS SUV, sat a Beech Air King. One engine was turning to keep internal power going. As we exited our vehicle, a man exited the airplane. It was the Governor of Texas.

"Dr. Reynolds, it's good to meet you. And this," he said, turning to Ellen, "must be the talented Ellen Reynolds. I've really enjoyed looking at your art."

Ellen picked up on the comment. "Thank you tremendously. By the way, it is for sale."

The Governor laughed. "After this is over, I may have to look into a purchase. Let's get inside where it's cooler."

He ushered us inside the plane and gave each of us a bottle of water. Ranger Matthews stayed with our vehicle. Another Ranger was in the plane.

"Let me introduce you to Ranger Elizabeth Moore."

Greetings were exchanged, and with that, the door was shut. The Governor looked me straight in the eyes and said,

"Tell me everything."

I told him most of the story. Not knowing how things would go, I referred to my students as concerned friends, which, technically, was true. The Governor listened intently, asking just a few questions. As I told the story of Domingo, his hands clenched his seat. His eyes went steely with anger. The man was fighting to keep his anger in check.

"Bastards," was all I heard him mumble.

Ranger Moore looked like a lioness wanting to attack, but she was the picture of self-control. After I finished, we sat in silence for about five minutes.

The Governor seemed lost in thought. It was a lot to hear and evaluate. Aside from DPS providing the forensic work, his hands were tied. Without an overt incursion, he couldn't bring in the National Guard. The federal government had already made it clear that any state seeking to beef up border protection would face the wrath of the Justice Department. Those wanting open borders were turning a blind eye to the cartels and insinuated racism whenever more efficient border patrol practices were used. The real world and the politically correct world do not interface well. Eventually one must die. At this moment the real world view was in pretty bad shape. After what seemed an eternity, the Governor spoke.

"Thank you for telling me straight. I wish I could give you more help. I will do this: From now on Ranger Moore is to be Ellen's bodyguard, shadow, and shield."

Ellen looked surprised. The Governor continued.

"Mrs. Reynolds, I'm asking you, no, begging you, to go back to your home in Fort Worth. Before you protest, hear me out. We can protect you there, along with assistance from Fort Worth Police Department, much better than down here. With luck you'll have Jack home in a week."

Ellen wasn't buying it. "What about Tabitha, Juan's wife?" "We've offered the same protection for her. She will be at her parents' home while the boys will be at Dr. Long's parents. We believe this separation offers our best plan for protection."

I sensed he was holding something back. "Governor, what are you not telling us?"

The Governor let out a long sigh. "Our sources tell us that Caesar has been using MS-13 as enforcers on this side of the border."

"Damn!" I was losing it. "This just keeps getting better. If Ellen stays in San Miguel she could get killed. If she goes home she could be killed. Do you see the common denominator in all this?"

Ellen took hold of my arm. "Calm down. Going all bonkers isn't going to help. Honey, I could trip getting off this plane and kill myself. Of course I'd rather stay with you. I don't know what I'd do, but I'd be there. The rational part of me says the Governor's right. Do I like it? No! But it will allow you to focus. I know you want to protect me." By this time, tears were on both our faces. Ellen continued "Leave that in God's hands. And I do believe Ranger Moore here can handle herself pretty well. So, Governor, you'd better keep my husband alive."

The Governor cracked a smile. "We'll do our best. Professor, do you have a gun?"

"Uh, no."

"Ranger Moore, give the professor that Baretta. Have you fired a gun before?"

"Once. It was a Smith and Wesson."

"This is lighter, and has greater stopping power. Consider it a gift, courtesy of the State of Texas."

I took the pistol and holster, and wondered how my world had gotten so crazy.

"Guys, we need to get you back, or I'll have a county sheriff upset. Ranger Matthews will drive you back to San Miguel. Ranger Moore will follow in the other vehicle. After Ellen packs, she and Ranger Moore will head to Fort Worth. You'll have a soft escort for the entire trip."

We both must have looked questioning.

"A soft escort is one or two unmarked vehicles keeping a moderate distance, but able to close in quickly. Now, I've got to get this plane back to Austin. This is not a state aircraft. It belongs to a friend who has a ranch, as well as a few other endeavors that bring in money. If I'd left in a state aircraft, questions would have come from Washington. Jack, Ellen, you've come into something very big. I wish we could have met under different circumstances. When this is over, the barbecue is on me."

"We'll hold you to that, Governor," I said as we left the aircraft. "I do have one request."

"Sure. You name it."

"Can Ellen and I drive one of the SUVs back alone, and Moore and Matthews follow in the second?"

The Governor's shoulders seemed a little more weighted. "How long have you been married?"

"Thirty-five years, Governor."

"David, will give you the keys. He and Ranger Moore follow." He turned back to us and said, "Vaya con Dios." With that, he went back in and took off.

CHAPTER 9

It was a quiet ride back to San Miguel. The only words I could think of were "I love you." There was no joking or playing around, just the somber reality that in the greatest crisis of our lives, we would be apart. Emotionally, we didn't want it, but we knew it was necessary. We had to talk about things we didn't want to. Where were the keys to the bank box? Where was the life insurance policy? Those are things we would prefer not to come up. God had brought us to this place, and for the moment we would be separated.

Packing went quickly at the ranch. When we arrived, Tabitha was just finishing. She was in tears, and Juan was fighting to maintain some degree of machismo.

"Give it up, dude. It ain't worth the energy," I said as I walked past him.

We all drove to town so both women could say what was, hopefully, a temporary goodbye. Juan and I stood on the steps as the two SUVs, one headed for Houston and the other to Fort Worth, disappeared.

"A real bummer."

"I couldn't have said it any better."

"I could use a drink."

"I've got a bottle of tequila in my desk."
I looked at Juan, surprised.
"Only for special occasions that truly, truly suck."
I patted him on the back. "Lead on, McDuff."
We adjourned to Juan's office, soon to be joined by Ester, Rosie, and Marquis. There was tequila enough for one paper cup per person, not enough for anyone to get drunk. It had been a long day with too many highs and lows, but at least there had been highs. I had Mexican comfort food at Sunne's Café: tamales, rice, and beans. She brought me a pitcher of tea and left me to my thoughts.

"Senor Jack, Senor Jack." Sunne was gently shaking my shoulders. "You fell asleep."

Groggily, I asked, "What time is it?"

"Eleven. Go home."

I shook my head to clear it. "I'm sorry."

"No 'sorry' necessary. You're tired and you miss your senora. I'm glad you could rest here."

I gave her a hug, left, and drove to the ranch. To my surprise, I slept well that night. I wasn't surprised to wake the next morning and find that Juan was not at the ranch. I called Ellen. She and Liz (Yes, they were on a first name basis now.) were tired, but had settled in. Our church was praying, and bringing food.

It was 11 am before I got to town. The impound lot was still a busy place. The "Thing" dominated the lot. That was what Penny, Jonas, and Barach had named their project. Already, the oil field truck had undergone a metamorphosis. All eight tires were aired up. Those big low pressure tires would give the vehicle traction over most any terrain. The mighty diesel, which Hassan somehow had rumbling like a sleeping bear, would supply ample power to the wheels. The single occupant driver's cockpit which had been surrounded by glass, mostly broken, was now surrounded by metal. Jonas and Penny had double-layered the scrap metal, leaving only three slit view ports. It looked as if the three of them had attached nearly all of San Miguel's junkyard to the Thing. The truck's bed held the most notable change. The derrick had been removed and, for lack of a better word, a turret now sat on the turntable. From one of the triangular sides, the multi-barrel Minigun poked out an angry snout. Several others had stopped what they were doing to marvel at the Thing. She was in the process of getting a coat of black paint. I didn't know if she'd see battle, but if she did, something said she would give a good account of herself. I was going to walk down to the church when Deputy Burton stopped me.

"Jack, could you see if you can get Juan to go home and rest? He's not stopped or even put his head down since yesterday."

I started to say something. Larry stopped me. "All of us have tried. Even Rosie got nowhere. He almost snapped her head off. Please, he'll work himself to exhaustion and be of no good to anybody."

"Why me?" I thought. Out loud, I agreed to give it a try.

I walked into Juan's office. He had several maps spread across his desk. Carlos was pointing out something when he looked up and saw me. I nodded at Carlos, and he left the room.

"Hi Jack." Juan didn't even look up.

"Are you going somewhere?' I asked.

Juan looked at me, puzzled.

"I ask because your bags are packed; the ones under your eyes. You look like you're planning for a long trip."

Fiddling with the maps, he said, "I've got a lot to do."

"Juan, you're going to be no good to anyone if you collapse from exhaustion. You've got a good staff and others here. They're concerned, and I…" was all I got out before he let loose on me.

"I'm Mayor and Sheriff. If anybody should put in overtime, it's me! I'll be damned if I'll let the S.O.B. across the river have one inch of this county or this town. If I die doing it, well, at least I've done my job!"

Now I was getting mad. "So you can't defend and protect Tabitha and the boys, and you turn all that on the town. Some good you'll be to "your" town if you're incapacitated by stroke, seizure, or because you're sleeping so soundly from exhaustion that no one can wake you up when the shooting starts."

"Back off, Jack! This is not your fight."

Juan had crossed a line. "My fight! Damned if you made it my fight when you asked us to come down here!"

"You can leave!"

"Like hell I can leave! Hey, my wife is gone too, or haven't you noticed? And someone greater than you told me to stay here. If I leave, before I reach the end of the town square, I'll know I screwed up. Trust me, facing you and your temper tantrum is nothing compared to having God tap me on the shoulder and ask me why I'm not where He told me to go. No way. I'll face Caesar before facing God, not having done what He said, which was to be here. So chew on that."

Juan was still angry. "Look, you don't have kids. How could you know how I feel?"

The worst thing anyone can say to a childless couple is, "You don't understand." The hurt it delivers is beyond description. You might as well tell them they're not complete human beings.

"Juan, that was low. That was beyond low."

"Well, you can't truly…"

With that, I grabbed a nearby chair and slammed it into the concrete wall. The wooden chair broke and splintered.

"Well, take your precious town and shove it up your ass!"

I stormed out the door, slamming it. I stormed out through the lobby. Everyone was staring, shocked and wide-eyed. Mike was standing by the front door, and without saying a word, he tossed me the keys to the department Durango parked outside. I caught them in mid-air, went out, got in, and tore southeast out of town. I needed to silence the demons of condemnation and accusation that tore my heart to pieces.

Four miles south of town, the road goes through a cut between two sixteen-hundred-foot peaks. Sam and the crew had named them the Twin Sisters, and therefore the gap between them was called the Cleavage. It was military humor, or rather male military humor. My emotions had started to wane as I got to the base of the Sisters. For some reason, I pulled over, got my canteen and binoculars, and headed up the west peak. By the time I reached the top I was exhausted, so I found a rock outcropping and sat.

I scanned the panorama before me. To the southeast, I could follow the river down toward Del Rio, its lights barely visible on the horizon. To the west, I followed it to the Big Bend area. To the south, across the river, was the reason all of us had been drawn together. It festered like a malignant cancer, seeking to destroy anything within its reach. Time up there became nonexistent. A cool breeze blew across the peak, its caress soothing painful memories and recent hurts. The tapestry of the Texas sky began to change. Tendrils of clouds fanned out from a setting sun, burning brilliant blues, reds, and oranges. I felt I was watching God paint a new masterpiece every second. To the east, the stars began to break through. With little ambient light except the harsh glow across the river, their brightness and sheer volume was beyond words, yet a song started to work its way into my mind.

"The stars at night are big and bright,
Deep in the heart of …Oh crap!"

I was no more than five miles from a drug cartel's camp, on a peak and very alone. I reached for my radio and pistol. Nothing. I'd left them both in the truck. I tried to tell myself not to panic, but that wasn't helping much. Getting back to the Durango; that was the first thing on my agenda. Then to the east, I heard movement, then silence, overwhelming silence. The coyotes and insects that had been serenading me had gone. To the north, I heard footsteps. My mind and body went numb, preparing for who knew what.

"You know, I'm glad we put GPS locators on our vehicles. You didn't exactly give us an itinerary." It was Juan.

I don't know how high I jumped or what the look was on my face. As happy as I was to see him, some of the pain came rushing back.

"Did you come to arrest me for destruction of county property?" I asked cynically.

Truth was, I was very ashamed of letting my emotions control me.

Juan spoke into his radio. "I've found him. He's okay. Carlos, I'll leave the keys high and dry and ride back with Jack." He signed off and let out a long sigh.

"This afternoon I did something stupid. I said one of the most hurtful things that could be said to a dear friend. All he was trying to do was give some wise advice, and all I could do was wallow in my own pain, not thinking that he was reaching out of his own pain to help. I'm sorry. I think on this interpersonal exercise I got an "F".

I walked over and gave him a hug.

"I forgive you, but in all honesty, the pain will take a little longer to dissipate. You're not the first person to say that, and unfortunately, you won't be the last. I'm sorry about the chair and the wall. I'll pay for repairs."

He cracked a half smile and jokingly shook at finger at me.

"You said years ago in class that we didn't want to see the grizzly bear side of you. It takes a lot to bring it out, but wow!"

"I'm sorry."

"No, don't apologize. As for the chair, I really didn't think anything could damage it. As for the wall, I think I'll leave it as a reminder to choose my words more carefully. Now let's get off this peak."

"Juan, did Carlos come with you?"

"Hey, man, we brought a fully armed patrol. I'm just glad we found you and no one else."

"Did Carlos and the patrol come around on the east side?"

"No, the west. Why?"

"We've got company."

All easiness evaporated. Juan got on his radio.

"Carlos, we've got company. Be alert. Jack said he heard something on the east side."

"Copy," was all Carlos replied.

"Let's get back to town. Oh, you might want this." He tossed me my pistol and holster.

Carefully, we worked our way back to the Durango. After a quick check of the vehicle, we headed back. Juan drove, while I sat, uncharacteristically quiet.

"Jack, your silence is unnerving me. Are we going to be okay?"

"We're okay. It's just the kind of pain that takes awhile to wear off. I'll be fine. Is everybody upset with me?"

Juan laughed. "Upset? Hell, you scared the crap out of us. None of knew that anger was there. For awhile we were scared of you, then we were scared for you."

"Let me off at the church, if you don't mind."

"I would, but I need you to come back to City Hall first. Everybody wants to see that you're okay. Can you do that for me?"

I turned. "Are they that upset?"

"For you, not at you. It took me ten minutes to get the door open after you slammed it." I was about to apologize again, but Juan stopped me. "No, don't apologize! By the time I got out, I thought everyone was going to lynch me."

"It's hard when people see a side of a person that's pretty well hidden. Many times they don't know how to react."

Juan patted me on the shoulder. "Compadre, the only thing I see is a man I admire, and he's human. But woe unto anyone who hurts someone close to you."

Juan's phone rang, and he answered it. The smile on his face became a frown.

"Something wrong?"

"Yeah, something to take care of when I get back. Oh, the deputies want to meet with you in the conference room."

We parked in front of City Hall and got out. Rosie came out and got me in a bear hug.

"You hungry?"

"Yes, ma'am, I am."

Rosie led me into the conference room where ten deputies waited. Marquis gave me a very firm grip on the shoulder and then followed Juan to his office. The faces around me were not smiling. I thought I was in trouble.

"Guys, I'm sorry…"

Ester raised his hand. "No, Jack, we owe you an apology. We weren't doing our job. It's our job to communicate to Juan our concerns. We've been unintentionally giving our responsibilities to you. We're sorry, and we're so glad you're okay."

"You're good guys and ladies, and I'm glad to be safe."

Rosie had come back with a plate of cheese enchiladas, beans and rice, which she put in front of me. "Eat," she said firmly.

I did. I was soon joined by Pancho Villa. The big tabby hopped up on the table started head-butting my hand.

"He has been one tense cat all afternoon. I believe he really missed you," Rosie offered.

The deputies filed out, all of them smiling. Each of them patted me on the shoulder. When Javier reached me and went to place his hand on my shoulder, he was met by a loud hiss, bared teeth, and an arched back.

"Whoa, big fella!" I looked at Pancho, and then at Javier. "It seems for some reason you two are on the outs."

Javier jerked back. "Hey man, I don't kno what's wrong. We're buds." He spoke to Pancho. "Hey, come on." Then he reached out to pet the cat.

I warned, "I wouldn't do that if I were you."

He didn't listen. There was a blinding movement from the cat and Javier jerked back a bloodied hand. He stood staring at it.

"Seems the cat has a beef with you." It was Marquis. He stood at one side of the door, with Juan at the other.

"It's said that cats are good judges of character. Isn't that right, Jack?"

Juan spoke to me, but the comment was aimed at Javier. I just nodded and began stuffing my face, handing off some cheese to Pancho Villa. Javier seemed rattled, but Pancho was calmly cleaning the blood from his paws before attending to the cheese I offered.

"Hey, I don't know what's wrong with that cat. I'd better go clean this and get some medicine." With that, Javier headed for the door.

With a speed that rivaled the cat, Marquis caught the deputy. He spun Javier around with one hand, while removing his gun belt with the other, then slammed him face first into the conference table. I jumped. The cat just purred.

"Hey man, what are you doing?"

Juan checked Javier's pockets and pulled out Selena's cell phone.

"What do you plan to do with this?" he demanded. Javier remained quiet. "Why, Javier?" Juan asked. "Why? What did they say? What did they offer?" The young deputy still refused to speak.

Marquis broke in. "What do you say, Sheriff? Shall we let Pancho Villa interrogate him?" He looked at the cat. "You want a piece of him?" As if he understood,

Pancho gracefully rose and started walking down the middle of the conference table. Javier's eyes grew larger and larger.

"Don't let him touch me! He'll claw my eyes out! This is abuse!"

Juan's voice had an edge as he replied. "Personally, I don't care if he rips your face off. What do you think Caesar would have done if he'd gotten Jack?"

I stopped chewing. Pancho was now a little over two feet from Javier's exposed face. He was crouching as if stalking prey. When he got a foot away, into a full crouch, and a growl began to rise, the deputy broke.

"They came to me in Del Rio. They said they wouldn't hurt me...us, if I gave them Jack! They said they'd help Domingo recover."

"And?" Marquis prompted.

"They wanted a radio. Get me away from this cat!"

Marquis hauled him up and Juan got in his face. "How long? How long?!"

"Yesterday. I took it yesterday and called. Then I left the radio at a location south of the highway."

I cleared my throat. "Juan, if he told them about our friends, the gig is up."

Marquis shoved Javier's face down on the table. Pancho raised a paw.

"No, man! I swear on the Holy Mother, I only told him that Jack had high-tailed it out of town. Please get me away from that cat!"

Juan lifted Javier. "Oh, you said they promised to take care of Domingo. Well, they did. The hospital called tonight. A nurse imposter slipped into Domingo's room. The police caught her, but not until she pumped a dose of digitalis into him. He's dead, and so is the real nurse the impostor killed before taking her identity. If we go down, so will you. No witnesses." He paused. "Put him in cell four."

Javier struggled. "Not four! No, not four!"

Marquis hauled Javier to the back of the building. I started eating again, feeding the cat cheese as I ate.

"Hey, Jack, how do you like being a high value target for a cartel?"

I swallowed hard. "I don't."

"Well, for some reason you are. As of now, I'm your shadow. Let's go home and get some rest." He turned to leave.

"One thing." I spoke up.

"Yeah."

"What is this with cell four?"

He chuckled. "This is an old building, and when we put in the jail cells, four was separate and against an outside wall. At times we find rats in there, setting up nests."

"Oh."

Pancho Villa was up as if someone had announced dinner.

That night, at the ranch, we kept both of Juan's German Shepherds inside, and guns under our pillows.

CHAPTER 10

It was eight in the morning when Juan stuck his head in my bedroom.

"Get up, sleeping beauty. Sunne has breakfast for us, and when Sunne says come and eat, you don't argue."

After quickly showering, we rode into town in Juan's truck. My days of going solo were gone. We parked in the impound lot and started to walk around the west side of the town hall. Carlos exited the back door and waved us over. His face told us he wasn't there to wish us a good morning.

"Jack, you were right. You did have company last night."

"How close?" I hated to ask.

"Close enough to take you out without firing a shot. Roughly fifty feet."

My legs got rubbery. Juan raised his hand. "You mean to say that whoever it was got that close and did nothing?" He looked at me.

"Jack, if they got that close, you shouldn't be alive." He turned to Carlos. "Analysis."

Carlos shook his head. "These guys are good, real good. They're not your run of the mill drug soldiers. They're pros. But they did leave this." He handed a small round object to Juan.

"It's Russian, at least I think so from the Cyrillic writing on it. I don't know the person. Do you, Jack?"

A pit was forming in my stomach as I took the medal.

"Jack, you look like you've seen a ghost. You know this piece."

I stood speechless for a few moments, as a flood of memories poured through my brain. Finally I spoke.

"Yeah, I know it. It's a medal of Catherine the Great, Empress of Russia. While she didn't invent sexual diplomacy, she honed it to a fine art." I looked back at the medal. "But how did this get here?" I looked at Juan and Carlos. We all knew it wasn't dropped. It was left intentionally.

"There are probably thousands of these in the world, but very few places in Texas sell them. One of them is closed now." My mind wandered back a bit. " I had a couple of these and I gave one to a Russian student." I fell silent, thinking that what I held in my hand was impossible.

"Come on, Jack," Juan said. "Sunne has breakfast for us. We can talk about this while we eat." He led me into the café, as I continued to think about the impossibility of what I held in my hand.

As usual, Sunne had a wonderful breakfast prepared. Her pan dulce would make a diabetic commit suicide. But my thoughts were locked on the Catherine the Great medal in my hand. Sunne had a television on in the corner, and it was set on a news channel. One story pulled my attention away from the medal. Thirty Central American immigrants had been taken by the cartel. All of those who refused to carry drugs for them had been tortured and executed. Juan was watching it, too. We looked at each other.

"Do you think they," and I waved my hand toward the lot where most of the activity was happening, "really know what the possible outcome is here?"

Juan slowly shook his head. "I don't know."

I looked at the screen again. "I think we need a meeting."

Juan nodded in agreement and keyed the military radio that we had started using for important communications since Caesar had gotten one of the department's radios. Communication on the department network was being kept to a minimum, just enough to keep Caesar listening.

"Sam, it's Juan. Round up all your people and be at Sunne's in fifteen. Critical meeting. Over."

"Copy," was the only reply.

I asked Sunne to put out some ice water, but she insisted on making iced tea, both sweet and unsweet. My students had become regulars, and she would treat them as such. In fifteen minutes everyone had assembled. Tina was almost late as she waddled in. She apologized and sat down.

I looked at them, and felt a lump in my throat. I was anxious to get this over with. I laid out the situation in as blunt terms as I could, bringing in the latest story to make my point. From the back someone shouted, "Jack, don't go all Alamo on us!"

The phrase stopped me mid-sentence. Then I saw the confusion on at least thirty of the forty faces. The meaning was lost on them.

I asked, "Seriously, guys, how many of you don't know the story of the Alamo, aside from it being in San Antonio?" Most raised their hands. I turned to Juan. "Your family was there. The floor is yours."

Juan rose and almost reverently recalled that pivotal point in Texas history. He included Goliad, where Santa Ana butchered those who surrendered. He was honest when he told the story of Colonel Travis' offering, givng opportunity to those who wanted to could leave. Whether fact or myth, his drawing a line in the sand had become history. For me, it was time to draw the line in the sand.

I watched the faces around me. These people were a part of history. Their eyes showed an acknowledgment of history. For them history was not colored over with political correctness. Juan spared no details. He also mentioned that the defense of the Alamo gained Sam Houston much needed time to find the right ground for a victory, San Jacinto.

Juan had finished. I looked around again. Tina, her bloated body carrying two precious lives, had tears streaming down her cheeks. She was the first that I addressed.

"Tina, you've done yeoman's work here, but you've got two lives to worry about. A battleground is a lousy place to go into labor. Your husband deserves a healthy wife and two healthy daughters."

"I'm sorry," she sobbed.

"There's nothing to be sorry for." Then I turned to Brad. "You and your wife have just had twins and you've got a growing church. The best thing for you is to go and take care of your family and church. All we ask is prayer."

A humbled Brad looked at me with tears. "You got it, Jack. Thank you, my friend."

"Brad, I'd like you to drive Tina back to Fort Worth. We'll give you a list of hospitals along the way, just in case."

I looked around, now addressing the whole group.

"Guys, I can't guarantee that any of you will come through this. We've got a lot of intel, but we still are lacking. You have all given more than anyone should ask for. If you want to leave, it's okay. No one will doubt your courage."

No one moved, but I saw the darting eyes of Lenny Grahm. Lenny had served two tours in Iraq, and received a medical discharge. Having two Humvees blown out from under him had left him traumatized. Miraculously, he had no physical wounds, but the psychological wounds of PTSD were severe. Any sound of gunfire set him to shaking. As everyone filed out, I pulled Lenny aside. He wouldn't look me in the face. I put my hand on his shoulder.

"Lenny, you've suffered enough. No one questions your desire to serve or your bravery. I can't imagine how you feel."

Sam had found Lenny in a Dallas homeless shelter. His wife couldn't handle his flashbacks and his inability to cope in the normal world. Their divorce was handled smoothly when Lenny conceded he might never be whole again. Few divorces end with the spouses hugging each other. Theirs did. I hugged my student who carried so much pain and fear and let him cry on my shoulder for awhile.

It was probably going to be at least an hour or two before anyone left, so a side trip to the chapel seemed like a good idea. Instead, Ester and Juan stopped me and
motioned me over. They had been discussing something and had shared a phone call. Sam came out to join us.

"We need to discuss a couple of things, Jack," Juan chuckled. "Well, maybe more than a couple."

"What?"

"We have to assume the highway is being watched and empty vans will not help our ruse, if it is still a ruse. There are also some items we need from San Antonio. The two big vans are rentals from the airport. The SUV that Brad's taking is from Fort Worth, so that vehicle is useless to us. We need more body armor and I know someone who can supply it.

Sam also suggested that we mount cameas with audio feed around the town, tied into our central command and control, to give us a continuous live feed. Whatever went down would be recorded and sent out."

"It might prove advantageous to us in a legal sense, if you get my drift," I added.

"Sounds good to me. Do what you need to." I turned to Ester. "What was the other issue?"

"Jack, I called my dad in Houston. He knows what's happening, and he has some well placed friends who are psychologists and psychiatrists. We want to send Lenny to Houston to stay with my parents and Tabitha and get him the help he needs. It's on my dad's nickel."

I hugged Ester. "God bless you and your parents. It could be a good solution, if Lenny is game. It's his call."

The deputy went over to Lenny and explained the offer. Lenny's eyes went wide and again tears flowed. A hug sealed the deal.

Ester rejoined us. "He doesn't understand why we want to help, but he'll take it. I'll call Southwest and have two tickets waiting for him."

"Why two?" I asked.

Ester chuckled. "Just so he doesn't have some fart next to him who wants to know his life's history or who smells bad."

We had a good laugh. I put off my visit to the church to see what Juan and Sam had planned.

PART 2

CHAPTER 11

As the small group planned its exodus, it developed into something of a comedy routine. To give the impression of more people, a number of full and partial mannequins were salvaged from two closed clothing stores. Since dummies need clothes to look authentic, those were procured from the same closed stores. Then someone noticed that all the dummies were white, very white. This problem was easily solved with brown and tan paint.

Some weighted empty boxes were placed in the vans to give the impression of a load. Zack was going to drive one van, while Deputy John Sexton drove the other. Since the vans were due at the airport the next day, Juan called ahead to re-rent them and sent along a cashier's check on the city of San Miguel, accompanied by a notarized letter. John and Zack's first stop in San Antonio would be a homeless shelter, where they would leave the clothes and mannequins for the shelter's resale shop. Then they were to go to a city dump to get rid of the boxes. Finally, they would split and go different directions. John's assignment was to hit up a local gun shop owner who did business with the military, and pick up twenty-five suits of Interceptor body armor, one of the newer and best types made. It weighed a third less than the standard body armor, but it could stop more. Ceramic plate integrated into the design would stop an armor-piercing round. Not cheap, but welcome, and maybe pickup some Dragon Silk body armor also.

Meanwhile, Zack was to go to an electronics shop owned by a friend of Carlos. Zack would bring back twenty First Alert P520 indoor/outdoor wireless security cameras to cover San Miguel. Juan put all of this on his personal credit card. There was an understanding that if any of said items were brought back he would get a fifty percent refund.

Once all that was done, both vans were to rendezvous at the Mercado by 4 p.m. After dinner they would return to San Miguel by I-10. They would take the San Miguel Road exit and come home the back way with no one the wiser. By ten pm that evening, the cameras would be in place. The preparations had been made. Brad, Tina, and Lenny had left, which was reassuring, but mildly depressing. I finally headed for the chapel.

Sitting on the front pew, I pulled out one of the prayer books used in Mass. That day's verses from Proverbs spoke to my need:

"Trust in the Lord with your whole heart, and lean not on your own understanding.

In all your ways acknowledge Him, and He will make your paths straight."

"Relax, I've got it covered" kept ringing in my ears.

Maria had joined me, sliding in as if she rode on the wind. She asked me if I wanted some ice water, and then left to get it. Even though she had left, something in me told me I was not alone. I stood and turned around.

There stood Selena, not the coughing, vomit-covered wreck I'd last seen, but the dangerous-looking cobra I'd seen in our first encounter. I noticed her deep brown eyes looking right at me, beckoning. Her lips were just the right shade to set off her rich brown complexion. Her hair had that slightly wild, but intentionally done look. Her blouse this time was only half tucked in, and every button was undone. Like any male, I couldn't help but stare.

The belt at her waist was hung loosely, as if to announce that it could come off easily. Then I realized that she was slowly and suggestively moving toward me. I tried to back up, but was pinned by the pew and kneeling rail. This mongoose was cornered.

"Senor Jack, you must think I'm an awful person." She moved closer. "I'm a lot like you said. I need a good man to help me."

The closer she came, the faster my heart beat, causing blood to flow to all the usual places. This was not good. She moved even closer.

"I can see you are a kind, loving man."

She said the word "loving" in the most "come to me" tone I'd ever heard. And she kept moving closer. She was close enough that her natural musk was filling my senses. She was about six inches from my face. My mind was going everywhere, some it good (to Ellen), and some very bad. All the images of every seduction I'd read or heard about flooded my thoughts. She took one of my hands and placed it directly over her right breast, separated from it only by the thin cloth of her blouse. She put my other hand on her face. Her lips were almost touching mine. She released the hand that was on her breast and placed her hand behind my head. Then she released my other hand, and started to reach for the zipper of my jeans.

"Back away, little sister, before you desecrate this sanctuary more than you have already." It was Maria, returned from getting water.

"Stay back, old woman. He is mine," hissed Selena.

Suddenly, Selena's presence was gone. I opened my eyes to see both women standing face to face, eye to eye. Maria had yanked Selena from the pew to the aisle. It was then I noticed the knife raised high in Selena's hand. But Maria had her by the wrist, and had pinned Selena's other hand that was balled up in a fist. The change from temptress to assailant was mind-bending.

"Leave now, little sister, before I have to add a greater desecration than has already been committed here today."

"I'll kill you, old woman." The younger woman was determined to destroy her foe.

Good versus evil, light versus dark, old lioness versus upstart lioness, or angel versus demon, it was a cataclysmic struggle and all I could do was watch.

"Little one, I warn you. I am part Mescalero Apache and my people are feared on both sides of the border," said Maria in even tones that struck with the force of a hammer. Selena suddenly tore from Maria's grip, and fled from the church, cursing. Maria then turned, picked up the glass of ice water, and threw it in my face.

"Here's your ice water," she said, smiling.

"Thanks, I needed that" was my only response.

After we had both calmed down, and I dried off, Maria brought me another glass of water. I tried to think through what had just transpired. One moment, I was in quiet
meditation, praising God and thanking Him for His care. The next moment, a woman was only seconds from

seducing me before the same altar. I was ashamed of my lack of ability, or desire, to fight back. As I pondered this, Maria never interrupted.

"Why me?" I asked, directed at no one in particular. Then I turned to Maria. "I'm not that good-looking, and I'm sure I'd be boring compared to her other conquests."

Maria just stared at me. "Are you that much of an idiot? Don't you see that she was going to have her triumph any way she could? If she seduced you, your credibility would crumble. You may not realize it, and maybe that's good, but you've become an iconic figure around here. Until your temper tantrum, which no one begrudges, it was as if you were the calm in this storm. You seem almost beyond human to some people. People draw from your peace, your clarity, your love, and your faith. The fact that you proved to be very human let people know they could be, also."

I listened, transfixed. "I'm just being me. I didn't ask for any acclaim." I shook my head.

Maria continued. "That's just it, Jack. You've been you; insightful, loyal, willing to call people into account, and not setting yourself above others. Selena wanted to destroy that. Had she succeeded in seducing you, everyone would have heard about your weakness. Her gloating, right or wrong, would have said that evil was triumphant. And if she hadn't been able to seduce you, she would have killed you. Either way, evil would have won." Maria sat back.

"Why did you give her a place to stay?" Now it was my turn to bring up another awkward point. Maria shook her head, and a few tears filled her eyes.

"I wanted to help her. Everybody in town loathed her, and not without reason." She wiped her tears. "I saw the broken little child and thought maybe, just maybe, the love of Christ could break through to her. I was wrong. Juan was closer to right in his actions after Domingo's family was killed."

I reached over and hugged the older woman. "You tried. But we never know what will happen."

"Not after our encounter here." Maria's doubt was clouding her vision.

"Maria, you fought a battle. You saved me, and possibly kept Selena from truly going beyond anyone's reach. And, by the way, I hope I never get on your bad side. Mescalero Apache, huh?"

She smiled. "Yes, somewhere back there. It comes in handy at times." Then we both fell silent.

My biggest concern was coming to the forefront in the silence. "For all our planning and preparation, we have damn little to go on. We have estimates of Caesar's forces, but very few tangibles. When does he plan to come? Maria, we're flying blind."

Even in God's house, those nagging worries persisted. The silence was deafening.

"If you will let me, maybe I can help you with those questions."

Maria and I looked up in shock. We heard a voice, seemingly from nowhere. But we were sure that God didn't speak with a Russian accent, at least not in South Texas.

"Professor, it is very good to see you again."

I knew the voice. It sounded a bit older, and filled with tiredness, but I knew it. So I answered. "Misha?'

A tall blond-haired man came out of the shadows at the side of the altar.

"Misha!"

I got up and ran over to my former student, and we hugged each other in a true bear hug. Holding him at arm's length, I looked over a very fond memory of my teaching career. Misha had seen a lot of rough road. Several scars marred the once fresh face I'd first known, but it was the eyes that revealed a deeper story. The once clear blue eyes were now a hard steel, seemingly emotionless, but a deeper look revealed pain, anger, and tiredness. I hugged him again. Spetsnaz uniform aside, it was my Misha.

"Maria, please come and meet one of my former students, Misha Antonov."

Still shocked, Maria came forward. She shook the younger man's hand, and then embraced him. Misha did not pull back, but took in the love of the hug. The big Russian's eyes were teary. Misha looked at me.

"If she," he said, pointing at Maria, "had not stopped that woman, I would have."

The lethality of Misha's words told me he meant them. Selena had come closer to death than she ever realized. We sat Misha down on the pew between us and I gave Maria the story of my first Russian student. Misha chuckled at the stories, and I saw some glimmer of life in the cold eyes. But for all the stories, here sat a killing machine. Even our own Special Forces respected Spetsnaz. Finally, I asked the question that was on my mind.

"How? I got your message." I handed him the Catherine the Great medal. How did you get from my class to here?"

The story he told would have any Russian author proud and sad. Misha had returned to Moscow after getting his degree. No longer doing black market selling, he found he was respected, but respect doesn't pay the bills. His dad, a high ranking officer in the Russian military, saw in his son the new post-Soviet Russia: well-educated, smart, and willing to prove himself. Officer training was nothing for Misha. Even physical training only encouraged him. His body matched his mind in quickness and strength. Nothing was given to Misha. He fought, learned, and advanced, becoming a Captain in a little less than three years. He had just been transferred back to Moscow for advanced training when he found a part of his life that had been missing.

Misha had been walking in Gorky Park when he saw a raven-haired woman. Such black hair was not a common sight. He saw a challenge, and went for her. Misha was always a gentleman, and it set him apart from some of his officer buddies. He spent more time with the married officers, becoming an "uncle" to their kids. But always an uncle. Sometimes people would try to set him up, but that usually ended with embarrassment all around.

Katia, the raven-haired woman who had caught Misha's eye, knew she was good-looking. Modeling was one way she'd made it through the hard streets of Moscow. She was also a fighter. More than one photographer had found himself with a broken nose, jaw, or worse injuries, after trying to take advantage of her. Katya was no wallflower, and had shared her bed with those she found worthy. Now in her late twenties, she watched mothers with their children, and felt an emptiness.

She had noticed the officer eyeing her from a distance, and had expected the usual try for the tryst. As Misha approached, she saw something different in his eyes than the expected lustful stare. She was taken aback when he politely asked if he could join her. She was joyful when he offered to buy tea and dessert at a little shop nearby. Two lonely people found each other. Love blossomed.

Even though both had been raised in an atheistic environment, they wanted to be married in a Russian Orthodox church. Spring broke out in a Russian winter for Misha and Katia. Misha's fellow officers made it a military wedding. Between his advancement in the army, namely Spetsnaz, and her modeling career, they made a good living.

When war broke out in Chechnya, Misha was called in. He and his officers found terrible command structure and they set out to reorganize units. What had been a stalemate soon became effective battle tactics. Misha became a major. One thing Misha tried to instill was taking out quality military targets and limiting collateral damage.

It was during this time that Katia had their son Peotr. Katya discovered there was a market for maternity models. Apparently people were very appreciative of pregnant Russian women. At times, they laughed at how good life was.

All that changed on October 23, 2002. Katia and other mothers had taken their children to Moscow Theater to see *Nord-Ost*. During Act II Chechen militants took over the theater and took 850 hostages. Misha was contacted in the field, and as soon as possible, pulled his team together. They knew the rebels, their tactics, and the best way to mitigate deaths. What they also knew was the incompetence of the command officers in Moscow. These were men who sat behind desks, and would use such an event to fatten their portfolios.

Their plane touched down at the closest airfield to town. Even before the ramp was down, they were headed to a waiting helicopter. Their hearts sank as the chopper sat silent. The general was there to meet them. The general, a family friend, could only come up and embrace Misha. These hard trained Russian Special Forces broke down at the news that Katya would never again brighten their lives, and Peotr would never call any of them "Uncle."

Misha paused for a moment. Tears and anger clouded his face. "Jack, they wouldn't even let me have their bodies." Then he continued his story.

Misha had asked to be taken to the temporary morgue close to the theatre. The Moscow NKVD, local police and former KGB, had cordoned off the area. It had become painfully clear that there had been a massive screwup. The Spetsnaz had pumped in a knockout gas. Most of the hostages killed were killed by that very gas. President Putin billed it as a great victory for Russia against terrorism, but as the truth leaked out, it was "Coprire il culo" russian for CYA time. No one outside the local force was allowed in. Local doctors were not told the type of gas used, so they did not know how to treat victims.

Misha and his team arrived in the general's command vehicle. At first, no one paid attention to the six heavily armed soldiers. At the entrance to the morgue, the group was met by an arrogant colonel. Even after Misha revealed who he was and his unit, the colonel was unfazed. The general, Misha's commanding officer, tried to reason with the stubborn colonel. Misha had life torn from him, and no one was going to deny him the bodies of Katya and Peotr. The arrogant colonel became a stupid colonel. He pulled his pistol on the grieving Spetsnaz officer. Within a moment, there was a loud crack, and the
colonel's hand hung limply from a shattered wrist, courtesy of the butt of Misha's combat knife. The

colonel's gun was in Misha's hand, pointed at the colonel's head. Misha's point made, he threw the gun across the room. He and his team went in to retrieve the bodies. The colonel, between surges of pain from his permanently damaged wrist, shouted at his men to arrest the warriors. They stood still. The colonel then turned his anger on the general, demanding Misha's arrest and court martial. The general replied,

"I saw nothing."

With the burial of his beloved wife and child Misha changed. The once jovial, talkative major became silent. The once bright blues eyes became steely and cold. After the burial Misha sold the furnished Moscow flat, taking only a few pictures of Katya and Peotr. He cleaned out his bank account, transferring all his money to Swiss territory.Misha's team in Chechnya had gained the title "White Death" for their ability to take out targets with minimal collateral damage. On the return to Chechnya, Misha himself started leading teams, not delegating authority to other capable officers. His team, in particular, took on deeper, harder, and more dangerous missions. His own commander only knew where they were when they returned and rebels were without another important leader. The reputation of the team, now called "Black Death," became as legendary as it was terrifying.

Misha's commander knew his best officer and team were even making waves in Moscow. Had this team not helped bring the rebel war to a close, they would have been forcibly separated and permanently hidden from view. This man, was the only man Misha still respected, asked his young officer in. It was as a friend. As best he could, he laid out the alternatives. To remain in the Russian Army meant eventual dismissal or court-martial. The alternative was to go independent, to be a mercenary.

Misha stopped and looked at me. "I really had no choice. We hugged, and as I left his office, he told me he hoped I would find peace. Then he gave me this." Misha pulled a small, worn, Russian Bible from his pocket.

"I wanted to give it back, but he insisted that I keep it as a memory of our friendship. He said I might find it useful. Jack, for some reason, in all my travels, I never let go of it."

Misha then returned to his story. After leaving Chechnya, he and his team gravitated to Afghanistan.

Misha chuckled. "The CIA pays very good." The Fall of 2003 he and his team took out key members of the Taliban. When the U.S. invaded, they pulled out, setting up shop in Istanbul, Turkey.

"I never, never, would fight against U.S. forces," he said. "The States held too many fond memories for me. And I never killed children or women, unless they were armed."

Misha and his team spent some time in the Sudan and Somalia. Even those hardened soldiers were appalled at the butchery of the Somali warlords. From Africa, they went back to Turkey, then moved to Venezuela. Chavez was getting new Russian equipment, and needed people to train his units. It paid good money, and all was well until Hezbollah showed up.

Chapter 12

"Hezbollah?" I asked.

"Yes, they have a full training compound outside Caracas. My group planned on leaving. We wanted to be nowhere near Muslim terrorists. We'd probably have killed them."

We were all silent for a moment.

Misha continued, "When Caesar contacted Chavez about assistance, we saw our opportunity to leave."

"You flew the Hind up here?"

"Regrettably, yes. "All we did was training for fights against the other cartels. All that changed when the terrorists arrived."

"Jack, Caesar has an official document saying that he has rights to this area. It's called the 16-16 Protocol. Apparently, it was worked out through U.S. Embassies in Syria and Lebanon."

"Misha, you said this document is official. How do you mean?"

"I'm no diplomat, but it looks official, and more importantly, Caesar believes it's official."

"And you say the Hezbollah terrorists brought it with them?"

"*Da*. We were going to leave when I heard of a particular stranger coming to San Miguel. Selena called you a minister, but one with no fear. Caesar has done his research. He knows who you are and he has a particular dislike for you. You've got to leave."

I pondered what I'd heard. "You've come over for more than just to warn me."

Misha hung his head. "Jack, you are the closest thing I have to family, you and Ellen. But you're right, there is something else." His hands were shaking. "I'd not opened the Bible my commander gave me at all until the other night. I had to. I couldn't resist. I opened it and read, 'Come to me, all who are weary and heavy laden, and I will give you rest.'"

There was a long pause before Misha spoke again. "When Javier called to say that you had taken off, I made sure my team came across. And you found my message. Now I'm here, and so tired. Help me."

His plea for help sounded like the student from years ago. Maria and I helped the wounded warrior to understand that God wanted to take all the anger and pain. Misha was a broken man. He could run and cover his pain and anger no longer. It all rolled out as he called for Katia and Peotr. Rage surged as he cursed the Chechen rebels and Moscow officials. The wails turned to sobs and his rigid features softened. He was finally peaceful, probably for the first time since his wife's and son's death.

A commotion in the back of the chapel broke the peace. It was Juan.

"Jack, I thought I'd find you here." Then he saw the sleeping Russian. "What the he..?" His hand flew up to cover his mouth to keep him from finishing the word.

Maria looked at me and said, "You go. I've got this."

I left Misha sleeping, snoring softly, his head resting on Maria's shoulder. I followed Juan outside.

"Is that who I think it is?"

"Yes it is. His name is Misha Antonov, and he was my student at one time, just as you were."

He shook his head. "Where's the next person going to show up from, Antarctica?"

"Not likely. That's the one continent I haven't had a student from."

Juan got serious. "Jack, cut the crap here. His presence is a real problem. For all we know, he's told Caesar everything."

Juan had had to endure almost everything, and this was a curve in the biggest sense. I had to play on our friendship in a way I didn't like. I had to force the point.

"I can vouch for him, but I know that doesn't seem to be enough. So I'm putting it to you this way: I've given all I can give, and asked nothing in return, and in the process become a high value target. Now I'm asking for something. I'm asking for a big favor. Misha is not the man we saw across the river. Yes, the one who saved Miguel is there, but he is a broken man, and wants, really needs, a place to call home."

"Home?!" Juan turned his back. "And where is he supposed to stay?"

"With us, for the time being."

Juan spun back around, eyes wide and fists clinched. I stared him down. "I believe Misha wants to help us, but if you can't trust him as I do, we'll have a divided camp. I'm not backing down on this. You either trust my judgment, which you have so far, or all we've done has been a sham. If that's the case, I'll take Misha and leave."

"Damn you, Jack. You are one royal pain in the ass!" Juan glared at me.

"Good. Now that we have that settled, we need to pick up Misha behind the church. I'll let Maria know what's happening."

Juan turned and stormed off.

"I'll be up there in a little bit." I waved.

After Juan left, I walked over and sat down on a low wall. All energy seemed drained out of me. From the near seduction, to Misha's return, to my argument with Juan, the gamut of emotions was as trying as intense exercise. I sat there, not knowing what to do next. From seemingly nowhere, Pancho Villa hopped up next to me and started purring. As I stroked the soft brown fur, the rhythmic purring drained my tension.

"What would you do next, big guy?" I addressed the cat, not really expecting an answer.

Pancho looked up, put a paw on my leg, and meowed softly. If you've ever owned a cat, after awhile you develop an understanding. He was right. I pulled out my phone and called Ellen.

"Hello," she answered.

"Hey, honey. How are you doing?" It was good to hear her voice.

"I'm fine. I'm anxious, of course. You sound a bit down."

"Well, it has been an eventful day."

I proceeded to tell her about the meeting, and those who had left. Then I got to the hard part. I let out a sigh, and told her about Selena's attempted seduction, and Maria's timely rescue.

"I don't believe I could have held out had Maria not intervened. I'm so sorry." My heart sank like a stone.

"Jack, the key is, nothing happened. As much as I may hate what went on inside of you, I doubt any other man would have fared better. The important thing is that she didn't succeed. I forgive you. Now forgive yourself. Don't let self-condemnation drain you. I love you. And by the way," she said with a chuckle in her voice, "thank Maria forme for dousing you with that glass of water."

"Yes it was needed. I love you."

"I love you, too, but had Selena succeeded, you'd be dead, and then I'd take her out."

We both laughed. Then I told her about Misha. She was speechless. Already this experience had so many twists and turns. Now here was another one.

We switched the conversation to other things. Ellen and her shadow, Ranger Moore, had gone to a couple of museums in Fort Worth. The Ranger had not been to them, and the fact that they were such public places was good. Ellen's faith and her art were keeping her going. She'd even started on a "San Miguel" series. No matter what happened, this small town would be remembered.

I closed my phone and got up to go in to tell Maria of our back door pickup. Pancho Villa literally jumped into my arms. He was heavy, probably about thirteen pounds.

"You may be the only cat in town, but you are well fed."

The purring machine and I entered the church. Pancho jumped from my arms and trotted down the aisle. He stopped long enough to get a stroke or two from Maria, then turned his attention to Misha. He was in the Russian's lap in a flash, headbutting Misha's chest .

Gently petting the big cat, the big Russian started speaking Russian to Pancho.

"I didn't know he was multilingual," Maria said, smiling.

"What's his name?" a much more peaceful Misha asked.

"He's Pancho Villa, after the Mexican border outlaw of the early twentieth century," I responded.

"Katia had two Siberians when we met. For awhile, I didn't think they would let me near her. We felt it was best that they have a new home when Peotr came." Man and cat were definitely enjoying each other.

After telling Maria the plan, I left for City Hall. As I entered, Rosie pulled me aside. "What's going on?" she demanded. When Juan came back, he was madder than a wet hen."

I could see the concern on her face. "Trust me when I say that something strange has occurred that could be of great help to us. After you get off work, find some reason to come by the ranch and all will, I hope, be explained."

About then, the guys returned from San Antonio, and the wiring of the town began. Juan and I left around 6:30 p.m. in the department's Durango. We quietly made a cruise around town, as was Juan's usual routine, and then came to the back of the church.

Juan was not speaking to me.

Misha placed a small duffle bag in the back and got in, still holding Pancho Villa. Juan cast a glance at the cat as if to accuse him of turning traitor. The cat ignored him. The first part of the journey to the ranch was silent. We were almost to the gate when Misha broke the silence.

"Sheriff, Operation 'Velvet Box' at Al-Qadisiyah was very professionally done. I bet the intel you got would have made WMDs."

Juan's knuckles on the steering wheel turned white, and he slammed on the brakes. Only his seat belt kept him from coming over the front seat into the back where Misha sat.

"Okay, damn it! How do you know about this so-called operation, and more so, what were you doing there, if you were?" Juan's eyes were as angry as I'd ever seen them. Misha never flinched.

"Sheriff, I was there, and I wasn't working for the Iraqis. Let's just say my men and I were on a retainer to someone who was just as interested as you were in that laboratory. You and your men did a job I admired. I only wish we'd had someone like the 160th SOAR. That operation was precision personified. The Russian Army couldn't even invade Georgia effectively. Now can you start to trust me? You and I were trained similarly. We don't become the best, or at least perceived as the best, until we prove it. I'm on your side."

I was intently watching both men, but I was really wondering about operation Velvet Box.

"Uh, guys, can I ask about..."

"No!" they answered in unison.

I just turned around and sat quietly. Juan finally turned around and drove to the ranch. After getting home, Juan showed Misha to a bedroom. I was ready for a shower. Apparently, Juan was, too. We ran out of hot water.

When we came out, a pleasant and unusual aroma permeated the house. In the kitchen, Misha was putting the finishing touches on dinner.

"I hope that you don't mind that I went ahead and fixed dinner. To be honest, I'm pretty hungry."

We were all hungry. Juan went to the fridge and got a couple of Shiner Bocks, offering one to Misha. Misha had cooked a fantastic meal. It was a little Russian, a little Tex-Mex, and a little you name it. After Misha finished his first Shiner, Juan offered him another. The Russian apparently appreciated Texas brews. I was detecting a thaw in relations when there was a knock at the door. Not wanting to interrupt the familiarization process, I got the door, knowing it was probably Rosie. It was, and I ushered her into he dining room.

"Hey, guys, I..." she stopped short when she saw Misha. "I don't believe we've met."

I did the introductions. By then, Rosie had recovered her composure.

"I brought sopapillas. I don't suppose you've had these before, Misha."

"Yes, ma'am, I have, but I'm sure yours are much better than the ones I've had. I'd guess they go well with a Texas beer."

Rosie spoke briefly with Juan, then motioned me to come with her out to the patio.

"What are you doing? I know you said you had an explanation, but this is beyond strange."

I gave the wonderful woman a big hug. She protected Juan like amother. She had to trust Misha as I did. If neither Juan nor Rosie trusted him, the deputies wouldn't trust him either. I gave her the brief version of Misha's story. She was silent for a few minutes, then began to wipe her eyes. The silence was broken by laughter from the dining room. We came back in to find the two warriors smiling. All the sopapillas were gone.

"Hey, man, you leave, you lose," giggled Juan. Misha was grinning, with a fourth bottle in front of him.

Rosie and I looked at each other and shook our heads in amusement. Rosie took her leave, and with her gone I could hear my bed calling me.

CHAPTER 13

It was Juan's turn to fix breakfast the next morning, and we feasted on chorizo, eggs, potatoes, and fruit. We laughed at the memories I had of both former students, years ago and in another lifetime when things were a lot less complicated. Then my cell phone buzzed.

"Jack here."

I sat up straight as a pronounced Russian accented voice spoke. I handed the phone to Misha.

"It's for you."

Both Misha and Juan had noticed my change in demeanor, and were alert. Misha took the phone and listened intently. The silence was broken by an occasional *nyet* or *da*. Misha was writing quickly on a napkin until Juan grabbed a pad and gave it to him. Misha turned to Juan.

"He needs to talk to you."

Juan was all business. He took the phone, and removed another pad from his shirt pocket. He listened, then replied,

"Yes, I know the place, by the river. Sit on the left side, second table. That will give you an ample view.

We'll be in a Dodge Durango with County Sheriff Department markings. Right." He hung up the phone, handed it back to me, and looked at Misha.

"That was Dimitri, my second in command. He and the team were supposed to leave yesterday. Something went wrong."

"What?" was quickly out of my mouth.

"He'll fill us in when we see him. Sheriff?" He turned to Juan.

Juan spoke. "Jack, we're taking a trip to Del Rio. Make sure you have your Beretta."

"Juan, I'm not licensed to carry outside of your jurisdiction."

"As of now, you're a deputy and consultant. I've got a couple of Kevlar vests. We're wearing those."

Juan got on the radio to Jenny, asking her to round everybody up. We would meet in masse at Sunne's at 10:30 a.m. We'd initially planned for the meeting to be later in the day, but things had changed. Misha's team's being compromised had changed the game. How much was yet to be determined. Sunne had gotten used to these meetings, so tea, water, and lemonade were readily available. She and her crew then made themselves scarce.

Everyone was there at 10:30, even Pancho Villa. He had not left Misha's side since the previous afternoon. There were a lot of surprised looks and some quiet side conversations as people filed in and saw Misha sitting with Juan and me. I took the floor, introducing Misha and telling of our relationship. Without going into extreme detail, I briefly gave the reason for him coming over to us. I emphasized his saving of Miguel, and how he could have kidnapped me, but instead left a greeting card.

"I trust Misha as I trust any of you. I believe I can say without reservation that he also has Juan's trust." I nodded to Juan, who nodded back. I couldn't help but think of the six empty beer bottles in the kitchen trash that morning. He and Misha had bonded.

"I believe Misha will be invaluable in our planning. He has plenty of reasons to hate Ceasar. Juan, the floor is yours."

The sheriff rose. "As of this morning, word came that Misha's team, who were supposed to leave Ceasar's compound yesterday, were compromised. Most of you know what that means. One member got away and contacted us this morning. Misha, Jack, Ester, and I will be meeting with the last team member in Del Rio at 12:30 this afternoon. We're going to a red alert status. Things across the river are heating up. We now know that Caesar thinks he has a legal right to an area ten miles by ten miles, and we're smack in the middle of it. Rosie will be passing out memos on what we know. Everyone keep your eyes wide open. Chico, you and John take the Highway 90 border watch. You two are my best at picking up on anomalies. All patrols will be in pairs." Juan stopped and looked at Misha. "Major, do you want to say anything?"

I was surprised at the gesture, but Misha wasn't. Juan's use of his rank gave his words gravity.

Misha took time to look around at everyone. "Thank you, Sheriff. I'm honored to be with those who've sat in class under this taskmaster next to me."

The tension broke, and most everyone chuckled and smiled. Only Zack was unmoved. If making me the butt of a joke worked, so be it.

"I'm also honored to be with those who have worn the uniform of the U. S. military. I want to help as I can. Jack left out a lot of my story. If any of you want to know me better, let us talk over some strong tea."

At that moment, Barach came running in. "Sorry to be late…"

The tension that had dissipated return in full force. I rose.

"Guys, let's get at it. Barach, can I see you?"

Everyone filed out quietly except for Zack, who muttered something about "that Russian." Damage control was in full force.

When it was just me, Misha, and Barach, I got down to basics. To Misha, I explained Barach's relationship to me, which school and when. To Barach, I did the same about Misha, specifically to explain the nature and surrounding of the death of Katya and Peotr. I told them I needed them both. The Palestinian and the Russian continued to watch each other as if sizing up an opponent. I knew Barach had a bigger stake.

"Barach, Misha has brought us intelligence that Hezbollah is working with Caesar. In fact, one of Caesar's lieutenants is Hezbollah. Be honest with me. If it comes to a firefight, can you go against another Muslim?"

Barach's muscles had tightened at the mention of Hezbollah. He took a deep breath before he spoke.

"First, to you, Misha, I'm sorry for your loss. I cannot imagine your pain and I would understand your anger toward me, albeit misdirected. I am sorry. Second, as for this Hezbollah pig: my youngest cousin was killed in an intifada in Israel. He was not killed by Israelis, but by Hezbollah murderers. They corrupt the holy word of the Prophet." He then turned to me. "As for your question, I appreciate your sensitivity, and here is my answer."

Barach removed his boot and hit it on the table, a Muslim curse. He then rose and extended his hand to

Misha. After only a moment's pause, Misha took it, smiling. Barach winced at his steel grip.

As we left Sunne's café, I noticed Zack griping to Fernando. Every other phrase was "that Russian." I told Juan I'd meet him in fifteen minutes. I went over to Zack and asked him to follow me. Fernando mouthed "Thank you" to me as the two of us rounded the corner of the building. I suddenly turned and grabbed Zack by the shoulders, pinning him against the wall. His eyes went wide with shock.

"Get this, and get it now! If you have a problem with Misha, then I've got a problem with you. He was in my class just as you were. Hell! He was a lot better student than you were, but that's not the point. The bottom line is this: if you can't work with Misha, I don't want you here!" I slammed him back into the wall for emphasis. "Do you understand me?"

Zack's shock had changed to pain. "Jack, I'm sorry. For years I heard my dad talk about having to deal with the Russians at Check Point Charlie in Berlin. He hated them. I guess I listened too much."

I fired back. "Don't give me this 'blame the parents' crap. You're a grown man, and if you didn't work with blacks, Hispanics, and Vietnamese, I'd call you a racist. Misha has seen more hell than either of us. Now, have you got the stones to man up and accept responsibility and put the bigotry aside?"

Zac's anger was starting to show. "Damn it, yes. I'll do my job, but it doesn't mean I have to love the guy!" He moved up into my face. "Don't you ever question my loyalty again!"

I laughed. Zack looked at me as if I was an idiot.

"I never questioned your loyalty, Zack, only your perspective. That's settled. I started to walk away when he caught me by the shoulder. "Yes?"

"You told us we didn't want to see you angry. Now I know what you mean." I gave him a hug and walked off.

Juan had the Durango in front of City Hall when I got there. He'd just finished loading assault rifles, Hook Mp5s.

"Expecting trouble?"

"Always. How about you? Trouble?"

I shrugged. "Babysitting."

Juan and Ester took the front seat. Misha and I took the back. Once we hit Highway 90, both men's attention was focused. Nothing was said until we crossed the county line. Juan broke the silence first.

"We've got company. Black Tahoe, about a half mile back, and they are not trying to hide their presence. Contact Prairie Chicken and see if he's in position."

Ester moaned. "Are you still using that code for him? You know he'd be mad as hell if he knew."

Juan smiled. "What he doesn't know won't hurt us. Just text him."

Ester's fingers flew over the Blackberry's keyboard. "He's a mile back." Ester moved his side mirror to check. "Oh, brother."

"What?" asked Juan, frowning.

"He's driving Chico's Impala."

When he wasn't in uniform, Chico was the stereotypical homey. His '65 Chevy Impala would have been at home in any Hispanic neighborhood in Texas. It was white with gold trim, with small diameter tires with whitewalls and gold spoke rims. All this was set on a chassis that was a classic low-rider. Chico was proud of his car, so he must have felt it was truly important to let it be used. It would definitely not be suspected of being a cop car.

Juan just hung his head, realizing that at times his control over his deputies was an illusion.

As we entered Del Rio, Juan thought it best to call the police chief.

"Henry, Juan here…Doing as best we can. I and three deputies are meeting an informant for a meal at Casa de San Felipe. Three of us are carrying outside, and we do have a tail. I know. Sorry for the late notice. No, no backup. Everything should be fine. All this just came together this morning. I leave it to you, but calling the restaurant might cause more tension. We've got our badges. I just thought you'd like to know. Give us a two block perimeter for your units." There was a brief silence. "I knew you'd help any way you could. Just have your dear saintly mother say a prayer for us…. You too." Juan hung up his phone. Law enforcement along the border was at times like family, especially with a shared enemy such as the cartels.

Casa de San Felipe was the quintessential Mexican restaurant. Fajitas were the big draw at this popular Del Rio spot. Still, since we arrived mid-afternoon, the place was nearly empty. Juan parked close to the building, where he could keep an eye on the SUV. A lovely young Latina met us, and after making eyes at Ester, led us to a table where a muscular brown haired man sat. If the waitress was nervous about the strange man, she was immediately calmed by our badges and sidearms.

Dimitri and Misha embraced, and Misha did the introductions. Chips and salsa were brought to the table. As drink orders were taken, I caught the waitress's eye.

"A bottle of your best Sangria, please."

"Si." She smiled and left.

Juan looked up. "I thought you didn't drink, except for that medicinal dose we had."

"I occasionally have a glass of wine or Sangria. Owing to the nature of the occasion, I think a bottle is appropriate to honor friends and allies."

Dimitri turned to Misha. "I see why you honor him as you do." He turned to me. "Professor, what about vodka?"

I put up my hands. "Only as paint remover." Even Ester laughed at that.

The door to the café opened, and two burly Latinos walked in. Dressed in black, there was no denying who they were and what they represented. The atmosphere chilled. The waitress approached the men nervously. They smiled as they handed something to her. Her smile was shaky as she left their table.

"Arrogant sons of bitches," murmured Ester.

Juan eyes kept darting from the men to outside the café.

"What's up chief?" queried Ester.

"I was sure there were three when they got out of the Tahoe. Where's the third?"

Two things then happened in quick succession that took the tension level up and down. Our waitress brought the Sangria and a fresh vase of flowers to our table. Her fear was palpable, though she struggled to hide it. Her eyes flashed from our table to the other. Misha started to say something, and Juan made eye contact and balled his fist. Misha stopped and went quiet. Just as Misha went quiet, the front door opened and in came Marquis. He was blinged out as only he could be. Bling was everywhere.

The cartel thugs looked at him in disgust. Marquis doffed his silk hat at the waitress and enchanted her as she led him to a table. With that distraction, Juan opened his cell phone and placed it next to the new centerpiece. Ester moved his hands and arms around as if making a point, all the while covering Juan's actions. The cell phone set up a feedback loop on the bug planted in the flowers. I almost chuckled as one of the thugs grabbed his earbud as feedback went through. Juan quickly removed the bug and started to drop it into the tortilla chips. He stopped and looked at Ester with a wicked grin. The deputy picked up on the grin and smiled. After closing his cell phone, Juan spoke.

"You know, I hear that Caesar gets it on with horses. I believe that's why he limps. A mare kicked him."

The Russians' eyes went wide with wonder.

Then Ester chimed in. "I heard that too. But he really likes to do it with sheep. Some people say he likes plugging his best guys before a hit, or before he kills them."

The two cartel guys had been munching on enchiladas and beans. They suddenly started to choke, and to jabber to each other. Their minds filled with images they didn't want. With that Juan dropped the bug in the chips and proceeded to mash the them. Both cartel guys yanked their earpieces out. Then Juan poured salsa into the chips. For all intents and purposes, the bug was now dead. With that, we were finally able to talk freely.

Dimitri's story was that the five of them had planted charges. Only Misha would have known where all of them were placed, because each man had a separate assignment. But as they started to leave camp, they were met by Caesar and some of his inner hit team. They had been betrayed.

Misha looked at his lieutenant. "Nikolai?"

"*Da*," was all Dimitri said.

"I knew it. He was always the one. Did he give a reason?"

Dimitri shrugged. "The same old thing; tired and wanting to spend money."

Misha's eyes burned with hate. He fell silent. I glanced over at Marquis, who was definitely making it with the waitress. He started texting. Ester pulled out his phone and showed the message to Juan.

"I found one of the homeys trying to leave a gift under the Dodge. Both package and homey have been returned to rightful owners."

The text included a picture of the bomb the guy tried to place on the truck, and a seemingly lifeless thug. The bomb was meant to be attached magnetically. From the looks of it, it was intended to be set off by cell phone.

Ester texted back. "Is the homey dead?"

I saw Marquis shrug and roll his eyes. He replied, "You hurt me, bro. You hurt me real bad. No, homey not dead, but may never wake up."

After showing the message to Juan and me, Ester pocketed the cell. Marquis had placed the "gift" on the cartel SUV and dumped the third guy in the back and covered him up. The cartel crew were starting to get restless. Their other team member had not shown.

At a nod from Juan, Marquis paid his bill, kissed the waitress, and started toward the door. As he passed the homeys' table, he blew the biggest kiss he could, and walked out. I didn't know if they would jump him or puke. Either way, he left them more than rattled.

Coughing from the other side of the table brought out attention back. Misha, having had a full view of what had happened, gasped, and nearly choked on his fajitas. We were still calming him down when Marquis pulled out of the parking lot, hip-hop blaring. The two killers left after that, not paying their bill.

"Major, you do have some unique comrades," Dimitri said with a straight face. Everyone smiled.

Our waitress was frustrated that the men had left without paying, but she was glad they were gone. Ester went to pay our bill and added the lost payment. The girl's eyes lit up, and she hugged the big guy. Our conversation then switched to Dimitri and his future. In an even tone, he told us that he wanted to go home to Russia, basically to retire. He had one last thing to do. He was going back to Caesar's camp to reset charges. Misha said nothing but nodded in understanding.

"You could come with us. We can use every foot on the ground possible," offered Juan.

"You are an honorable man, Sheriff, but I'm not doing this for my team. You, Misha and your town need someone behind enemy lines. Trust me, Sheriff. I do plan on making it home." He handed Misha a small radio.

"I'll be listening."

The two Russians hugged each other. Good friends with years together, they understood this could be a last meeting. Dimitri handed five memory sticks to Misha, shook our hands, and left. As we left, I mentioned the bomb in the cartel vehicle. Juan explained that the cartel wouldn't set off the bomb in Del Rio. It would be too public, and too quick a response by local police would not achieve the desired effect. However, if our vehicle exploded across the county line or in town, the message would be sent.

We headed out of town. After four blocks, we noticed Marquis putting on the "why pull me over?" act with a black and white.

"You know," said Ester, "These guys will never respect us."

Juan grinned. "As long as Marquis is our best utility man, I don't care."

"True," Ester nodded.

Juan explained that getting pulled over by the black and white was a way to bring the locals up to speed. Plus, while the homeys thought the weird black guy was being shaken down, Marquis could give a description of their vehicle, its occupants, license number, and tell them it had a bomb on board.

CHAPTER 14

Juan took the barest streets he could find. Soon the black Tahoe was trailing us at five blocks. Once we hit Highway 90, it stayed a half mile back. All was quiet until we hit the county line.

"Here we go," murmured Ester.

I had a sudden thought, and just blurted it out. "What if there's a second device?"

Three sets of eyes went wide, and Juan slammed on the brakes, hit the side of the road, and we dove out. At the same moment the cartel SUV went up in a fireball. The metal was peeled from the back of the roof forward. The vehicle rolled for about 200 feet until the tires blew and became a funeral pyre.

During our exit from Del Rio, Ester took a call and a text with picture. Nothing
was said, but Juan just hung his head for a moment and drove on.Now as we walked back to the burned out SUV, I asked Ester about the call.

"John and Ramon found what's left of the Major's team, and I do mean what's left. You don't want to see the photo. We'll be there shortly."

Marquis, now in uniform, pulled up on the opposite side of the wreck.

"Boss, I've got a call in to DPS. They're going to be busy today."

Juan tried to wave him silent as he turned to Misha. "Misha, I'm sorry about your…Oh!" Marquis looked as if he would like to crawl into any hole available.

Misha looked hard at Juan. "What does he mean?"

"Misha, two of my deputies found the rest of your team. They're just down the road at the cut off."

"And you were going to tell me this when?"

"Look, I'm sorry. There was a little matter of a bomb to deal with." Placing his hands out toward Misha, he continued. "I'll get you there as soon as DPS can take this over."

Misha just turned and started walking toward the San Miguel cutoff. Juan radioed his deputies that Misha was walking towards them. They assured him they'd watch and that the DPS Forensic Unit had been called. They were coming by helicopter from San Antonio.

I walked around the charred wreckage after the fire was out. The two bodies were fused to the dash by the intense heat. The driver's body had been blown apart when the heat caused the airbag to deploy. The third was essentially vaporized since his body basically cradled the bomb. Marquis was right. The third guy would never wake up. Any compassion I might have felt was mitigated by the realization that those bodies could have been ours.

After an hour, we drove on to the cutoff. It was a good twenty miles to the location, yet Misha was nearly a third of the way there. He climbed back into our vehicle and rode with us the rest of the way. Three Sheriff's vehicles, three DPS cars, and a civilian vehicle let us know we were there. Juan pulled over and Ramon met us.

"We found them about noon. They hadn't been there long. We've got the people who found them cleaned up, and have been questioning them. Just four college students from Alpine. They thought the heads were jokes, but when they looked close, the smell hit them. They puked and peed on themselves." He paused. "I don't blame them."

Juan just patted the deputy on the back. Misha had walked up. When a DPS officer tried to stop him, Deputy Sexton let him through. So far I thought I'd seen the worst. I was wrong.

On metal stakes driven into the side of the road were four decapitated heads facing east, intestines stuffed in their mouths. I turned, walked back to the Durango, and let go of my lunch, breakfast, and probably last night's dinner. This sadism was beyond my imagination. How long I puked my guts out I don't know, but when I was done, someone was offering me a bottle of water and several paper towels. I looked up and saw Ester.

"Here," he said. "You can probably use these."

"Thanks, bro. Sorry for the scene."

"Hey, this gave me a reason to come back here. I wasn't too far from joining you."

After washing my face and drinking what was left in the bottle, I moved to where I could see Misha. Juan was talking with the DPS officer.

The downblast from helicopter blades set dust swirling, and, thankfully, the stench of death. The DPS

Forensic team even halted momentarily when they saw the gruesome sight.

I overheard one saying, "I've seen all kinds of wrecks, killings, and mangled bodies, but this…There's got to be a special place in hell for someone who does this."

I couldn't have agreed more.

Juan spent a lot of time talking to the head of the forensic team. All the time Misha went from head to head. Juan moved over to the Russian, spoke a few words, and Misha nodded. The sheriff came back to Ester and me.

"Once forensics is finished with Misha's team, they will be taken to St. Francis Mortuary in San Antonio. I know the owner. He'll prepare the remains properly and then proceed with cremation. The urns will be returned to us, and we'll give them a proper burial in the town cemetery."

"Nice touch," nodded Ester.

Sometimes different worlds, maybe universes, come into contact, and good can result. Our contemplation was broken when Misha came over and said evenly,

"Give me the radio."

Juan didn't hesitate. He reached into our vehicle, retrieved one of the compromised radios, and handed it to Misha. Misha moved from the line of sight of the DPS officers, but stayed within our hearing. Ester started to say something, but Juan waved him off.

Misha spoke. "Caesar, I know you're listening, coward that you are. His volume stayed even, but the tone had the cut of a buzz saw. "You send your underlings to do what you're afraid to do. Right here, right now, I challenge you to face me in the town square for all to see, just me and you. I know you won't. You've always cowed before me. For the lives of Sergei,

Markov, Ivan, Nicolai, and Dimitri, I call you to face me, if you're man enough."

Misha then said something in Spanish and tossed the radio back to Juan. Then he strode a little way down the road and shot a bird over the RioGrande.

"Did he just call Caesar what I think he did?" Ester asked Juan.

Juan let out a big breath. "Oh, yeah, that he did."

I must have looked as curious as I felt. Ester turned to me and said, "Let's just say our Russian friend insulted Caesar's manhood in the worst possible way. Besides that, everyone in his camp heard, or will hear."

"Gentlemen," said Juan, "Misha just threw down the gauntlet, not on the ground, but in the big boy's face, and did it publicly. If he doesn't respond, his image is damaged. His machismo is gone. Hell, I'm kind of glad he did it. I'm tired of this SOB hiding across the river. I'm ready for a fight."

Ester agreed. Even though I had misgivings, I had to admit I wanted this over. To quote a former BP executive, I wanted to "get my life back."

As we rode up the road to town, we could tell the team had been at work. Here and there were cleared areas, barbed wire where it hadn't been before, and hundreds of other things that only a trained eye could see. Especially around the Sisters, there was more wire, and fresh dirt here and there, hiding something. With the wind blowing, the evidence of fresh work would soon be erased. As we crossed Harkell Canyon, I could only imagine what nice surprises lay waiting.

When we reached San Miguel, Misha asked to be let off at the church. Maria was waiting outside, like a mother worried about her child. She knew what had occurred.

City Hall was a beehive of activity. Everyone sensed things were coming to a head. They were also glad we were alive. I was slow getting out because something was nagging at me. Why did Misha include Dmitri in the litany of his dead team members?

"He did it to give Dmitri time and cover." Juan's words brought me to reality. "It's an operational procedure. If Caesar thinks that his boys got Dmitri before we got there, he won't be looking for the shadow in the mist."

Juan shut the door and went inside. I was learning firsthand about things I'd only read about. It was exciting. These lessons were also unnerving. My students were teaching me.

Inside the big conference room Sam, several Rangers and several SEALs were going over a big topographical map of the area from 90 to the town. Mike Nguyen seemed exceptionally proud of a series of approximately ninety squares along the road in a dragon's teeth pattern. I then noticed Juan standing beside me, taking it all in.

"Okay, you scoundrels, what have you done to my county?"

Fernando Trevino, a former SEAL lieutenant, responded, "Just setting up defensive positions, Sheriff."

The group seemed particularly pleased with their handiwork. Juanwalked over and looked over the map with a critical eye.

"How many mines?" "Eighty, mostly anti-personnel, with ten vehicle mines waiting to beset," responded Consuela, a captain and chopper pilot with experience in recon and hand-to-hand. She'd ridden with the 82nd Airborne.

"How many feet of barbed wire?"

"Two miles wrapped around the base of the Sisters, set ten inches high. The four strands are approximately three feet from each other. You trip on one and fall into the next. They're good and rusty," responded Casey Martin, Marine Captain and SEAL Black Ops Specialist.

"What are these round points?"

Jerry Patton, the only Air Force Special Ops guy in the room, responded. "Sheriff, we noticed you had sixty fifty-gallon oil drums. Those that weren't already full of used oil we filled from leftovers at the closed auto parts store, and Sunne's leftover cooking oil. She had almost two hundred gallons." He paused. "We loaded these up and placed them where you can't see them. They're primed with blocks of C-4. Call it a poor man's napalm. Some are buried, and others are on top of the Sisters, where we can punch holes in them and roll them down on the road, setting them off with C-4 by remote. And for good measure, we placed a couple tied in with Claymores in Harkell Canyon, in case the bad guys want to come in that way."

"Good set," said Juan, "But to circle through the canyon means crawling over cactus and climbing through thick mesquite trees. Those thorns will do a great deal of damage. Add a little oil fire and flying steel balls, and I think you might dissuade anybody from coming that way…What are these boxes?"

Everyone looked at Mike Nguyen, who had a big grin on his face.

"Well?" asked Juan. By now Misha had joined us.

"Sheriff, do you remember something from Vietnam called a tiger pit?"

"Yes. Pits four by six by four, covered on the bottom with punji sticks or sharpened iron stakes covered with crap. Sometimes there were much deeper pits that contained a hungry tiger. They were death by deep multiple stab wounds or by being eaten. A questioning look crossed his face. "But we don't have some of this stuff."

Mike's pride was palpable. "We call these scorpion pits. They're four by six by four. We used the town's backhoe to make them. We covered the bottom with prickly-pear cactus."

I winced. The local variety of the cactus had very strong thorns, one to two inches long.

"Also," Mike continued, "We came across hundreds of scorpions. You know those things glow under a black light? Anyway, we tossed them into most of the pits."

Juan interrupted. "Big ones or little ones? The little ones are more dangerous."

"Oh, we found lots of the little ones."

Juan interrupted again. "You said you put scorpions in most of the pits. What about the other ones?"

Again Mike smiled. "We called those viper pits. You have lots of rattlesnakes out here, so we gave some of them new homes."

"You didn't put snakes and scorpions in the same pits? They'll kill each other."

"No, Sheriff, they are separated."

"And damn angry," I heard Marquis murmur behind me.

Mike looked quizzical. "What was that? Oco…Oco…Ocotillo. They work real well as covering."

"Kill and maim them. It works for me," I heard Ester chime in.

Juan stood looking at the map, pondering. "Good work. In two years, sand, water, and cactus will fill in the pits. Lethal and biodegradable; it works for me." Then he turned and left the room.

I turned to walk away and saw Misha staring at the map. I could have sworn he looked pale.

"Aren't you glad those weren't finished when you came looking for me?" I inquired.

"*Da*," he replied softly. Just when I think I have you Americans figured out, you scare me." He turned and left. Only Deputy Sexton remained looking carefully at the map.

"What's up John?" I asked.

"That area just south of town, and I mean just south of the square. They could regroup or disperse messing our defensive set-up" He kept looking...."I believe have just the solution, Foo gas. " He left and I went to find Juan.

Chapter 15

Juan was in his office, boots on the desk, head back and eyes closed. Ester was in his usual seat, cleaning a weapon I'd not seen before. A closer look showed it to be a USAS-12 shotgun. The weapon is a wicked beast. This particular one had a 30-round detachable magazine. Ester cleaned and wiped the weapon like he was caressing a beautiful woman. It was a 12-gauge, but the ammo made it especially destructive. The ammo was a Remington SP-12 F-20 Beehive Flechette. The shells deployed blades which added stability and lethalness. They could penetrate three inches of wood, nearly a quarter inch of metal, which meant they could also pierce body armor, at a range of over 450 feet. Ester looked up at me and smiled.

"Big man, big gun."

Juan leaned forward, raking his hand through his hair. "Big man, big gun, scorpion pits, barrels of fire… but hell, they're nothing unless we know when Caesar is going to cross the river."

It was the dark cloud of a question that lingered over the room. Would the cartel leader take Misha's challenge or blow it off? My ability to stay here was slightly open-ended, but my students had only another four days at most. Some didn't have that option. They had jobs, families, and lives to get back to. I sat down and got out my laptop. I felt prompted to do a little research on our adversary. We needed to know our enemy.

Juan had just propped his boots on the desk again when Rosie stuck her head in.

"He's on the phone."

Juan looked up. "Who?"

"The devil himself," she replied.

Ester sat up as Juan punched on the speaker phone.

"Sheriff Cordova here. To whom am I speaking?"

Caesar's voice was smooth. "Sheriff, such formality. We are almost like neighbors by now."

"Neighbors don't try to blow me up and slice my friends into pieces."

"True, Sheriff. You do have me there. You realize that a man in my position must, shall we say, maintain appearances." His voice was filled with arrogance.

Juan was impatient. "Cut the crap, Caesar, and get to the point."

"Ah, a man who doesn't mess around. The point is, Sheriff, I have legal right to your town and a ten-mile by ten-mile area of your county."

Silence hung in the air for a moment. Then I spoke up. "Caesar, I'm Reverend Reynolds."

Juan looked at me with a look that said "Be careful."

"I'm counseling the sheriff on this matter." There was a pause on the other end.

"Oh, so you are the Padre my Selena told me about. You're advising the sheriff to hear my words. By the way, I've not heard from Selena. You don't happen to know her location, do you?" His voice was losing its smoothness.

I handed Juan a piece of paper on which I'd written "deflection." My presence had put the drug lord slightly off his game, and I hadn't even brought out my ace.

"We've not seen Selena for awhile, but that's not the point. You say you have a legal document giving you the right to this area. Why should we believe you?"

Caesar was now angry. "Padre, don't impune my honor."

"Caesar, if you are a man of honor, why did you change your name from Paco Gomez?"

We heard someone laughing in the background. The laugh was quickly silenced by two gunshots and a curse in Spanish. Then Caesar spoke again.

"Sheriff! This Padre does you no good. Your town is mine!"

Juan straightened up. "Not so fast, Paco. Until I see that document, you're just pulling a bluff. If you cross the river in force, it will be considered an invasion and will accordingly be repelled."

Caesar was grumbling to someone, then he came back to the conversation. "I grow weary of this chatter. My legal staff, who happens to be a graduate of a prestigious American law school, has assured me of the document's legitimacy."

We looked at each other. Was it possible that the document was legal? The ramifications were astounding and catastrophic.

"Caesar, we'll need to see the document and let our legal crew see it. We can save a lot of bloodshed."

Juan looked at me like I'd gone mad. He started to speak, but I held up my hand to stop him.

"Ah, Padre, you are a man of reason. You and the sheriff should come to my camp and we'll settle this like gentlemen over a fine Texas wine."

Juan cut in. "And get sliced to pieces? No thanks. You meet us here in my town tomorrow at noon."

I was glad Juan was on the phone.

Caesar continued. "Sheriff, I will see you tomorrow, but at my time, 11 pm You don't trust me and I don't trust you, but I will see you and I will take what is mine. And furthermore…"

Juan had heard enough. "Bye, Paco," he said, and turned the phone off. Then he turned to me. "What the hell are you doing? I'm not giving up any of this county or town, even if the damn document is legal."

I gave a moment for the steam to settle. "Did you not learn a thing in my class on persuasion? Caesar is the one having to prove something. If you noticed, his voice, volume pitch and tone changed dramatically. No one, aside from Misha, has ever stood up to this guy. We both have the same end in mind. Make him show his hand long before we reveal ours. Ceasar is also a student of Adolf Hitler and has read 'Mien Kampf.' Hitler said the greater spirit overcomes the lesser in the dark. It's a paraphrase, but that's why he picked a night meet "

Juan leaned back again, and laced his fingers behind his head. "In the words of Wellington and Houston, 'we've set the battlefield.'" Juan smiled.

"That was a pretty cool play for someone who doesn't play poker. What are you trying to find on your computer? By the way, the 'Paco' thing was brilliant."

"Praise the Lord for the Internet." I looked at Ester. "Big man, do you still have the photos from our excursion to the river?"

"Sure."

"Find all the ones that show the people standing around Caesar. I believe his 'attorney' may be in that group. Misha?"

"Yes, Jack."

"You said the document was worked out in Syria and Lebanon. Do you remember the name of Caesar's lieutenant?"

"*Da*. It was Afaz al-Assad. As much as he tried to blend in, he was usually more tanned than olive-skinned. His hair was dyed black." He chuckled. "His blond roots would show, and though he spoke English, it had a distinctive cadence, or flair, or…"

"Dialect," I offered.

"Yes, that's it."

"Any idea what part of the country? South, northeast?"

Marquis interrupted. "Blond hair and tanned would, to me, indicate California."

My fingers tapped on the keyboard while Juan put in a call to the Texas Rangers to check Interpol for Afaz al-Assad. Fifteen minutes later we hit pay dirt.

"Michael Williams, law student at UC-Berkeley Law School, kicked out after wanting sharia law incorporated into the curriculum."

"I thought Berkeley was liberal," intoned Ester.

"Liberal, yes, but when you tell a female law professor she should be arrested and punished under sharia law for her attire and attitude toward males, your welcome is terminated."

Juan pondered out loud, "So Caesar's legal counsel is a law school dropout. I bet Caesar doesn't know that. A fake law degree is easy enough to come by."

Rosie came in and handed Juan a sheet of paper. He perused it briefly.

"Yep, it appears our boy is on Interpol's suspect list."

We sat there for about fifteen minutes examining and discussing what we had: a drug lord with a "legal" document supposedly giving him carte blanche to U. S. land, and a lieutenant who was an expatriate working with Hezbollah and billing himself as a graduate of a well known law school. Now, what were we missing? Probably a lot, because this situation got more confusing.

"Damn!" shouted Juan. We all jumped.

"It's so simple, ingenious, and diabolical." We were all ears.

Juan went on. "The cartel wants to set up shop without interference from law enforcement. There's probably a non-violence clause in the document for towns in Texas on either side of the area. This means better flow of drugs, but no killing in Texas border towns. In a roundabout way it relieves Mexico of one cartel. That makes for good relations. But if Hezbollah put this together, they're using Caesar as a Trojan Horse. Hezbollah will send across fighters, and at some point they'll break off and attack targets in Texas. Once they start attacking, Caesar will be blamed, and the feds will come in with force. It makes the administration look good politically. While the politicos are patting their backs, Hezbollah will launch attacks. Do you realize how many oil wells there are between here and Midland-Odessa? Most of them are out in the open and unguarded. Hell, they never had to be. They could blow up wells with a little C-4 or a stick of dynamite. Law enforcement would be called out to vast areas, and away from cities like Houston, Austin, and Dallas. Divide and destroy, sow confusion, which allows for more attacks. Most Texas towns are small, and their police departments aren't equipped for terrorist attacks."

Juan paused for a moment, his mind racing. He caught his breath, and continued.

"Jack, you're from Fort Worth. Think of all those gas wells, hundreds of them, most in residential areas. You start lighting off a few of them, and you have panic. With the small attacks drawing attention, they would then try to hit a major refinery. Oil prices would spike and the economy would be in shambles. Panic and confusion; just what the terrorists ordered."

Juan's words had cast a pall over us. Ester broke the depressing mood.

"And we're the speed bump in the road to jihad paradise."

The mood started to brighten. "I think it's time this speed bump became someone's worst nightmare," put in Marquis energetically.

Juan stood up. "No one takes one inch of our town, county, or country on my watch. Sam, round everyone up except those on patrol. We'll meet in the council room in ten minutes."

"Gotcha!" Sam responded.

With our target in sight, and a better understanding of the enemy, we all felt some pick up after a very hard day. We still had to see that document and make a copy, and there were still some big questions. How many troops would Ceasar bring across the river? How many of them would be Hezbollah? Would we have enough of an element of surprise to somewhat even the playing field? Most importantly, would any help come once the gunfire started?

Philippians 6:4 says, "Be anxious for nothing, but in everything, by prayer and supplication with thanksgiving, let your requests be made known to God." I laid all these questions on God's altar as I made my way to the council room.

The council room was packed. Juan took the floor, and laid out what had been discussed. He followed up with orders that left no doubt they were to be followed.

"It's currently 1900 hours. Sam, all your crew will bust their butts until 2200 hours, then call it a day. Guys, you've come and done more than anyone could ask. Your sacrifice will not be forgotten, but as of 2200, the protectors of this town and county are me and my deputies. It may be the last full night we have her, so she is ours alone. Get some well-deserved rest, and be back at 0800 tomorrow."

Juan's phone buzzed. He looked at it, put it back in his pocket, and resumed speaking.

"To all of you, my sincerest thanks. I couldn't have served with any better group. Now go!"

Everyone filed out with a new sense of urgency and purpose. I noticed Sarah and Chico slip out the back door together. They were definitely becoming a team; a team of lovers.

Juan motioned for me to come with him. He told Sam to get Dominique and follow us. Rosie, ever vigilant of her boss, came along. Once in his office, he told us all to take a seat. Juan looked at his phone message, dialed a number, and then put it on speaker phone. Juan's friend in the Governor's office answered.

"Dude, it's Juan. I've got you on speaker. Tell everyone here what you just texted me."

Juan's friend explained, "I'm sorry to be the bearer of more bad news, but word is, the Attorney General of the United States will, on Monday, accuse you and your department of arms smuggling."

"What the f...?" shouted Rosie. We all turned to look at her, almost as shocked by her outburst as by the message.

"Sorry," she meekly said, very red-faced.

Juan's friend continued, "I have to agree with her. We both know the Feds are aware of the intercepted arms shipment, considering they basically kidnapped the driver from the hospital. Juan, is there any way you can get those arms packed for us to get tomorrow, or no later than Sunday?"

"No can do, my friend. Caesar is coming over tomorrow evening, probably in force. We couldn't round them up in time, and if we could, we would be defenseless. By this time Saturday, San Miguel and most of us may not be alive. Can the Governor go to bat for us?"

There was brief silence on the other end. "He's been apprised of the situation, and I've never seen him madder. Our A.G. will be attacking the charge, but with the information you just gave me, the picture has become a bit clearer. Give me fifteen minutes to bring the Governor up to speed, and I'll call you back."

Juan turned off his phone and looked at us all. For a man facing overwhelming odds from two directions, he was surprisingly calm. He turned to Dominique.

"Dominique, as you can, analyze the legal aspect of our response."

"On it, Sheriff," she replied. She smiled and said, "I think we can beat this." She turned and left.

"Guys," he said to the rest of us, "Keep this under your hats. We've got enough to be concerned about, but I felt you needed to know. We'll cross one bridge at a time. Sam, get your work done and get some rest."

Sam nodded and left.

Juan looked at Rosie. "No tears. I need you at your strongest." Rosie hugged Juan and left.

"Jack, my friend, it just gets more fun. At 2200, take Misha and go to the ranch. Get some rest."

But something was nagging at me.

"Spit it out Jack."

"Maybe it's coincidental, but doesn't it seem strange the demand for our 'extra' weapons comes just prior to Ceasar crossing the border. Like I said, maybe it's coincidental."

Juan eyed me. "Do realize the implications of that assumption?.. Misha?"

"In games like this, I don't believe in coincidences."

"Me neither. But let's deal with the devil we know, and not the devil we don't know. Jack, get some rest."

I left Juan to his thoughts and duties. For the time being, I thought it best to get out of the way and let the professionals work. I was wrong. Less than an hour later, my radio sounded. It was Deputy Smith, saying I needed to get back to City Hall.

Chapter 16

I walked into the communication and computer center, still marveling at what Sam and the crew had turned it into in four days. The only thing we didn't have was radar. Given time, this crew would have figured that out. Sam and Misha were staring intently at the computer screen. Another student with a background in intelligence had earphones on and was writing feverishly. Juan was looking on when I walked in. He motioned me over.

"We've broken Caesar's encryption code. It was an old Special Forces algorithm used in the first Gulf War. We gave it to the Mexican Army after the Russians broke it."

"What have we got?" I asked.

"Nothing good." He let out a sigh. "We were right to expect him to cross in force, but it's the force size that's a problem. None of us will get much rest tonight."

Sam handed me a readout from all we'd garnered. Misha had the base deployment at twenty-five hundred. Half of those were in maintenance, production, shipping, and protection from the Mexican army, which had been getting closer to probing the cartel's southern flank. That left over a thousand active members available to cross, putting the odds at nearly twenty to one. No battle plan survives the first encounter. Ours was having to be revised hourly.

"Why such numbers?" I asked.

"Overkill, machismo, pageantry? Hell, Jack, I don't know. We've got to figure out a way to keep part of that force from crossing the Rio Grande. Up until now, I really thought we could even the odds, or maybe handle odds of five to one. No. This means we've got to find a way to limit the interdiction." Juan was worried.

"Sheriff, why not drop a couple of mortar rounds on the bridge once it deploys?" came one idea.

"No, they've got to fire first." I saw the light turn on. "But if we get them to fire first, we're in the clear. Texas has the Castle Law. If someone invades your house, you can kill the bastard. Now, I'm greatly enhancing the scope of the law, but if we can get them shooting, at anything, we have provocation."

"Sheriff?" It was Mike Nguyen. "I hate to play devil's advocate, but we've never discussed ROE."

Rules of Engagement were the guidelines troops had when going into battle. Many in the room had had one hand tied behind their backs by the Pentagon's ROE.

Juan straightened up. He knew ROE could be profanity in a war zone. He'd seen it first hand in Iraq.

"Sam, everybody got ears?"

"Roger, Sheriff."

Juan put on the headset. "Attention, everyone. A pertinent question has been put forward about ROE. Aside from getting the cartel to fire the first shot, here is the bottom line. We face an enemy that is ruthless and shows no mercy. We shoot to kill. I don't need to remind you of what happened to Domingo's family and Misha's team.

All of you will be given plastic handcuffs in case an enemy surrenders. Cuff them and leave them. They'll be gathered after the event. Caesar has shown every intention of taking this area no matter what, and I don't want you hampered in defending yourselves.

We now face an enemy vastly larger in number than we expected, but with a little bit of skulduggery, maybe we can lower the odds. He paused. We must face the possibility of being overrun. Should that time arise, Sam, Jack, or I will give the call sign. It's going to sound hokey, but seeing our situation, it's appropriate. The evacuation call sign is 'Alamo.' Those in town will evacuate north to the airfield, wounded being carried by school bus and truck. Teams 1 and 2 manning the Two Sisters, meet me at 2300 hours for your evac orders." He paused again, taking a deep breath.

"Hopefully, in about thirty-six hours we can get rip-roaring drunk and laugh at this. If there are any questions, feed them to Sam, and he'll get them to me. Thanks, all of you."

Slowly Juan removed the headset and gave it to Sam. Some of my students outranked Juan, and in war he'd be taking orders from them. Their trust was in him now and what he said was law. I don't remember who said it, but someone broke in, asking if in that weapons load there had been starburst mortar rounds. I saw that sly grin cross Juan's face. We might have just found the way to get Caesar's men to fire, and disrupt the crossing.

We called it the "greeting cards." Our two forward observation teams would each have 60mm mortars. They would fire three starburst shells after thirty vehicles had crossed. Hopefully, the unexpected would cause confusion and disruption in the crossing. The two teams would then hunker down and wait. They were our eyes and ears as to what crossed the river. If battle started, it would be their job to take out the north end of the bridge. They would remain covered. If worse came to worse, they could get their collective asses out of there. One team would move east to the Pecos River and the other would parallel Highway 90 until they were clear. Then they would radio DPS.

When time came to meet with the teams on the Sisters, the orders were the same. Team S1 on the western side and on the biggest of the Sisters would be manned by Army Rangers. Team S2, on the eastern side of the road, was the smaller. The SEALs, along with our one Air Force Special Ops person, would hold it. Both hills sat six hundred feet above San Miguel Road and were our best and most important outposts.

The "cleavage," or the road between the sisters, was a choke point. Five miles north of 90 and four miles south of town, it was the only defensible point before town. But the very things that made them important also made them targets if a firefight broke out. The two teams between them probably had fifty-five percent of our firepower. They'd made those hills a death wish for anyone to take, yet I still couldn't help but worry.

Juan called Jerry Patton, Air Force Special Ops, aside. Of all the weapons unloaded from the truck, one box remained unopened. Juan took Jerry over to the box and opened it. Jerry's eyes grew wide.

"You guys on S2 are less in number. I wasn't going to pull this out, but I believe your team could use it."

"How?" asked Jerry. "This is an XM25. They just started deploying these in Afghanistan."

The XM25 is the first ever programmable grenade launcher. It uses microchipped ammunition. Its full name is XM Counter Defilade Target Engagement System. With a range of up to 2,300 feet, the weapon could put a 25mm air-bursting grenade over the top of an obstruction, killing those behind it. Less than a mortar, it was a precision-guided weapon. S2 would have a range north and south of their position covering close to a mile. Jerry looked as if he'd gotten an early Christmas present.

"I'll put it to good use. I tested a prototype before I got out. It would have saved some lives in Iraq." His face clouded. "I don't even want to consider what the cartel would have done with it."

Juan patted him on the shoulder. "They didn't get it. We did. Now don't tell my Army buds where you got it. They might think I'm going soft on 'fly boys' and 'squids.'" Jerry repacked the weapon, then sat down to read the operations manual.

By 11p.m., activity was at a fever pitch. A review of our defensive layout revealed a critical weakness. We had a "dead spot" a mile south of town and a mile north of the Sisters. Mortars from the Sisters could reach that area, but that would mean leaving the south side open. We now had to hope Deputy Sexton's Foo Gas would work. We had few bodies to spare, and all but a few mines had been deployed. sixty tons of weapons seems like a lot, but with the forces we were facing, it was not enough to give us a margin of comfort. Even with plenty of weapons, we still lacked skilled bodies. We'd deployed twenty between the sisters and twenty in and around the town. Three of those were manning "The Thing," and Sarah would be perched on a crown southeast of town. She would have a clear field of fire for her M107 LRSR. Other team members were helping in communications and medical. We didn't have enough, but you work with the hand dealt you.

I'd had too much for one day and was ready to leave when Misha came by to get me. For all the Russian had been through in two days his eyes were as clear as the Texas sky. We reached the front door when we overheard Deputy Sexton talking to Juan.

"They won't leave, Sheriff. I've got Chico and Rosie trying to get through to them that they could be killed."

"And?" replied Juan.

"They're tired of running. This is where they stop. They know we're short-handed."

"But we don't have weapons for them." Juan was sounding exasperated.

"They know. They'll use their own guns."

"John. When it gets dark we won't be able to see them. We could just as easily shoot one of them."

"They know that, Juan. That's why they are going to put silver duct tape on their sleeves, in crosses."

Misha and I headed on out. Those in the town knew we wouldn't shoot them, but that silver duct tape would make them targets for the cartel members. Our hearts were heavy as we drove to the ranch. These people who had lost almost everything to the cartel and fled here, saw others sacrificing themselves. Now they were willing to give the last thing they had, their lives.

I sat on the porch that night, looking at the bright stars, a small glass of Jack Daniels on the table next to me. I'd never prayed before while sipping whiskey, but I felt God was close.

"God, don't let me be afraid," I prayed.

"I won't," was the reply that entered my thoughts. Somehow sleep came easily that night.

It was ten o'clock the next morning before I rolled over. Juan and Misha were gone. When they had left, I hadn't a clue. Today was the day. I put on my desert camo pants, military style boots, and a black short sleeved shirt. I'd brought them because they were good for desert hiking, never knowing they'd come in handy otherwise.

The one way I'd found to be helpful was to wander around observing, asking questions, and then letting my students either comment or ask questions themselves. The questions were not about military strategy. They were personal or spiritual. That was my role, so it wasn't out of the ordinary that I went over when I saw Rick sitting by himself, looking at his smartphone. As I got closer, the concerned look on his face caught my attention.

"Can't get a call out?" I inquired. Cell coverage was spotty in this part of Texas.

Rick looked up. "Jack, I can't do this."

"Do what?" Now I was perplexed.

"All this." He waved his hand around the impound. "This is senseless. This fight is not right."

"How do you mean that? We didn't pick this. It fell in Juan's lap. We're just helping a friend, and people in need." My mind was grasping for what to say. Where could he be going with this?

"The drug war is a farce. Everyone knows that. Let Caesar have this spot. It's time we became honest about the drug trade."

"Where are you coming from? We've got a drug lord coming across the river tonight. If you want to leave, I can respect that. I'll even drive you to Del Rio, and you can catch a plane back to Houston or wherever. Heck, I'll pay for your ticket. But I've got to be here tonight." Where was Rick going with all this?

"Jack, I can't let this happen." A strange look crossed his face. "I've got everything we've done here: plans, weapons, locations of traps, mines, all of it recorded in here." He held up his phone. "One press, and it all goes to my Facebook page and YouTube. I'll do it because this whole situation is nonsense." A sullen look clouded his face.

"What about the butcher of Domingo's family?"

"The old man went across the river. It was his own fault."

Shocked, I kept pressing. "What about Misha's team. I saw their heads on stakes."

Rick's attitude changed to arrogance. "They deserved it. They were mercenaries."

"What about the people who fled the drug wars and came to this town? They're planning on fighting. They're not going to run anymore."

His arrogance was now on full display. "Not our problem," he said as his thumb hovered over the send button.

"Rick, please don't do this. If you do, Juan has to give up our help in defending his county and town. You'll give Caesar intel. He'll sit until we're gone, then cross and kill everyone here."

"Not my problem." His change to personal pronoun said there was more going on here.

I tried again. "What about Hezbollah? You'll be allowing them access to our country."

Rick laughed. "Hezbollah, my ass. That Russian told you that to get in good. It's probably one big story."

I had to struggle to contain my anger. Rick's extreme selfishness was infuriating.

I paused to think, then asked, "Rick, have I ever lied to you?"

Rick looked puzzled now, and not so arrogant. "No."

"Do you believe me when I tell you that in fifteen minutes, I can get you proof of Hezbollah's presence?"

Now he was puzzled and conflicted. His arrogance and selfishness was running into his trust in me.

"Well?" he said.

"Give me fifteen minutes, and please don't push that send button. This is just between you and me. After I give you the evidence, you still want to do this, I can't keep you from it."

My mind was racing. I could get the evidence. That was no problem, but should I tell Juan or Sam? No, I needed to focus on right now. If he was going to do it, there was no stopping him.

He shrugged his shoulders. "Okay."

"I'll be right back." I turned to leave, but thought I noticed movement behind me. Suddenly I felt blinding pain, saw an intense flash, then everything went dark.

CHAPTER 17

The throbbing in my head woke me up, along with the pain in my wrists and ankles. I realized I was in the back of one of the rental vans, bound with plastic handcuffs. Painfully, I raised myself to a sitting position. Thankfully my hands weren't bound behind me and I wasn't gagged.

Rick was driving Highway 90 at close to 90 miles per hour. As best as I could tell, we were headed east, either to Del Rio or San Antonio. I had no idea how long I had been out.

"Did you hit me?" I asked Rick.

"Sorry, Jack. You mean a lot to me. I didn't know if you'd tell the others."

"And the evidence might have made you change your mind.

"Jack, when I joined the military, I was looking for action, and to be honest, girls. But I was good at materiel and supply. I never even shot a gun except the range. So as my time to leave drew close, I wanted to shaft the people…"

"Whom you felt shafted you." I finished the sentence for him. Anger was now overcoming my pain.

"I started releasing little tidbits of info to various blogs." He chuckled. "Suddenly I was important. People were clambering for my work. Then all this fell into my hands and I couldn't let it pass."

"How much have you let out," I demanded.

"You're not my professor anymore. Don't use that tone with me," Rick flashed back.

I told myself to calm down. "Sorry, but seriously, how much?" I was worried.

"I haven't let anything out yet!" His anger was rising, but at whom?

"Rick, were these really necessary?" I raised the handcuffs.

"I didn't know if you'd fight me. Sorry if they're too tight."

I rolled my eyes. This was as ridiculous as it was scary. "I won't fight you, but I do have to pee."

Rick seemed to ignore me. It was then I saw that we had crossed the county line and were heading east toward Del Rio. Good, I hadn't been out all that long.

"Seriously, Rick, I've got to pee. There's a convenience store about five miles from here. I promise you I won't run. Just let me use the bathroom."

Rick tilted his head. "How do you know this stretch of road? I thought you weren't from here."

"We came this way to meet…a friend. He had intel on the cartel." I wasn't going to mention Dmitri. "It was about here the cartel homeys pulled close to us to set off the bomb."

"Bomb?! What bomb?!" Rick almost drove off the road.

"While we were meeting with the informant, the cartel planted an explosive device on Juan's vehicle. Marquis found it and transferred it to the cartel SUV. That dark spot you saw on the road a few miles back was where they set off the device, which, unknown to them, was in their vehicle."

"I didn't know this. Do the others?"

I had him thinking. I had to play this carefully. "Only Sam knows. There was no reason to worry everyone else. There are a lot of things you don't know, Rick. It's not that we withheld it from anyone in particular. It just wasn't something that everyone needed to know." I paused. "Man, I've got to pee." I really meant it.

The Flying K truck stop appeared ahead. Rick pulled in to the side of the building. He came around and opened the van door, then took out a knife and cut my leg cuffs. He stepped back.

"Go."

I sat right there, my anger rising. I turned and looked him straight in the face. Let's get this straight, I'm not budging one bit until you cut these cuffs off me. Then I'm going to the bathroom. You can watch me pee if you wish. Then I'm going to get me something to drink and eat. I'm damn hungry. Then and only then I'll get back in the van with you. I'm sure you left my phone back in San Miguel, but did you at least leave me my wallet?"

"Yeah." He seemed genuinely taken aback by my anger. He cut the plastic cuffs from my wrists.

"Thank you." I rubbed my wrists and got out of the van. I turned and put my hand on his shoulder. He started to jerk back. "Chill," I said calmly. "Rick, I'm going to tell you something else, and I want you to ponder it. Then I'll shut up. Back in town, you said it wasn't your problem, those that fled across the border. Do you know that the illegals who cross into Arizona are sent back across at Presidio, Texas?"

He shook his head.

"ICE and Border Patrol don't repatriate people across the Arizona-Mexico border. If they did, the cartels would kill them?"

Rick's eyes went wide. "Why?"

"Because when they came across the first time, they didn't bring drugs with them. Cartels don't give a second chance. They're butchered as a message to others. You see, Rick, there is a lot you don't know." I turned and headed to the restroom.

Much relieved, I got myself a pack of crackers and a medium drink. I asked Rick if he wanted anything. He shook his head, but I got him a Coke anyway, which he readily accepted. We came back to the van, and he opened the side door.

"Something wrong with me riding up front?"

He just shrugged, so I got in and he shut the door. As soon as the door shut, I saw a .357 pistol pressed against Rick's temple.

"Hands up, and don't move a muscle. You as much as jerk, and I'll remove the top of your head." I could tell Marquis meant every word. Ester moved in to handcuff Rick with real handcuffs. Then he opened the door.

"You okay, Jack?"

"A bit of a headache, that's all."

"I guess we can add assault to kidnapping, unlawful detention, and auto theft. Richard Goldberg, you've got some jail time facing you."

"Hold on for a second, Marquis," I asked. "How did you guys find me?"

Ester chuckled. "Since you almost got taken that night, Juan and Sam thought it best to place a tracking unit on you. I guess you could say we Lo-Jacked you."

"Thank you, I think."

Rick looked surprised and genuinely concerned. "Who tried to kidnap you, Jack?"

"The Santos Diablo, Rick. Because I came to help the people of San Miguel, I'm now a high value target, as is Juan. Our families are under the protection of the Texas Rangers, because we won't run. My life and Ellen's will never be the same again. You see, there's a lot you don't know.

"But why, Jack?" He sincerely wanted to know.

"Because God said to do it, and if my students need assistance, I'll help them if I can. It's called friendship."

Rick dropped his head. Marquis took him to the unmarked unit. Ester was talking to Juan, assuring him of my safety. I asked Ester for the phone. Juan was happy that I was okay, but not about what I was asking.

As I returned the phone to Ester, he frowned. Marquis had just put Rick in the unit when Ester told him what Juan had said. He was not happy. They both looked at me as if I was an idiot. Maybe I was.

Ester took an M16 from the back of the car and put it in the van. He left, headed for San Miguel. I grabbed Rick's stuff and put it in the trunk. Marquis took Rick out and removed the handcuffs. Rick looked at Marquis, then at me. "What are you doing?"

"I'm not pressing charges, and Juan agreed to waive the others. Now get in the back seat."

Confused, he complied. As I started for the passenger's side, Marquis held up Rick's smart phone. "You want this, Jack?"

"Not right now. I'll take it later."

Marquis had been driving for ten minutes. As we entered Del Rio, Rick finally spoke.

"What are you doing and where are we going?"

I turned to look at him. "We're taking you to the airport. I'm going to buy you a ticket to anywhere you want to go in Texas." I turned back around.

"Jack?"

I turned again. "You're giving me pain in my neck to go along with my headache."

"Why? After all I did to you, and threatened to do, why?" He couldn't comprehend what was going on.

"It's called forgiveness."

Rick was quiet when we got to the airport. As we got out of the car, I told Marquis to give him back his phone. He looked at me again as if I was an idiot, and handed the phone to Rick.

Rick put out his hand. "You don't need to go in with me. Thanks for the offer to pay, but I'll do it." He lifted his phone, and pulled up all the information he had gathered. As he scrolled through it, Marquis' eyes went wide. Rick had it all in one folder, ready to send. He looked at both of us, then pressed the delete button. He even rechecked his files, and whatever was left, he deleted that also. Then he picked up his duffle.

"There's a lot of things I don't know. Take care and be careful, Jack. Deputy. He shook our hands and headed for the ticket counter.

"You know, Jack," Marquis said as he watched the young man walk off, "one of these days, your hunch is going to be wrong."

"Yep, I know."

"It could get someone hurt or killed. Possibly you."

"Yep, I know."

"Is that all you've got to say?"

"Nope. I'm hungry. Let's get something to eat. And we're not going to Casa del San Felipe."

Marquis rolled his eyes. "But hey, that was a mighty fine Latina."

"Get in the car."

We hit McDonald's, then headed back.

We arrived back in San Miguel at about 3 p.m. Marquis had strongly suggested that I should get Mei to check me for concussion. Thankfully, I just have a hard head, and there were no signs of anything else.

Mei had prepared as best she could for the night ahead. Devon, an army captain and trauma physician, had assisted, but he would be called on for only the most serious injuries.

"You have anyone helping you in here?" I asked.

"Maria has some training, and Devon will be available," she replied. "Jack, I'm scared."

"How's your Teddy Bear?"

Mei blushed. "He's nervous. He admires all of you; your military training and your calmness."

I put up my hands. "Hey, he has more training than I do. I've just studied a lot of this, and I practice some kendo. I believe it comes down to what a pastor friend of mine said after 9/11: "If it's not on God's timetable, I'm invincible." That doesn't include doing something stupid to test that statement. It's just that I see my timetable as being set by God." I gave her a hug and went to find Juan. He was in his office, so I just walked in.

"Welcome back, my prodigal. What was Mei's assessment?"

"I have a hard head and I'm fine. You Lo-Jacked me."

Juan looked up, smiling. "If you weren't such a problem child, I wouldn't have to do it. Have a seat and rest awhile." I did just that, and promptly fell asleep.

I slept for an hour before Juan woke me. "Hey, sleeping beauty, what are you planning on packing tonight?"

I little confused and still waking up, I asked, "What do you mean?"

"Well, when Caesar arrives, it will be you, me, Ester and Marquis that meet him in the square. All the supporting cast will be in their places. I'll be carrying an M4, two Glocks, and multiple clips. Ester will be carrying that monster shotgun with a thirty round clip and a backup M16. Marquis, aside from who knows how many blades, will have a P90 with an MP5 as backup. So, what are you packing?"

"My Beretta. I didn't think I'd need anything else. I'm better at talking than shooting."

Juan shook his head. "You and I hope we can resolve this peacefully, but we both know that's highly unlikely. If it comes to a firefight, I'll have Marquis toss you the P90 with clips. They're fifty-round clips that snap on the top. The thing is light, but powerful. Its bullets will penetrate most body armor. I'll have Marquis give you a quick lesson."

Ester entered the room. "You rang, boss?"

"I did," replied Juan. "Come on in and shut the door."

As Ester shut the door, Juan got up and unlocked a file drawer. He removed three shirts, tossing one each to Ester and me. They were black, with a distinctive logo on the front.

Ester's eyes went wide. I looked up, humbled. "Is this...?"

"Yes it is," replied Juan. "It's the unofficial logo of the 160th Special Operations Aviation Regiment, otherwise known as 'Night Stalkers.'"

The logo was a pale Pegasus mounted by a Grim Reaper holding a sword. This was set against a night sky background. The horse's eyes glowed red, as did those of the Reaper. A yellow band ran across the top of the logo which read, "Death waits in the dark." At the bottom were the words, "Night Stalkers."

"That saying at the top has a double meaning," said Juan. "The death in the dark could be your enemy's or it could be yours. I'd like you guys to wear these tonight. I saved them for just the right, or maybe the wrong, time."

"I'm honored, bro." replied a proud Ester.

"So you were on that mission in Iraq?" I inquired.

"Al-Kadysha? Yes. Those guys, the 160th, took us in and heaved our butts out. I wish we had them tonight." We all fell silent in agreement.

It was decided that we'd suit up about 8 p.m. There was no need to don all the gear until as late as necessary. We were all in our own worlds. When I glanced at the clock, it said 5 p.m. It was the traditional time for evening mass at Catholic churches. To say the day was already filled was an understatement, but on the eve of a potential battle, before God was a great place to be. I gave that honored shirt back to Juan and told him to keep it until tonight. Something else was more pressing. Juan smiled as if he had read my thoughts.

"I may join you," he said.

"Count me in," added Ester.

With my mind focused, I walked through the building and out across the square. Oblivious to the world around me, I headed for the church. I hadn't been there since Selena's seduction attempt.

CHAPTER 18

With the time established for the meeting with Caesar in the town square, the world felt like it was spinning out of control. Selena's seduction attempt was the farthest thing from my mind as I entered that wonderful place, although I did look twice on entering.

Maria was kneeling in prayer as I entered. She rose and turned. There was no need for an apology for my interruption.

"I knew you were coming," she said. "What other place is there to be on the eve of a battle than before God?"

"You've gotten to know me well. I hear you'll be assisting Mei with the more seriously wounded…" My voice trailed off at the thought of people dying.

She smiled. "In my younger days, I was a triage nurse. Little could I have known that God was preparing me then for this, tonight. Jack, you're bearing burdens you're not supposed to. Come, pray and give those burdens to Christ."

I managed a smile back. "Are you trying to preach, Maria?"

We laughed. God does have a sense of humor. He created this irony: a college professor and Baptist minister praying and sharing burdens with a Catholic holy woman. Yes, God has a sense of humor.

"I only have one request, Jack."

"What's that?"

"Do you mind if I sit to the side and listen to you pray? You have an intimacy with the Lord that I find restful and encouraging."

I was taken aback, not because I wear my faith on my sleeve, but because I treasure those quiet moments of talking with God. But here was a woman whose faith had been keeping God's house ready for someone for years. There was no way I could say no.

"It will be fine."

I removed my camo hat and positioned myself before the altar. I entered the throne room.

"My Lord and my God, I'm scared. From the beginning of all this, You've kept drawing me back to Psalm 43:10, 'Be still and know that I am God.' In that You mean, 'Relax. I've got it covered.' You do have it covered. You've provided us with all the things we need to fight. I'm not a warrior, yet I'm surrounded by warriors. I'm humbled. Lord, help me to relax.

We face evil tonight. You know the intent of Caesar, and Hezbollah. You know their plans. Lord, confuse and confound them. We have used the best plans of men to work the battle, should it come to that, and I believe it will. Daddy, I invoke the words of the prophet Elisha: 'Greater are those who are with us, than those who are against us.'

Would it be so, my Father, that as in Egypt, the Angel of Death would cross through Caesar's camp.

We face what seems to be the worst form of evil.

Hear the cries of the women and children he and his men have slaughtered. Let them not go unavenged.

Daddy, I look at my students and I am both proud and sad. I am proud of their friendship and service. I am saddened that once more they don the armor of war. Some of them do not know you, and I pray for their souls. Draw them to you. For those of us whose names are written in the Lamb's Book of life, may we not fear death, for even in death we are victorious. For those who aren't here; our families, wives, children, parents. Place a hedge of protection around them, and may no weapon formed against them prosper.

Father, grant all of us wisdom: the right decisions, the right words, and the right time to say them. As I look around this beautiful church that Maria has so lovingly kept for You, I ask You to bless her and bless this place with Your protection.

Father, I ask forgiveness for those in our own government, who, for whatever reason, have sought to leave this town and these people to be slaughtered. I ask forgiveness, but I also ask for justice. I ask that they be held accountable.

Daddy, carry me in Your arms. Hold my hand and walk beside me. If I live or if I fall, may Your name be glorified. In the beloved name of Christ Jesus my Lord, Amen."

My solitude was suddenly rattled by a quiet chorus of "Amens." I stood up to look. What had only been Maria and me was now a full church. Students, the sheriff, deputies, townspeople, and even my atheist students were there. They looked expectantly at me. I hadn't planned on a prayer service.

Maria drew close and said, "I think these are appropriate." In her arms were the elements of the Eucharist, or the Lord's Supper, as I was accustomed to call it. She even had the priest's vestments, or whatever they're called. I looked at the vestments questioningly.

"Jack, you are a man of God. It is right for you to don the priest's vestments."

I walked behind the altar table and Maria carefully placed the wafers and the chalice of wine in front of me. I kissed the vestment, and with Maria's help, dropped it over my shoulders and around the back of my head and neck. I then turned to face the people who, at this moment, were my flock.

"It is not unheard of over the millennia, that before a battle, people make peace with their god. What we share today is the Lord's Supper. Jesus Himself instituted it the night before He was crucified. He spoke of the bread as His body, broken for us, and we partake of it in remembrance of Him. This cup of wine, the blood of Christ shed for our salvation from sin, we drink also in remembrance of Him. It is for the healing of His people, His church. I would wish that all of you would partake, but that is between you and God. For those of you who do not believe, I would ask you to accept the mantle of peace we feel right now as those who wish to partake do so."

I now looked at the elements. "Holy Father, Lord Jesus, bless these the bread and the wine to our communion with You, and to the healing of our souls. May You be honored. In Christ's name, Amen."

With that, most of those present came up front. They took the wafer, then drank from the cup. As each one finished drinking, I said the words of blessing, "The Lord bless you and keep you." I couldn't help but wonder who would not be alive tomorrow.

My atheist students stayed in the back, seemingly in deep reflection. Out in the vestibule, Barack had put down his prayer rug, pointing toward Mecca, and prayed. It was beyond words.

As time went on, I realized wafers had changed in texture and consistency. In fact, they looked and smelled like Nilla Wafers. I glanced at Maria and she shrugged. She looked a little sheepish when we finished. I took off the vestments, turned, and said to her,

"Oh taste and see that the Lord is good!"

She stifled a laugh, and punched me in the shoulder. "Shut up!"

"Hey, you work with what you've got." I seriously doubt God was offended. Some of those who were there later commented that those were the best communion wafers they'd ever had. Humor: a bit of lightness in the midst of darkness. How many of those people would be alive the next morning? That was in God's hands. With my unexpected pastoral duties done, I headed off to a shooting lesson with Marquis, a lesson I wished I didn't need.

PART 3

CHAPTER 19

The town square was rigged with cameras and lights. When the meeting went down, all lights would be on. Targets would be easier to predict, but as soon as the shooting started, all lights would be out. Our crew had night vision goggles, so the transition from light to dark would go faster. For Caesar's men, the transition would, hopefully, be confusing, providing an advantage for us.

Sunne had cleaned out her café. Her last meal, hopefully temporarily, would be for us that evening. It was a cornucopia of food with plenty of carbs for a long night. Sunne was hugging everyone, tears in her eyes. She and Byron would go out of town and camp out until it was clear what had happened.

By 8 p.m. our forward teams had deployed, and the Sisters were locked and loaded. Sarah came by and gave me a hug, then grabbed the heavy sniper rifle and headed southeast of town. City Hall had gone from looking like a hacienda to a fortress. When Juan and his dad had expanded and remodeled the place, they had added something becoming common on the coast, Kevlar window shades. While they were quite decorative, they were built to withstand anything a hurricane could throw. Having seen ominous signs across the river even a few years ago, they had decided to install somethinfunctional as well as decorative.

Back in the locker room, we suited up. The newer body armor used was ceramic in its construction. It was lighter, yet harder to penetrate. I put mine on, wishing it wasn't needed. I put on the "Night Stalkers" tee shirt with a sense of honor. A group like that would be handy here. The odds at the Alamo were nearly fifty to one, and ours weren't going to be much different. There were so many intangibles and so many ifs. Too many. It was now 8:30 p.m.

As I passed the conference room, I saw Misha looking intently at our layout. I stopped.

"A penny for your thoughts?"

My Russian student looked at me with a peace in his eyes I'd never seen before.

"We've got a good plan, with the resources at hand. This spot here is my one concern." He pointed to the area south of town and an equal distance north of the Sisters. "It's a live zone, versus a dead zone. They can fall back and regroup, even wait for reinforcements once the canyon fires are out. I don't like it, but you dance with the one who brung you, as you Texans like to say. Another crucial factor are the choppers. Hopefully, Dmitri can at least damage them. The Hind is an especially nasty beast." He smiled. "I've flown them. In good hands, they can be real trouble."

"But we've got the Stingers," I responded.

"*Da*. But only two that work. Use those and our anti-aircraft capability is quite diminished. Jack, I sent five memory sticks to Ellen. If I don't make it through the night, make sure they get to Juan."

I was stunned. "Surely, Misha, you of all people should come through this fine."

Misha chuckled, relaxing. "You are a good man, Dr. Reynolds. But I've learned in battle, nothing is sure except death. I couldn't do what I do if I didn't accept that." He looked at me. "Now just don't do something stupid and get yourself killed. If that happened I'd think you're not as smart as I thought. No, we've got a good plan, good people, good leadership, and you can't ask for much more than that"

"I noticed you didn't say 'luck'. I take it you don't believe in luck."

Misha had gone back to studying the map. "Da."

We'd settled on "Covey" as codename for the city hall/ command center. All in the field would be "Quail", Quail 1 to Quail 20. Sam was Quail 1 or Quail Leader. I was "Doc" (very original) and Juan would be "Justice". Juan joined us at the map.

"Worried about that spot?" He pointed to our area of concern.

"We've done all we can do….Jack, are you ready to meet the Devil himself?"

"You want the correct answer or an honest one?" Both men chuckled. "Honest."

"I'd rather be anywhere than here, but more precisely back in Fort Worth with Ellen…Oh, and by the way Juan, never contact me again for advice."

He laughed.

"You'll do fine, not perfect, but fine. If the shooting begins, just hit the ground and stay there

About that time, Sam radioed that F1, Forward One, had noticed the assault bridge being deployed. The greeting cards were prepared for delivery.

Juan looked at me and Misha. "Showtime!"

"Would 'break a leg' be inappropriate right now?'

"*Nyet*. It would be good as long as you said both arms, both legs, and a few necks, also," Misha intoned. At that, we left.

We would limit the crossing to the initial thirty vehicles, then release the greeting cards. The forward positions equipped with 60mm mortars, easily set up and broken down. The Sisters had the 81mm and the road was all theirs. With the ROE set, it would not be a problem for our people to protect and defend themselves. We hoped.

The news from the river was that numerous Humvees, narco tanks (many mounting heavy machine guns) were coming across and interspersed within were SUV's and pickup trucks (some with modified sides to allow shooting from within). We averaged, conservatively, seven to eight armed men per vehicle. Hopefully we could keep the initial group to about two-hundred soldiers.

As the thirty-first vehicle hit the Texas bank of the Rio Grande F1 and F2 released the greeting cards. Caesar's men were so self-absorbed, and just a little bit high, they missed the distinctive "whoop" of the mortars. The star shell burst took them completely off guard. The sky lit up like Texas thunder storm and darkness became light. Vehicles immediately scattered expecting gun fire, and others on the bridge slammed on brakes causing those behind them to bunch up or try to turn to avoid crashes. The result was total chaos. Ten vehicle wrecked or tumbled into the river effectively closing the bridge, at least temporarily.

The second round of star burst shells spooked the cartel members even more . Shadows became perceived enemies and sporadic gunfire broke out. Men were deployed from the remaining functioning vehicles and fanned out about ten yards along the road. Our teams had deployed anti-personnel mines starting a mile up the roadway, and now they started their welcome to Texas. About the time the last star burst shell went off, the first mine was stepped on. What had been restored to a somewhat orderly deployment went bananas.

A few more mines were stepped on in the confusion, killing not just the unlucky cartel soldier, but anybody close by. A dying mercenary's AK-47 fired as he fell sending a string of bullets into a nearby SUV and igniting its gas tank killing all on board. Initially. the cartel picked up its wounded, but as more mines exploded, and stray bullets found marks, they left the wounded to whatever fate wound befall them. The same happened to those who fell into the scorpion and viper pits. They'd step on the ocotillo falling onto the cactus spines and very angry snakes and scorpions. The cartel members would scream and cry trying get out, poisonous bites and stings everywhere. Others would attempt to help them, only to be bitten, stung, or pulled into the pit also. Finally, if someone fell in, they were just shot then and there Turkey buzzards, despite all the noise were starting to circle in the sky.

Caesar did not seem seriously concerned and the column continued toward the town. Even as they approached and passed the Two Sisters, they didn't seemed concerned, even after finding our barbed wire set-up. They remained alert but never even checked the prominent hill tops. We were monitoring their radio traffic and while anxiety was in the air after our greeting cards, Caesar had the column press on. We did learn that the assault bridge wouldn't be passable for another half hour.

Juan, Ester, Marquis, and I took up our positions on the edge of the parking lot. The two Deputies took up posts about five yards behind us and about three yards outside our line. We wanted a clean field of fire if things went bad. All around the square twenty people were positioned, and our ace was sitting in wait, the "Thing."

Juan sent out six deputies to patrol the county. They vehemently argued to stay and fight if it came to it. They were under strict orders not to get bogged down or engage anyone. They were to report the problem, but remain flexible if they were needed. No deputy wanted to be away, but Juan wanted only his most experienced in town.

"Where's Mike Smith?" I asked about the grizzled deputy.

"Look at the top of the building at out eight (meaning back and to the left). He wanted that heavy fifty all to himself. I'm just hoping he, that gun, and all that ammo doesn't crash through the roof."

Where Mike had made his machine gun post slightly behind a sign and he had a clear range of fire over the entire square.

"It took him the better part of two hours to get all that crap up there and set up," deadpanned Ester.

"He fell in love with that fifty as soon as we unloaded it."

"That's no worse than you cradling that shotgun cannon you got as if it were a fine woman, and you were planning a romantic evening." Marquis chimed in.

Ester gave him that 'I'm going to kill you' look.

"Alright gentlemen. Quit playing firepower envy, and focus on the job at hand." Juan looked at me. "See what I put up with in the best of times."

We both smiled wishing it was the best of times.

""Quail leader, where are Quails 15,16, and 17 located?" I asked.

"Doc, they're located just off the square and ready to go if all goes ape…Once the square is secure I'll send them down the road, where we need to cover that 'live' area." Responded Sam.

"Copy that, Quail leader, Doc out.

Now all we could do was wait.

Between the star shells, bridge accidents, and mines, Caesar's original thirty-one vehicles had been slimmed to twenty. Fifteen vehicles rolled into the square parking lot and the rest were funneled down the road south of town. If anyone had tried coming through the abandoned buildings south of the square they would have encountered several claymore mines. None went off. There was one Hummer conspicuous by all the antennae , leaving no doubt which was the command and communication vehicle.
Juan keyed his radio,

"Mike, see that Humvee with all the antennae. If this goes hot, render it a non-factor."

"Copy." Was the only reply.

The vehicles that rolled in to the square were similar with no distinctive markings to distinguish one from another. In some ways they could have passed for a National Guard convoy in the states, although the narco tanks did look a little strange. But between the Suburbans , Expeditions, Hummers, Humvees, and pickups, lethal as their loads were, maybe the point was to blend in. But for now they were not hiding.

I glanced to see if any laser sights were trained on us, for the moment not yet. Caesar and his lieutenant emerged from one of the lead vehicles. At six feet and two hundred and forty pounds, there appeared to be no fat on the man, it was all muscle. In some ways he almost appeared benign, like a bar bouncer in San Antonio, threatening, yet not. Evil is like a coral snake, alluring , but deadly when it strikes. This was Caesar Cortez.

But it was his lieutenant that caught the eye, Afez el Assad, aka Michael Williams. He stood straight, unlike many of Caesar's men, his eyes darting back and forth. He may have been raised in California, but from the dark tan to the kaffiyeh tucked in around his neck, he fit the image of one gone totally radical. How funny it was that he held the druglord in utter contempt, but he was still Caesar's lieutenant and chief legal adviser. Both men hated each other and only saw the other as a means to an end. Assad was very uncomfortable, while the cartel leader was very much at ease.

"Sheriff, Padre, or should I say Professor Jackson Carson Reynolds, holder of numerous doctorates, and tenured faculty at one of Texas fine universities, and ordained Baptist minister." There was contempt in his voice and it showed we weren't the only ones doing our homework.

"Your greeting, shall we say, was 'interesting'. It just reinforced my understanding that you have my weapons. But I won't hold that against you. It was rather ingenious if I say so myself. I will accept the costs as part of doing business. You do realize the bridge will be cleared and the remainder of my forces will come over. So let us conclude our business before I lose more costly material and you lose your lives."

Juan spoke up, "You said something about having legal grounds for this area."

"Si, Sheriff, you will soon realize all this gunfire and blood wasn't necessary."

Caesar turned to one of his men and spoke in Spanish. "Diego, bring the case quickly."

A squat ugly man reached into the Humvee and hurried up to Caesar with an aluminum brief case. I heard a growl come from Ester. Diego had been one of the men who sadistically brutalized Domingo's family.

"Calm down there big fella. I see him." Acknowledged Juan.

I knew if this thing went south who Ester would be gunning for first. I just didn't know who'd get him first, Juan or Ester. Hell, even I wanted to take out the son of a bitch. Caesar opened case and withdrew a legal folder.

"Your copy." But he stopped before he handed it to Juan. "By the way, how is the beautiful Tabitha? Staying with her family in Houston I presume. River Oaks is a beautiful area. It must pain her to be separated from you and especially the boys. What they find fascinating about shrimping and shrimp boats I fail to understand, but I do love eating shrimp." Caesar rubbed two fingers together as if he were popping a morsel in his mouth.

Pasadena is pretty in the Spring, but not the fishing boats." He paused and looked my way.

"Ah Professor, your wife Ellen is truly a magnificent artist....Her use of colors and texture for fuller depths is far beyond my humble understanding and appreciation. But it is beautiful. Isn't it amazing how so many artists become famous after their demise. I assume Ellen and Ranger Moore have become quite close by now. It is good to have people around when times are 'hard.'"

The threats were pointed. My mind reeled and my stomach tightened. How could Caesar know so much? A glance at Juan revealed only a slight tightening of his grip on the M-4. In my earbud I heard somebody say, "Son of a bitch." Caesar seemed to have all the cards.

What seemed like an eternity went by, but it was only a couple of seconds.

My cell phone went off, "Excuse me while I get this."

Juan looked at me "really" was all his face said. Caesar was truly taken aback and confused. Admittedly I was as confused as anybody. One moment everything I hold near dear is being threatened, but I didn't know anything else to do but answer .

"Jack here."

"I've got the shot Jack. Let me take it." It was Sarah perched on the crown of a hill southeast of town, "Let me blow the bastard's head off."

My mind pictured a fifty caliber round taking off the head of this monster.

"Hey dear, it's good to hear you voice too. Yea, I hate all this stuff also, but everything will work out."

By now everyone is looking at me like I'm crazy. I kept smiling, holding my hand as if to say "give me a minute."

"Damnit Jack. Just give me the word and that bastard won't have another thought, much less hurt Ellen."

Sarah had met Ellen and the two had developed a strong bond.

"Yes honey, I know it's important and critical and you want to do it yourself. It will set for the moment. When I get back we'll start the process and get it done. I love you too, but I gotta go…..Bye." I hung up.

An exasperated Caesar shoved the file toward Juan. He took the file and glanced at the document. He flinched ever so slightly, and then handed it to me. Too many things already had caught me off guard, but this about gave me a heart attack.

The document I saw was on U. S. State Department stationary and carried its seal. It had been prepared at the

U. S. Embassy in Beruit, Lebanon. But it was also signed by the Secretary of State, the Vice President, the U. S. Attorney General, and the President's Chief of Staff. A brief glance revealed that it gave Caesar the right to an area sixteen kilometers by sixteen kilometers, or ten miles by ten miles. He was to meet no state or federal resistance. Our own government had sold us out. I heard Juan swear.

"I can assure you amigos it is quite legal. My own legal staff helped in it's drafting." The cartel leader smiled like a poker player holding all four aces.

"You'll forgive us Caesar if we would prefer our own legal adviser check it over. Seeing that ours is actually an attorney and licensed in Texas. Dominique."

Caesar seemed puzzled by the word "actually."

Dominique came out of the Town Hall took the file and gave it a cursory glance. Her eyes widened .

"I'll be back in five minutes with my opinion." As she turned to head back, I heard low whistle come from Caesar.

"Mi amigos, I must say your legal advisor is much easier on the eyes than mine. If she wants a new employer, I'll be glad to give her an 'interview' and check out her credentials"

He chuckled as did a few of his men.

"She'd cut your stones off and hang them out for the birds to eat." Growled Ester.

"Oh, the slave speaks…Ester Long, Senior Deputy and former NFL linebacker. Tabitha is your sister, no? You must hate not being there to protect her and your family. Your mother's heart condition is not good, si? But since your wife Mei is the doctor here you must feel torn…So much to lose."

Ester started to take a step.

"Deputy, stand down!" ordered Juan.

"Yes, yes, do listen to the plantation master." Caesar looked around amused as he was loving pushing all the button.

"But who is this 'boy' in men's clothes back here?" He spoke to Marquis.

"Sheriff, have you gone to Somalia and hired children to play law?

Marquis didn't move and didn't say a word.

"The 'boy' has no tongue amigos." He chuckled. "Sheriff, you having to hire mutes now?" Caesar laughed as did his men.

"Marquis", Juan broke the revelry.

"Yes Sheriff", Marquis replied in cold tones.

"You want to talk to the man?" Juan was laying a trap.

"Gladly." Marquis didn't move but his words held death.

"Careful 'Paco'… where I come from we take homies like you slice them up and feed them to our pitbulls. The only problem is the 'pits' would get sick and puke you back up…They got better tastes."

Anger flashed in Caesar's eyes. Marquis had the knife in and now he twisted it.

"Remember your 'homies' you sent to take out our people in Del Rio? Well it was this 'boy' who found your toy and gave it back. Yep right up their brown butts. Sad thing was, after the explosion and fire, even the vultures and the bugs wouldn't have anything to do with the bodies. They have better tastes."

I couldn't help but crack a smile. Marquis had humiliated the drug lord in front of his own men. There was rage in Caesar's face and time seemed to stop.

CHAPTER 20

Suddenly the silence was broken by a screaming Selena as she came running from the east side of the square. She looked like an animal. Her hair was matted and wild, her clothes were dirty and ragged, and she had a crazed look in her eyes. She ran up to Caesar. I steeled myself for what might come next.

(In Spanish)

"Kill them! Kill them all! Kill them all!"

Even Caesar was taken aback by wild appearance and screaming.

"My love, kill them in the most horrible and terrible way. I hate them" She spit. Then she pointed a shaking finger at me. "I want his head and his wife's to hang on my wall, and his heart for me to eat."

Selena had definitely had a psychotic breakdown. I heard Marquis on my earbud.

"What did you do to get on her bad side, and I do mean 'bad' side?"

I whispered. "It's complicated, but I can't even understand what she's saying."

Selena was just jabbering and pointing at me with a demonic rage.

"Trust me Jack," said Juan. "You don't want to know.

She was now whimpering on Caesar's shoulder.

"Kill them, kill them all….." was all that came out.

The look on the druglord's had gone from devoid of expression to that of a lover. With one arm he held her and with the other lightly removed her knife

(In Spanish)

"So you want me to kill them my Selena?"

"Si."

"And why would you want me to do that…?"

With a flick of the of the steel blade the top button of her blouse flew off.

"Because I love you." Selena's tone was changing.

Another flick and another button flew off.

"Because I love you and you love me." She nodded.

But Caesar's tone was devoid of emotion. Two more flicks and two more buttons were on the ground. Her black lace bra barely holding her heaving chest was clearly visible. It was like we were witnesses to some sick S and M fantasy being played out before us. Selena hands moved to remove her lover's shirt. Caesar's men had relaxed and watched rapt fascination. This was not an isolated occurrence. It had been played out in front of them many times before. The thought of it was repugnant.

Flick, the bra was now cut.

"And why should I kill them?"

The voice was now cold as an Arctic night.

Her chest was heaving and her groans had grown animalistic.

Breathlessly, "Because you love me." It was child's voice seeking to please.

The blade slid down toward her jeans, but stopped right at her navel.

"I could never love an animal like you."

Selena's eyes went wide with shock, as if a great realization had come to her. A moment later Caesar slide eight of the ten inch blade into her stomach. He then let her go.

Selena crumpled to the ground crying loudly as she tried to remove the object that violated her. I was just about to give Sarah the word to shoot when Maria and Rosie ran in and cradled the wounded woman. Caesar started to move and Juan was ready to give the command to bring hell when Maria stood and faced the druglord like an avenging angel. Her voice was clear, loud, and strong as if God Himself were speaking.

(In Spanish)

"You son of the devil and fortress of evil, you've destroyed enough! You are a cesspool of vipers whose soul was cast off years ago. By He who sets on the throne of Heaven, Jesus Christ, back away or die where you stand. Hear this! Caesar, you will be in Hell by morning!"

Maria then bent back down and with the help of Marquis and others carried Selena to Mei's care.

Caesar's eyes registered fear I'd never seen before. He stumbled backward falling against his Humvee. The faces of his men went ashen, with many of them crossing themselves, as they fearfully looked around. One could only imagine the terror that swept over them. I was reminded of the words of the Old Testament prophet Elisha, "Greater are those that are with us than those that are with them."

I heard Juan say, "Holy mother of God!"

I was brought back to my senses by Sam telling in my earbud.

"Jack, the document is illegitimate. The signatures appear to be authentic, but it lacks a congressional seal and a Presidential signature. The congressional seal is crucial for any treaty giving away U. S. territory. Even with a presidential signature it's invalid without a vote from congress."

"Get me a copy with note in two minutes."

"Copy that!" Sam signed off.

I leaned over to Juan and whispered in his ear in case he hadn't caught what Sam had said. A look of hope spread across his face. Caesar was just about recovered when Dominique handed me the copy with a note as I had requested. Caesar had straitened himself up and bellowed.

"You think some woman spouting some holy words will intimidate Caesar Cortez!.."

His words were there but the voice was shaky, something had rattled his chain. Even his use of the words "holy words" were tinged with fear.

"I will take care of her as I have done so to many priests and nuns." He then noticed the file in my hand. "I see you have the document . I sure you now realize all this area is mine courtesy of the U.S. government.

But I'm a fair man. I'll give you professor the Sheriff and his deputies three hours to vacate the area. BUT the townspeople stay!...Many have come across without my permission. There is a penalty to pay for such insolence." He smiled. "My men will even escort you to the county line. All safe and sound my compadres." His men laughed

Even if the document were legit and we had to leave, we would have never made it out of the county. But now it was our show.

"Caesar," said Juan. "after due inspection of your so-called 'legal' document, put together by your so-called legal adviser, I'm happy to say it is not worth the paper it's written on."

Caesar was dumbstruck. Afaz looked very nervous and Caesar's men seemed confused. The whole premise of their incursion was based on that document.

"You see," I continued, "The document is baseless on several points. Whereas the signers maybe authentic, the document lacks a presidential signature and, more important, congress did not vote on it. It doesn't carry the weight of law, because only congress can approve the dispensing of any American territory to a foreign entity, or individual…Like I said it's not worth the paper it's written on….But then again I'm sure your pseudo-attorney knew this all along. I am right am I not Afaz? Or should I say Michael Williams?"

Afaz was now very edgy, and cringed when Caesar glared at him.

"You see, Caesar, Michael was kicked out of the law school at UC- Berkley for threatening a professor. Oh, we're sure he has very convincing falsified documents proclaiming he's an attorney. But even if he was, he's not licensed in Texas and therefore unable to do a contractual agreement that would be binding in this state.

Someone has played you for a fool. When this document came to light I'm sure you were told not to share it with anyone, and the 'signers' can claim 'plausible deniability' saying the signatures were lifted from other documents. Welcome to the American political and judicial system…What you really need to ask is why was Hezbollah was so eager to get you this 'document?' You see, you and we are the fall guys."

Caesar's face was growing redder with rage. Afaz tried to say something to him, but the druglord snapped at him, and then he ordered his men to surround the "outsiders." Apparently this was the term the cartel was using for their terrorists cohorts.

"Caesar Cortez, as sheriff of this county and leading law-enforcement officer representing both the sovereign state of Texas and the United States, you are accused of of making an armed incursion across state and national borders. You've killed or wounded innocent citizens and destroyed both private and public property....It is you who are leaving. You will either lay down your weapons and immediately return to the Mexican side of the border, or you will be arrested and your weapons and vehicles confiscated...."

Juan's words were interrupted as a livid Caesar made a cutting motion with his hands and a shout,

"Enough!"

(In Spanish)
"Luis, bring me the boy and my machete!"

A man appeared dragging Miguel, Domingo's grandson that Misha had saved. There was duct tape over his mouth and his eyes were wide with fear. His hands were bound with a rope. The man also handed Caesar a machete The blade glistened in the lights of the square. There was no doubt the blade was sharpened to a fine edge, but it also seemed wet and to drip something.

Taking the boy the enraged cartel leader ripped the tape from Miguel's mouth. The boy's scream could be heard to echo around the square. Holding the boy tightly with one hand and the machete in the other, he placed the shiny metal at Miguel's throat.

"Amigos, I grow tired of playing word games. My men already outnumber you and more will be coming across the river as we speak."

It was true. F1 had radioed the bridge was clear and more vehicles were dashing across.

"It is you who will leave or die, and the boy will be first. This blade will not only take his head off, but it is covered with a poison similar to that used by the Aztecs. One nick and the boy dies within moments....This game is over! Document or no document, this town is mine. Sheriff, I will enjoy making you half a man." Caesar then turned to me. "To you professor or padre, I will particularly enjoy hearing you screams for mercy as I place one part of you at a time in container of acid." (Defiantly) "Not even God Himself can keep you from such pain and the sound of my laughter."

I was frozen. All Sarah needed was the word to shoot and this personification of evil would be gone. Caesar realized he'd achieved surprise and leverage. All I could see were Miguel's fear-filled eyes.

"Release the boy, Caesar, and I might shoot out only one eye."

The heavily Russian accented Spanish came from my right. I turned and saw Misha with his Tokarev pistol leveled at the druglord's head.

"But if anybody so much as flinches, it will be your head that splinters."

Caesar sneered, "So the Russian cur comes crawling to the Americanos...Why did I not kill you long ago?"

"Because you couldn't." Replied Mesha in perfect English.

Misha was a good forty feet from Caesar, but everyone one knew he wouldn't miss.

"Answer me a question, Russian. Why did you and your friends leave? I would have made you rich."

"We decided to leave after you decided to incorporate these Hezbollah pigs into your group...Especially when you made this particular sow your lieutenant...oh, and by the way (shouting) release the boy!"

I looked at Afaz and he was glowing with rage. An infidel could call a Muslim nothing worse than a pig or a dog. Afaz had now become the focal point. Caesar was a man that could control himself. Afaz was allowing rage to dictate his actions.

Cortez pushed the boy to the ground.

"Deputy Sexton, come get Miguel," Ordered Juan, and in moments the boy was out of harm's way.

"The child is nothing, but you, Russian, I will enjoy making you scream just like I did with your compadres." Caesar still believed he held the upper hand, and was driving it home. But it was Misha who spoke next.

"My men, except for Nikolai, died fighting, and my guess is when Nikolai died it was a cowardly act by you... I will avenge Nikolai, Ivan, Markov, and Sergey." growled Misha.

Caesar laughed, "You are so frightened you forgot one of your own men."

"Oh, I didn't forget Dimitri....You see he is very much alive and returning the 'gifts' that my men had placed, but Nikolai revealed to you." A wicked grin spread across Mesha's face. Caesar's face registered shock as Misha raised a small radio to his mouth.

"Dimitri?"

"Da."

"Good luck and 'Katia.'" Misha dropped the radio to the ground, its use completed. A moment later the sun rose nine miles to the south as Caesar's base went up in numerous fireballs.

It was a good eight seconds before the roar of the explosions reached us, but in the particular moment all in the square witnessed Caesar's empire disintegrate. Drugs, ammunition stores, vehicles, gas, oil supplies, and drug labs, anything combustible was gone or being consumed. About the only area untouched was the helipads as the birds had taken to flight, bu one of the smaller choppers was a little slow on liftoff and was sucked into a fireball, destroying it and killing its crew.

Caesar was consumed with rage but it was Afaz that reacted first. With a shout of "Allahu Akbar" he raised his AK-47. Misha, ever aware of any movement, shifted and put two bullets in the terrorist's eye socket. He was dead before he hit the ground. But Caesar was unbelievably fast raising his pistol and getting off three shots at Misha. Misha had adjusted and gotten off two before he crumpled to the ground. One hit the cartel leader mid sternum where his body armor kept it from penetrating, but the other came in just under the left clavicle, shattering bone and severing an artery. Caesar had the strangest look on his face. He'd never suffered any injury, but if Misha's bullet hadn't done the job, Sarah's fifty caliber did. Her first shot entered Caesar just right of his spinal column shattering his ribs which in turn sent shrapnel all through his thoracic cavity. The bullet then exited the front of the startled drug lord. Her next shot ended it all as Caesar's head exploded like an overripe melon being hit with a sledge hammer.

As soon as Misha had fired, Juan gave the command and the square became a killing field. Juan grabbed me and threw me to the ground covering me.

"What the hell are you doing? Get off of me." I shouted over the roar of gun fire.

"I'm not about to let you get wounded and have to face your wife. So shut up and fire like we taught you."

The problem was, with Juan on me I couldn't get my Beretta out to fire, but I really didn't need to. The cartel did not expect the onslaught of well aimed high-powered weapons, and had we been concerned about the 10- 15 fighter-filled vehicles just south of the square, we needn't be. Deputy Sexton's idea was working quite well.

CHAPTER 21

After our review of defenses, he had seen the weakness and addressed it with Foo gas. John had gone out around the town and rounded up all the PVC pipe he could find, about five hundred feet. He then had the townspeople assist in drilling small holes every six inches inches. The holes barely went through, and this was critical. John and his gang then buried the pipe along side the side of the road going out of town. There were two hundred feet on either side, buried about three inches deep. The they flared out another fifty feet at a forty-five degree angle with the end capped off. Once that was started, he began making the witch's brew called Foo gas. He combined two hundred and fifty gallons of gasoline, oil, used oil, and soap powder. The viscous material was then poured into a feeder pipe when the cartel reached the parking lot. There were two reasons for waiting this late. One was so that the mixture wouldn't leach out. The second was so the cartel guys wouldn't smell the brew.

At Juan's command, the deputy set off the ignition. Nearly three hundred feet south of town became a literal tunnel from Hell. The flammable mixture burned at somewhere between seventeen hundred and two thousand degrees Fahrenheit, and because because of it's sticky nature it stuck to everything and everyone. Anyone walking within fifty feet of the road had the oxygen ripped form their lungs as the 'poor- man's napalm' consumed it all. If they could still take a breathe, all they got was super heated air which immediately seared their lungs. Those that didn't die instantly would die very soon from asphyxiation and searing pain as their epidermal skin layer was burned off not to mention their eyes cooked in their sockets.

Those inside the fire tunnel went quicker and in just as ghastly a manner. Anything that wasn't metal melted or vaporized immediately. Those inside Narco tanks felt a sudden rise in temperature just before their bodily fluids boiled and the bodies burned like torches. Those outside in backs of pick-ups or SUVs with the windows down went the quickest, never knowing what killed them. The fires were feed by the vehicles themselves. Gasoline and diesel spontaneously went from liquid to boiling to gas to igniting, blowing apart the tanks and vehicles, and sending shrapnel in all directions. Even troops a good hundred feet farther back were knocked to the ground by the concussion. The carnage was also going on farther south.

Mortars from the Sisters rained down on the cartel vehicles and men both north and south. Our teams started rolling down fifty gallon barrels of oil and diesel with C-4 charges attached. This made the 'cleavage' a valley of fire. In Harkell Canyon, when some of the cartel troops sought to flank the town, booby-traps went off igniting fuel oil, claymores, and C-4 charges, turning Mesquite trees and thorns into burning, piercing shards.

On the river our forward units let go with 60mm mortars that straddled, then hit, the bridge. One shot was one-in-a-million hit that went through the top of a packed Humvee and detonated on the bottom plate. The bridge twisted and buckled as it was torn from its moorings on the American side. The Rio Grande had been running strong from recent flooding rains. The bridge finally couldn't stand the strain and rolled over dumping men and machines into the waters.

In the square, everyone was putting their new toys to work. Mike Smith was raking the parking lot with the heavy .50. He made mincemeat out of the communications Humvee. As soon as anyone close tried to raise a weapon, Ester hit them with flashetted shells from his automatic shotgun, usually tearing off an appendage or blowing a hole big enough to see through. It sounded like a cannon behind us. Sarah, from her distant raised perch, took her time before putting a .50 caliber round in to someone. A cartel member or terrorist might take cover behind a Humvee or an SUV, only to have Sarah's round go through the metal like paper. More times than I could count, a terrorist would rise to fire and then grab his face or throat where Marquis had sent one of his seemingly endless supply of blades.

"Damn it Juan! Get off of me. I won't do anything stupid."

"Damn straight you won't, because we're in the middle of full stupid. Anything you do could get you killed. And I'm not facing Ellen." He then rolled over letting loose with another volley from his M-4.

Suddenly, from the west side of the square, the roar of a diesel was heard and out of a side street charged the "Thing". The former eight-wheeled oil field truck came on like a monster. Barach had built a small single man armored gun mounting right next to the driver's position, which was also armored. Barach's 240B SAW cleared a to path for the vehicle. But the real teeth of the "Thing" was the minigun housed in a small turret mounted where the crane used to be. Penny had the rotating barrels spouting fire like dragon's breath. She raked the minigun over the cartel, shredding both bodies and vehicles. Somebody did get a grenade tossed, but it just bounced off and back among the bad guys creating more chaos. A pickup mounting a heavy machine gun barreled in to the square just in front of the rampaging "Thing." Barach tore it apart with the SAW and Jonas just gunned the beast and and it literally rolled right over the demolished pick-up.

Once it had crossed the square Jonas turned the behemoth around to once again continue the carnage. An RPG flew toward the "Thing" but it cleanly passed between the turret and the driver's cab. The man who shot it was rewarded by being shredded by Penny's minigun.

Action was going on everywhere, and anytime Juan and I tried to move to the cover of the masonry fountain, bullets licked the ground around us. I looked to my right and saw a terrorist fighter aiming an RPG our way.

"Juan! RPG at 2 o'clock!"

The former Ranger rolled and sent a short burst into the gunner. As the terrorist fell, the RPG arched skyward seemingly headed directly for the City Hall. Fortunately it missed the main part of the building but slammed into the the northwest corner, the jail cells. Javier had now received punishment for his treachery, the rats being the least of his worries. The Hezbollah fighters were no longer hiding their Keffiyehs The black and white design was quite easy to make out by the numerous fires in the square. Another fighter came running for us from the left, but he suddenly grabbed for his throat as another of Marquis' blades found a target.

Several times I saw a person ready to fire only to grab their face as if to pull something from it. Their distracted moment allowed a bullet or shotgun shell to end their existence. It's amazing what goes through your mind when life hangs in the balance What were these guys grabbing at? I momentarily removed my NVG's to scan the square and saw a fleeting dark shadow run across.

"Damn!" I thought. Even Pancho Villa had joined the fight. God bless that cat.

South of town two Stinger missiles arched into the sky. They appeared to hit each other, but such was not the case. The cartel's remaining Hughes Defender had crossed the river and was heading north to the fight in the town. But its pilot hadn't realized we had surface to air missiles, and so he flew straight not moving around to be harder to hit. The missiles came from the Sisters, one from each peak, and impacted the chopper at the same time resulting in a fireball. For the moment we ruled the skies.

Ester had dropped to one knee as he continued firing the massive shotgun. When the firing stopped we looked back. Ester had emptied two thirty round drums and he'd discarded the shotgun to go to his M-16. Suddenly the big deputy cried out in pain and fell to ground clutching his side. Several rounds, possibly Teflon coated, had caught the seams on the side of his body armor and penetrated. The way he was flinching and cursing meant it was bad.

"Marquis!" shouted Juan.

"I've got him boss...Jack, take these and use them."

I reached out and caught the P-90 with five more clips tied in a bundle.

"Can you use that thing?" Juan looked at me.

"Just watch!" I rolled over, slide the safety off, and sent a burst under the vehicles in front of us. Several fighters rose up to avoid my shots, only to be taken out by Juan.

"Not bad for a rookie." My former student gave me a quick smile. "But if we don't find cover we won't be around much longer to compare totals." he added.

Juan was right. For all the carnage and destruction in front of us, the remaining cartel and terrorists were turning their attention on us. A bullet hit close to us and Juan groaned.

"You hit?!" I yelled.

"It hit the ground and then my armor. But damn it hurts." he was gasping for breath.

I looked around, for all the world feeling very helpless.

Out of the darkness another loud diesel sounded. The department's big F-250 Super Duty came barreling out from behind City Hall. It made a sliding turn, bounced onto the square and stopped right in front of us. Chico jumped out of the cab.

"Need some assistance?"

"Damn straight." I yelled.

We both grabbed Juan and hightailed for the fountain. We just made it behind the fountain when an RPG tore into the Ford, making it scrap. I hit the ground, almost landing on Ester. Marquis had been unable to get the wounded deputy inside due to heavy fire. Now, with the truck being a distraction, Marquis grabbed Ester and moved into City Hall. Gun fire was coming from the wrecked trucked when Juan landed next to me. Chico hit the ground hard next to Juan. Juan looked at me and gave me a high-five and then turned to do the same for Chico. But Chico was gone. His lifeless eyes stared straight ahead, and small trickle of blood wept from his mouth. For both of us everything stopped. Had it not been for the bravery of this young deputy, Juan and I could have been dead by now. Tears burned our eyes. Juan would have gladly traded places with his deputy. Juan gently closed Chico's eyes, kissed him on the forehead, and then crossed himself. He then reached in his vest and pulled out a frag grenade.

"This is for you, mi amigo."

Juan pulled the pin and tossed a perfect arc, the grenade landing just past the F-250, exploding just as it landed. Screams were heard as it went off and ignited diesel fuel. He then let loose with a full clip from his M-4. He was down to two clips and I was down to one.

Chico was dead. Ester was badly wounded as was Misha. Once Misha went down he lay there in the square for a few moments until Zack came running out and grabbed him by the collar. "Damn Russian" was all I could hear Zack say, and then he went down shot in the knee. Two others had raced out and pulled them to safety. But we were losing people. All around the square lay bodies with silver duct tape crosses on their sleeves. Simple people who wouldn't run anymore. And then it got worse.

The comms came to life.

"They've got another assault bridge....Damn it, they've got another assault bridge!... Instructions!"

Another assault bridge Why hadn't Misha noted that?

Sam was on the radio, "Do you have anymore 60's you can drop?"

"Negative, repeat negative." was F1 and F2's reply.

Juan came on, "Sam, have them bug out of there....'Alamo' I repeat 'Alamo.'"

"Copy, F1 and F2 'Alamo' repeat 'Alamo' and good luck."

"Copy Quail Leader, take care of yourselves."

"Quail Leader , this is Doc. How are the Sisters on hardware?" I steeled myself for the answer I knew was coming.

"Doc, bullets and grenades they got but nothing heavier. The store is running out."

What had seemed to be momentum on our part had totally vanished. Ammo was running low and casualties were multiplying. Juan looked at me and keyed his radio.

"Quail Leader start removing the wounded. Evacuate as many as you can to the airfield. Do you copy?"

There was a long pause.

"Quail Leader do you copy?'

"Justice, we cannot repeat cannot evacuate. That RPG that hit the jail sent shrapnel in to the bus. Radiator, belts, hoses, and power steering were shredded... The pick-up we're going to use ......"

Juan cut him off, "It was the one Chico used to save our butts."

"Roger that...sorry."

Juan switched frequencies. "Sheriff to all deputies, fall back to the town ASAP. We've got a town to defend and casualties to protect. Juan out!"

There was moment of silence between Juan and myself. We knew the odds were long, but we really thought we might pull it out. We were at our low point when the bottom really dropped out.

"Quail Leader, this is F2, the Hind is on the loose, repeat the Hind is on the loose....Good luck guys, we're bugging out."

"Copy F2, Godspeed," replied Sam.

"Doc, Justice, you heard."

"Affirmative Quail Leader." The knot in my stomach grew much tighter. The Hind was flying tank.

"Quail Leader, do the Sisters have anything they can throw at that bird?"

"Negative, and the 'Thing' is down to three tires. It's mini-gun could work, but they'd be a sitting duck."

"Doc, Justice," it was Penny, "I know what this gun can do to that thing.....we'll hold.."

Juan cut her off.

"Can it!?....You are a target and pretty much a stationary one."

"But we...."

"No buts!....Get out and abandon the vehicle...'Alamo' is in effect for you also.....Don't try to be heroes!

"Copy...bugging out."

Juan and I looked at each other and suddenly had the same thought, the Sisters. Sam was thinking the same thing.

"S1 and S2 abandon your position, repeat abandon your position....'Alamo' in effect...Set your charges and move..You are prime targets."

Silence, and then rockets and cannon fire were heard. The western big sister went up first, like a volcano. It was only moments later the eastern little sister followed big sister. Had they gotten off? The radio crackled.

"Sorry Quail Leader, we were ahead of you. We've pulled back but left calling cards. It appears our uninvited guest found them."

"Did the bird get damaged by the blast?"

"Negative...This guy stood off and fired. I'd say Misha trained him well."

Copy that." replied Sam.

Suddenly tracers laced upward from south of town toward our demon.

"Damn it! Was Juan's reply.

"Penny get your butt out of there before we have to pick you up in baggies."

The firing stopped but moments later the Hind's guns tore the 'Thing' to pieces. We could only hope she made it out safely.

Sarah came on,"Guys, looks like the Hind is headed your way, and I'm now hearing cheers from that 'live area' north of the canyon. The bad guys are regrouping to move on the town. You'd better get out."

"Copy," we all replied.

CHAPTER 22

There was only one problem. There was no way to "get out." Already the Hind was chewing up the south side of town, destroying what little was left. Mike let go with the heavy .50. It was a gun that could damage this bird, but the pilot was good and immediately started shifting faster than Mike could adjust and re-aim.

"Get off there now!" Juan yelled into the radio. The firing stopped, but the death angel had found his target. Two mini-rockets and machine gun fire reduced the store to a pile of ruble.

The sound of the Hind's twin turbines and rotor blades filled the square. It was like an enraged beast determined to destroy any life it could find. I can't describe the way we felt hidden behind the fountain. At any moment, the Hind would open up on the City Hall making it rubble and killing everyone in it. I took out a small note pad scribbled a message and handed it to Juan.

"Don't ever ask for my advice again." it read.

He read it, chuckled, and yelled, "Maybe."

"Will this guy get it over with and stop stalling." I said to no one in particular.

Juan and I peaked over the top of the fountain grateful for the moments reprieve. The big helo was hovering south of the square, yet he was rotating as if to find something. It was Sarah. I saw sparks jump as she tried to find a vital point on the Hind. But soon it would either go after her or just return to destroy the town... we thought.

Suddenly the air was filled with a ripping noise as four missiles came in from the north. Sarah's distraction had kept the pilot from seeing the smoke trails racing toward him until the last second. He responded by yanking the big chopper up, but instead of the missiles hitting the turbines they tore into the twin cockpits. The Hind continue to rotate going inverted, before it hit the ground in a massive explosion.

New sounds now filled the air as multiple choppers screamed in from the north. Four AH-6's, armed "Little Birds" crisscrossed the square. Six MH-6's carrying troops swooped in disgorging their contents by rope just outside the square. Other MH-6's, snipers perched on side pods, crisscrossed the town looking for anything that tried to respond. If something did, it didn't again. Heavier blade sounds now came across, three MH-60L's DAP Blackhawks charged south like wolves after prey. They were immediately followed by an AH-60 or S-70 Battle Hawk, and this hawk was going to destroy anything it wanted. The Hawk's chain guns seem to literally rip the air. It was a sound I'd never heard before. It was magnificent. A Blackhawk rotated in and touched down in the impound lot. Seconds later it was off and more Blackhawks dropped heavily armed troops east and south of town. Now the ground began to shake as six MH-47 Chinooks flew over heading south...the cavalry had arrived.

"Hot damn!" shouted Juan. "Now that's what I like."

Moments later footsteps ran toward us. We turned, guns ready, a soldier raised his hands and knelt down next to us.

"Captain Manuel Sabine, Texas National Guard Special Forces. The Governor thought you could use some help....Are you Sheriff Cordova?"

Juan nodded and slapped the Captain on the shoulder. There were no words we could say. The Captain read our faces.

"It's our job now. What do you need from me and my group?"

Juan seemed at a loss for words. He really didn't know what to do next.

"Go, go, go and take care of home base." I gave him a shove.

He gave me a quick smile and left with the Captain and his squad. I was suddenly alone. After a night of chaos and people I was by myself. For the next fifteen minutes I waited, watched and listened. There seemed to be fire fights all the way to the river nine miles south. The evening had been a cacophony of emotions from anxiety, to fear, to excitement, to dread, to hopelessness, to elation. For the moment I didn't know what to do.

I looked at my cell phone and thought about calling Ellen to let her know I was okay, but something told me not to. I looked at my watch and it was 2 am. We'd starting talking to Caesar at 11 pm, and now three hours later the Santos Diablos was history. Hezbollah's incursion into the U.S. was stopped before it could get started. A lot had happened in three hours.

I pulled myself upon the lip of the fountain, set down the P-90, and removed the NVG's from around my neck. My eyes continued to adjust to the the darkness. The only lights came from the fires in and around the square. Vehicles were destroyed or burning, buildings reduced to rubble or damaged beyond repair, and the bodies. The cost of victory had been steep..very steep.

A scream, or something like it, carried in from southeast of town. I surely doubted any coyote would even be near, so I let the thought pass. I left the P-90 on the fountain as I got up and walked back toward the square. Pausing, I picked up Chico's Glock .45 from his hand. He'd never need it again. The young deputy looked as if he was asleep. I prayed he was at peace. Telling Sarah was not something I looked forward too.

I pulled the bolt back to make sure a round was in the chamber, caught the one ejected, released the clip, reloaded the shell, and returned the clip to the gun. My own Barreta was still securely in it's holster. Even the snap was still in place. Walking toward what was left of the F-250, I noticed something on the ground. It was a snake stick. Many of the deputies kept four to five foot walking sticks in the their vehicles. If you needed to check out something in the bushes or cactus, you didn't use your hand. Thorns, snakes, or some other critter might not like your intrusion, hence the snake stick. This particular stick was four feet long and had the same weight as my bokken, a wooden sword used in Kendo.

Handling the stick loosely with my left top two fingers and using my right hand for direction, I was back in the dojo. Kendo toned the mind and body. It, at least for the moment, took my mind off the destruction around me. Almost imperceptibly, there was the noise of gravel moving to my left. My grip tightened. Turning, I brought the stick around by instinct. A groan was heard as well as the breaking of bones. My would-be assailant's knife flew off into the darkness. There before me was a very shocked Hezbollah fighter, his Keffiyeh plainly visible. Instinct was in full play as I brought the stick back, hitting the terrorist in his right temple. The blow stunned him. White hot rage flew through me as I came back again to deliver a blow to the left side of his head. I let the stick go, and with my free right hand, pulled out my Air Force survival knife. With my left I grabbed the terrorist and jammed the entire blade of my knife up through his jaw and into the brain, twisting it as I did. I'd literally lifted the man off the ground with the blow. He struggled only for a moment and went limp.

"How dare you try to kill me." I whispered into dead eyes.

Pulling my bloody knife from the body, I wiped it on the dead man's clothes and returned it to its sheath. Everything was on automatic now as I pulled pulled Chico's Glock from my vest. All movement and all sounds were being analyzed. My peripheral vision picked up something to my right. Turning, I braced the Glock in my left hand and squeezed off two rounds. At almost the same moment, I saw several quick flashes and a semi-truck slammed into my body with red hot searing pain tearing through my left arm. The gun went flying and I was on the ground trying to breathe, crying, and cursing all at the same time. Waves of pain overwhelmed my brain making me forget another shot could be coming. It didn't, but it might have been a relief to what I was feeling.

My right hand went to my left arm and it felt something wet and warm. It hurt too much to touch, but now my hand was covered with blood.

"Is this what it's like to die?" I thought. "Ellen is going to be so pissed that I got killed."

Funny thoughts go through your mind when you think you're dying. I heard voices, probably coming from my radio. I crawled toward the fountain. It hurt so bad, more waves of pain flowed over me.

"God, you didn't say it would end this way." were my thoughts. "I'm tired, so tired. I just want to sleep....Ellen is going to be so upset with me."

I curled up on my right side and the darkness came.

In the thirty minutes or so since Juan had left much was going on inside. The TNG Special Forces came in with their commander and a brigadier general, they plus ten other men, were being briefed by Juan.

"That's the basics as of now, let me introduce my logistics and tactical adviser..."

"What the Hell?" said the Colonel. "Sam? Sargent Major Samuel Lawrence. Why am I not surprised to see a son of a bitch like you in the middle of this."

"Colonel Travis! I never thought I'd see you again, but just the same I'm not telling you to leave. You saved out butts. ..Sir, we have friendlies out there, all the way to the river."

"It's covered Sargent, we've got your people painted."

Sam was worried. To "paint" someone usually meant targeting them.

"You need to remember this isn't my first rodeo. We've been watching this thing unfold for almost four hours. You guys have friends in high places. A Predator drone has been on station catching the whole drama on camera. The Governor's office and DPS got the feed and therefore we did.

We know the bad guys and are taking them out.... Sheriff, what were your ROE's?"

"Colonel, if they surrender cuff them and if they don't, kill them."

"Good enough for me." replied Colonel Travis.

"Sir," it was Sam. "The assault bridge?"

"Don't worry, that's the primary target of the Battlehawk...Not a bullet will cross the Rio Grande...Sam, Sheriff this General Jim Spivey. If it weren't for him we'd be sitting on our hands at the airstrip, and you would be...dead."

Sam saluted and then shook the General's hand.

"Glad to meet you sir, but what does the Colonel mean?"

General Spivey shrugged his shoulders," It's complicated. By the way, is there a Dr. Jack Reynolds close by?"

"Yes General, I'll...."

Pistol and automatic weapons fire echoed into the City Hall and everybody flinched.

"Damn it!" It was the Colonel. "Sargeant, I thought the square was secure. Get it done!"

The Sargeant and four others headed out. Everybody eased up.

"Sheriff, wasn't Jack with you? The General was asking about him." It was Sam.

"Yea, we were hunkered down by the fountain when you guys rolled in. He told me to get in here with Captain Sabine, and I left him.....The gunfire, the square!... He's still out there!"

Juan bolted for the door yelling for Marquis. General Spivey and Sam followed. Sam was yelling into his comms.

"Jack..Jack.. do you copy?!" Silence.

Sam joined the group at the fountain. Juan was staring at the spot where he left me.

"He was right here when I came in...Marquis, Sam spread out from here and find him." Juan was near frantic. "I shouldn't have left him."

As they fanned out Marquis was the first to find something.

"Sheriff! Look at this. I don't remember this guy being here..this close."

He bent down to examine the dead jihadist. "Damn, whoever killed him did it well. It was a knife through the jaw and into the brain, If it was Jack, there's a side to him we didn't know about."

"Look at this." It was General Spivey holding up a wicked dagger, not unlike what ISIS used when beheading people. "It was his." He nodded toward the dead terrorist.

"Jack was in hand to hand combat, but where the hell is he." Sam was calling everyone back in focus. It was then Juan found the snake stick. There was blood on the end.

"Jack took Kendo, and it looks like he used it." General Spivey glanced around. "But Jack, where are you?"

Marquis moved to the east side of the square, everyone had their flashlights out now. A prone figure caught his eye.

"Juan, Sam, General Spivey, I've got a dead Hezbollah guy here. Two rounds dead center in the forehead." He reached down and felt the barrel of the AK-47. "AK is still warm. This had to be the weapon's fire we heard. Damn, Jack, where are you?"

Juan then noticed a pistol on the ground by itself. He did a quick check.

"This is Chico's Glock and it's been recently fired. The last time I saw was in Chico's hand when we..... Jack had to have used it."

Shining his light back toward the fountain, in the shadow of the lip of the fountain he saw a prone figure. "He's here guys!"

Juan, Sam, and General Spivey sprinted to the fountain. Marquis shook his head and just mumbled.

"No, Lord no."

The General and Sam got down close to the very still body. They both noticed a soft noise coming from the prone figure. General Spivey had a quizzical look then started to chuckle, the other men seemed stunned at the General's reaction.

"It's Jack alright....He's sleeping. I know this guy. He can sleep anywhere. He's wounded though. Sam, help me to get him sitting up where we can check him."

Gingerly, both men got me upright, and then saw the blood, a lot of blood covering my upper body.

"Get medics out here with a stretcher! Tell Devon we've got Jack and he's wounded." roared Sam over the comms.

Sam touched my left arm, and with a quick breath, I was back among the living.

I had been in my own dreamworld, which was really more of a nightmare. I kept wondering when Heaven would appear. I heard people calling my name, but I was too tired to answer and just wanted to sleep. My dream world evaporated when Sam touched my left arm. I woke up, agitated and fearful, eyes darting back and forth, waves of pain rolling over me, and breathing rapid shallow breaths.

"Calm down, Jack, it's Sam. We got you now...Where are you wounded?...You had us scared to death."

My agitation seem to grow when a long familiar voice touched my mind.

"Calm down big guy....You're among friends....Try to slow your breathing....You're in good hands."

My mind continued to lock on to that soft familiar voice. A friend.

"Jim....Jim Spivey, what are you doing here? Tell me I'm not dreaming."

"You're not, my friend, but you're hurt pretty bad. We need to get you inside for medical treatment." He put a light hand on my uninjured shoulder. "How I got here can wait for a little bit....Guys, handle him carefully."

A medic had arrived and three Guardsmen put me onto a stretcher. The medic kept checking me all the way into the City Hall. Everywhere had been turned into a medical center. Devon Akers met us at the door.

"Medic, what have we got? Get me an I.V. started over here. Put him on the table."

"Preliminary check shows a through and through to the left arm. But I think he may have several shots to the left upper chest area," was the medic's report.

"Have you done any morphine?"

"No sir, not knowing the full extent of the wounds."

"Good, but have me 2cc's ready to go when I ask."

"Copy that sir."

"Sam, Juan, help me get his body armor off, carefully. Jack, this is going to hurt, but I don't want to give you anything until I can fully see the extent of your injuries."

CHAPTER 23

Sitting me up, Sam and Juan started removing my gear. Every movement brought more waves of pain, my eyes wide open. Juan was trying so hard he was having trouble. Jim stepped in and took over. They got the body armor off, but Devon looked quickly at Juan.

"Did you double vest him?"

"Yeah I did.... I didn't want to take any chances..."

"You did good brother. We got three rounds to the left and upper quadrant. One vest might not have stopped them. Scissors... we got to get this shirt off...It's a wonder his heart didn't stop beating from the impacts."

I mumbled, "Not the shirt. It was a gift."

"I'll get you another. Cut it." said Juan

When they cut the shirt off everyone either turned their heads or their eyes went wide. Only Jim kept a calm face.

"What? I moaned.

Marquis was the only one who said anything. "Jack, if your chest and shoulder were any darker, you'd be darker than me." No one smiled.

"Devon?" I asked.

"Tell him," said Jim, "or he'll just keep on asking."

"Well Jack, from your waistline up to your neck and

shoulder, and over to the sternum you've got a massive contusion, a very big deep bruise. Even if there is no lasting tissue damage, the ribs are probably bruised also, a subperiosteal hematoma.. You're going to hurt for a month or more...With what I gave you, is the edge coming off the pain?"

"It is, Devon." I was breathing easier. It was then I notice nearly everyone in the triage area was looking at me. I then caught a glimpse of myself in a mirror. "Oh my....." My head suddenly became foggy and things started going blurry. I slowly fell back on the table.

"BP's dropping fast Doc." It was the medic.

I vaguely heard Devon giving commands to raise my feet and bring some kind of panel to shield me from the rest of the triage and concerned eyes, and then I was out. When I did return to the land of of lights and sounds, I heard the medic say I was coming to. Jim Spivey's face was the first I saw.

"Are you through trying to die on us? Welcome back."

"How long?"

"About thirty minutes. It was long enough to get your wound cleaned, stitched, and bandaged. You had us going when your BP dropped."

"It sometimes happens after extreme stress situations, and I caught a look at my bruise."

"You did lose a lot of blood, and were lucky we had your type, kinda rare."

"I know....Jim, I had to kill tonight...I've never done that before."

"Did you enjoy it?"

"What?"

"Did you enjoy it, killing someone?"

"No! I didn't think I'd have to."

"Good...It's okay my friend. It was kill or be killed, and you handled yourself well. Just because you and I are ministers doesn't make us exempt from defending ourselves or others...It's just harder to get past, and you are wounded and traumatized."

I still hurt for the killing even though my friend was right. I tried to raise myself up.

"Now where do you think you're going?"

"These are my stu....friends and I need to check on them."

Jim pulled up a chair and sat down next to me. "They're your former students...I know. The Colonel doesn't and I'll keep to to myself...But you should..."

"What Jim? And thanks for not telling the Colonel...Yes these are my students and they came to help....But God in Heaven how many did we lose?...I've got to check on them." Jim assisted me to stand It wasn't easy.

"Jack, you shouldn't be up." It was Juan. "But I can tell you're not going to stay....Let me get one of Ester's t-shirts for you You're attracting attention. We need to put it on and cover that..(he shook his head) It hurts me to look at it."

Putting on the shirt took about five painful minutes, and I was under strict orders from Devon to go slowly and sit down whenever I could. But first I needed to be updated on our casualties. I had seen numerous townspeople lying dead in the square. They had to flee, but no more. Now would never have to flee again.

"As to your question, we took it pretty hard." Juan fought to compose himself. "Chico's gone. Rosie and Ester have been medivaced to San Antonio. Mike, Ramon, Larry, and John have various injuries, some more serious than others, but none life-threatening. We lost at least thirtty townspeople."

"What about Penny? Did she get out of the Thing?"

He shook his head. "She barely cleared the vehicle when it was attacked. Barach and Jonas stabilized her as best they could. She's in serious condition from shrapnel, the concussion, and several bullet wounds. Right now it's touch and go. TNG's trauma surgeon is stabilizing her for transport."

Rosie was on my mind as I made my way to see the wounded. Rosie was back here. What had happened?

The first person I saw was Zack. His shattered knee was heavily bandaged. He'd limp the rest of his life.

"Hey, my man, thanks for coming after Misha. But why? I didn't think you really cared for the guy."

Zack gave me a questioning look. "Just because I don't like someone doesn't mean I don't care. I couldn't leave the guy out there, although my knee would probably disagree. But I had to get him after what he did to that Hezbollah bastard....Damn Russian." And with that the pain meds took over and Zack drifted off.

There was a bunch of activity around a table. Medics and doctors were trying to help the individual, but there was resistance. I saw that the curled up figure was Sarah. I got the docs attention and leaned over our heroic sniper. She was in a fetal position and whimpering. A TNG corporal stood guard at the head of the table. Doctors told me she was shot in the leg, but she wouldn't let them cut away the pants. I got a chair and sat down next to her.

"Sarah, Sarah, it's Jack. These doctor and medics need to treat you." She just shook her head and curled up tighter. The corporal motioned me to the side. "What happened?", I ask.

"Sir, she's every bit a warrior. My squad was working our way up to her position. She was firing and we saw no reason to stop her. Then the rifle stopped, but we heard a pistol fire, and muffled yell, and then a fight. We rushed up to her position. One of the goons had circled behind and come up on her. He shot her in the leg, kicked the rifle away, and straddled her."

"Oh my Lord, no wonder....."

"No sir, he never got a chance to. Apparently as he was trying to....Sir, I got a wife the same age....Well, in his haste, he let go of one of her arms. She got her knife out and gutted him like field dressing a deer. He let out this ungodly yell, and was rolling on the ground trying to hold his guts in. He died quickly, but she's a fighter. If you don't mind I'd like to keep watch on her."

I knew this corporal would not leave her side.

"Sarah, it's Jack. You're okay and safe here. You even have your own personal guard. Let the medics take care of you."

She had stooped moaning and opened her eyes to look around, and then she looked at me. "You're wounded."

I had to smile at that. "Yea did something stupid and got wounded, but you kept that Hind preoccupied. You did great...Now let them take care of you."

"I want to see Chico first." She looked around. "Where is he?"

Now was my turn to hurt. All I could do was shake my head. She started to shake her head and mumble "No."

"He saved Juan and me. He was as brave as you....He'd be proud of you...Now please let these people care for you."

Slowly the child/woman/warrior uncurled and they were able to treat her. As I looked up, another sheet was pulled over someone. I made my way to the clinic where the most serious had been brought. Only one body was there, it was Misha. Mei was curled up in a ball in the corner. Shock had overwhelmed her. Maria gave her an injection and cradled Ester's wife. I moved to Misha's side where I was joined by Devon. "How bad?"

Devon just shook his head.

"We're trying to relieve the fluid build up." He nodded toward a jar filled with reddish fluid. "There was massive internal damage and resulting bleeding. The bullets were only slowed by the vest and shattered as they entered the chest area...I'm astounded he's still alive.. Its' like he's fighting to stay alive to see someone. Probably you."

"Why wasn't he medivaced in the first group? " I demanded.

"He wouldn't let us. I'm sorry. We've done the best we could." Devon shrugged.

"I'm sorry Devon. I know everyone did their best. Forgive me." Misha started to move, so Devon left us.

"Jack?" he opened his eyes. They were still bright but tired. I don't think his skin could have gotten any paler.

"I'm here." I gently took the Russian's hand. He looked at me and smiled a weak smile.

"Did you go and do something stupid?"

"Yea, I did," I could hardly bear the grief I felt. "I'm sorry my friend. I never wanted this...I."

Mesha's hand tightened.

"Did we win?'

"Yes we did.

"Good." Hid breathing was becoming more labored.

"Jack, thank you for being a friend....and you too." Maria had joined us.

"I just regret I didn't get to see Ellen."

"I'm sorry." I said again.

"Nyet, don't be..." he smiled. "I'm home. My friends and God brought me home. I'm happy and at peace, and I'll soon be with Katia and Peotr."

Juan joined us. He was fighting a losing battle at holding the tears in. Misha looked at him.

"It was a pleasure fighting beside you, Captain. Take care of your town."

"The honor is all mine Major. This town will always be your home." With that Juan turned away. Misha looked at me once more.

"Thank you for everything. " With that my friend, my student, my child went home to be with God.

We were quiet for a while, when I felt a hand on my shoulder. It was Jim, watching me as only a friend could.

"Yours?"

"A student of mine from early in my career."

"Spetnaz?"

"Long story that I can't talk about right now."

Jim squeezed my shoulder turned to Misha and gave last rites. Aside from being a Brigadier General, he was also a chaplain. I turned to Juan.

"Can you take care of Misha? Trying to explain a Russian Spetnaz officer to...."

"We got it Jack. Misha is..is...is our home boy now. The Colonel won't know."

"I found a chair and sat down wondering how many more of "my kids" had gone down, or were seriously wounded. Maria sat down beside me, eyes red from crying.

"What's the story on Ester and Rosie?"

"Ester was the worst. Mei stopped the bleeding but he'll still need major surgery for the shattered ribs and much rehab for the chest muscles."

"What about Mei?" I nodded toward the sleeping figure on the floor.

"She's a trooper," answered Maria. "It was only after Devon came in with the Guard docs and medics the full impact hit her, and the shock set in. I gave her an injection of a sedative laced with Valium. She sleep for a while."

I looked at Maria questioningly. "Is that concoction legal or safe?"

"Legal, no. But administered correctly it allows the trauma patient the ability to rest and start to recover."

"Rosie?"

"She thought she heard something out back and went to check. We heard a single shot, but not from her pistol. Pancho Villa had been in here with Misha and he raced out of here like his tail was on fire. We then heard two more shots. Those were from Rosie's gun. Apparently that bas... person thought he'd killed Rosie. His shot to her shoulder area did a lot of muscle damage, but it wasn't a kill shot. She recovered and killed him, not that Pancho Villa left much of his face intact." She chuckled and smiled. "She left a message for you."

"What?"

"I killed him, I killed him good....Now mind you she was pumped full of morphine."

I tried to chuckle but broke down in tears. There was a place I had to go. I got up and headed out the door toward the square. Juan started to intervene but Jim restrained him.

"Let him go, he'll be alright."

CHAPTER 24

As I headed out into the square, two Sargeants, Thomas and Michaels, drew up beside me.
"I'm okay guys. (I wasn't) I don't need a guard."
"We're assigned to you sir. That's our orders."
I knew arguing would do no good, so I accepted my body guards. There were a few fires still burning ghostly shadows dancing a ritual of death. Bodies lay everywhere, some whole, and others like Caesar's, not so much. In many of the vehicles you could see the charred skeletal figures. Some of these had been burned to death in their seats. You could tell by the forever death scream that results when a person is burned alive. Their final moments seared in a permanent yell as the muscles tightened with extreme heat and flame. Even in autopsies after such an event the bones were so fused the only way to close the mouth was to break the jaw.
Part of me said I should have felt some pity, but I didn't. Those figures could have very well been us. I was reminded of a quote by Robert E. Lee that went something like this:

"It is well that war is so terrible, otherwise we should grow too fond of it."

I thought of my current students, many of whom play video war games. Would they still play with the same eagerness after seeing what I was seeing? How would God take all this into account when I stood before Him? I just knew I needed to head for the church. How had the building fared and how much damage had resulted. When I reached the small church, I was taken aback. There was no damage.

I wandered all the way around the church fully expecting to find bullet holes, shrapnel hits, any kind of collateral damage. There was none. My faithful guards walked with me, not saying a word. They were both strange and soothing. I made my way to the front door. There in the heavy wooden doors I found one bullet hole It was probably made by an AK-47. In all the carnage, death, and destruction, the symbol of God's presence had taken one bullet. With a strange mixture of joy and sadness I entered again expecting some disarray. My faithful guards took up positions outside the doors. Not even a candle was knocked over, and the alter beckoned me. Only hours before I had delivered the elements of the Holy Communion, but outside appeared anything but holy.

Once up front, I sat down on the floor. I had so many questions and felt so much pain. I sought God to ask my questions and patiently listen to my cry. But those questions fell away as my distressed body and spirit clamored for rest. I leaned my head back on a pillow in a pew and fell asleep. Dreams and flashbacks clouded my mind. I even dreamed of eating something and drinking a sweet green liquid. Both were refreshing. How long I was out I had no clue. When I finally opened my eyes and begin to stir I was rudely reminded of the abuse my body had taken. There beside me was a small plate of fig bars and a bottle of sports drink. So I had eaten, and it wasn't a dream. Light was filtering in the stain glass windows.

"Morning glory." said a familiar voice. Maria was setting on the steps to the alter. Apparently she had slept a little also, pillow on the floor was evidence. She still had on her scrubs.

"Thanks for the food and drink." I said as I took some more.

"You're welcome. The fig bars will give you energy and the sports drink will hydrate and replace electrolytes....How are you doing?"

"Crappy, but alive." It was an honest answer.

"I appreciate an honest answer. Now these are for you." She pulled out two loaded syringes.

"That's not that witch's brew you gave to Mei is it?'

"I could be offended but I won't be, given your current condition. No these are from Dr. Akers. He figured the first round would be wearing off when you woke up, or I woke you up. I'll be gentle."

This wonderful powerful woman of God gave the injections and I didn't even feel them.

"You need to head back toward City Hall before they come looking for you."

After some assistance in getting up, my head quit throbbing. I headed out the door. My guards from hours earlier were gone, but I didn't need them. Colonel Travis, Gen. Spivey, Sam, and Juan stood watching over an army of people carefully going over the burned out wreckage. Sam saw me coming went inside a brought back a chair...I didn't refuse.

"Afternoon sleepy head." called Juan. "If you feel as bad as you look, you feel terrible."

"Thanks... I love you too....By the way, you're not exactly a sight for sore eyes either."

I carefully sat down.

Jack, this is Colonel J. B. Travis Texas National Guard Special Forces unit."

I extended my right hand. "Thank you, Col. Travis?...." The Colonel just rolled his eyes.

"Please just let it go....It's good to meet you Professor Reynolds...One of my men found this. I believe it belongs, or belonged, to one of your crew."

I cringed. It was a cloth badge from Misha'e Spetnaz uniform.

"Now Professor, I don't, repeat don't, want to know how this got here. But I think the young man who wore it would want you to have it." I quietly took the badge and put it in my pocket.

"Colonel, I'm not trying to look a gift horse in the mouth, especially one that saved my life. But how did you guys get here. I mean we truly believed we were on our own. Could you settle my curiosity?"

The story that unfolded was mixture of perfect timing and being in the right place at the right time. The Unit had planned for months to do an extensive exercise in far west Texas. It was to simulate an incursion by terrorist organization or a cartel. The Colonel only realized it was for real when they were ordered to carry full armament loads and fuel. What had been evolving at San Miguel had become a focal point. Surprisingly they had received up to date satellite imagery of Caesar's camp. So when things started to happen, including the attempted bombing of our vehicle, orders changed. When Caesar crossed the river aviation units left Martindale Army Airfield flew around San Antonio to Camp Bullis, special forces base of operations. They were on the ground for five minutes and then back in the air. It was there that General Spivey "caught a ride."

"If he hadn't threatened to pull rank on me, I wouldn't have let him come," the Colonel continued. "But if he hadn't been with us we wouldn't be here and you'd be...dead."

Jim just shrugged his star emblazoned shoulders at myself and Juan's quizzical looks. The Unit had forward based at the airfield in the northern part of the county. They had a ringside seat to the goings on from both the drone feed and the fact, which I had forgotten, Sam was streaming everything on the internet. That feed had not sat well with somebody. They'd tried to shut it down several times. But as they did another feed picked it up. Sam was good. When all hell broke loose the Governor gave the order to spin up and deploy. He was on a direct link to the Colonel. They were moments from liftoff when another communication came in from the White House Chief of Staff.

"Stand down."

But it wasn't just "stand down." It was coupled with the threat that if a single chopper took off toward the town, not only would the Colonel be courtmartialed, but every officer and enlisted man would be also. The Colonel was literally caught between two superiors. He pleaded with Washington that "Innocent people were being slaughtered." But the bureaucrat's response was "I don't give a damn about who's getting killed, you are to stand down and wait further orders."

It was at this point that General Spivey intervened. Jim had been listening to the same feeds as the Colonel and he had had enough. Jim reached over, turned off the radio, and said this:

"As highest ranking active duty officer on site, it is my responsibility to order this unit to press the attack and save fellow United States citizens and repel a foreign incursion."

The Colonel just looked at Jim and said "Thank you." He then turned on his comms and gave the order,

"Scorpion flight, this is Scorpion Leader tally ho, we got got butts to kick and lives to save."

I looked at Jim, "Aren't you suppose to retire soon?" He'd seen thirty years of service.

"Yea, two weeks. So what are they going to do, fire me?"

"General, thanks is not enough." said Juan.

"Hey, a General has to throw his weight around sometime, and this seemed like the right time." Jim just smiled.

The sun was high into the sky when a hobbling Marquis brought a lengthy report of what had been found. To be honest it would take days to go over every vehicle that lay between the town and the river.

"My man Jack, good to see you. You do look a shade better than last night."

"Back at you brother. Others around here say I look like crap, but then I consider the source...But what happened to you?"

The deputy looked a bit embarrassed .

"Blade man here," intoned Sam. "after the battle was over tripped on a curb and cut his calf on a burned out vehicle. Seems pretty man here had not had a tetanus shot in fifteen years. He avoids bullets and shrapnel only to taken out by a curb."

Marquis seemed to glow a bit red, not anger, blushing.

Juan let out a low whistle and then gave the list to the Colonel.

"And this is just the beginning Deputy?"

"Trust me boss. We're cataloging everything as we find it, and there is no way we've found it all. We're moving what we can to the impound area where we can guard it. Thanks, Colonel, for the guards." The Colonel just nodded. "We have been surprised at every turn. Thank God DPS showed up in force and they're flying in forensic teams from all over the state."

"Thanks Marquis. I knew DPS Region 3, 6, and 4 commands were not going to be left out of this party." said Juan.

The story behind the the Department of Public Safety (DPS) was almost as crazy as the National Guard's story.

When everything went south Region 6 Command out of San Antonio, Region 3 out of McAllen, and Region 4 out of El Paso deployed in force. Region 4 Command having the longest distance, had forward based as much as they could in Presidio. Region 3 came in on highway 90, forward basing out of Del Rio, and Region 6 came I-10 and came down from the north. Their only delay had been the National Guard, and that was quickly remedied. The same could not be said of Regions 3 and 4.

As their vehicles came in from the east and the west they encountered backed up traffic, but the DPS crews were given the right of way by regular people. The real problem came when they each reached the county line. The roads were blocked by the Border Patrol. Considering this was an incursion by a cartel such actions were not out of the norm. But this time they wouldn't let DPS through, at gun point.

Now DPS has a reputation of taking nothing off nobody, but this presented a dilemma. These were fellow law officers, and it soon became apparent that there was more going on here than protecting citizens. All this did was make the DPS commands even angrier. Both 3 and 4 contacted Director Hollis, and his order was direct.

"If they don't move, take you APVs and run a damn hole through their barricade. Get to San Miguel!"

The road was immediately cleared of onlookers and the commands brought up their APVs. Since the Border Patrol had no anti-tank weaponry, they were not going to stop them. When faced with that option the Border Patrol cleared the way.

Meanwhile, the Texas Navy was not having any problems. DPS had been faced with how to stop the cartels from moving contraband across the river. Not only were the cartels using anything that floated, their firepower had gotten greater. Enter the Texas River Interceptors. From north of the second assault bridge and from the south came the DPS answer to the cartels. These were gunboats plan and simple. and they were fast, armored, and well-armed. The boats were specially built for Texas with a length of thirty-four feet, powered by three three-hundred horsepower blueprinted Volvo maritime engines that pushed them to a speed in excess of seventy miles per hour. They mounted six FN M240B 7.62 mm machine guns (two bow mounted guns in single mounts and two dual mounted guns mid ship), and retractable ballistic panels. They were manned by tactical crews with extensive training. The boats owed a heritage back to the riverine craft that were very effective in Vietnam.

Two came from the north and two came from the south, and they weren't playing nice. In the darkness, they had crept up close in near silence and then opened fire. Turning the engines wide open, with skilled hands at the wheel, they were able to direct fire onto the bridge and the Texas shoreline. Again the cartel was caught by surprise. On two of the boats someone had grenade launchers and put them to use. Vehicles were crashing into each other, tumbling into the river, and blowing up. Reinforcements for the cartel elements across the river would never arrive. When the Warhawk AH-60 arrived the bridge was totally eleminated. What TNG Special Forces didn't get the DPS did. While Region 6 had a little easier task going south from the town, Region 3 and 4 Commands would find the San Miguel road north of Highway 90 a road of death. It would take the better part of two days to work their way up. But now everyone was here and picking over the wreckage as group of vultures tore apart a dead animal.

CHAPTER 25

General Spivey asked for the report. He just shook his head. "If I hadn't seen this I wouldn't have believed it. Those guys had 'balls.'"

He handed the the document to me and my eyes must have bugged out. If I hadn't known who was doing the research and cataloging, I might not have believed it. Aside from the mountainous number of weapons it was a cartel/ terrorist wishlist.

9 tons of cocaine

2 tons of fentanyl

8 tons of crystal meth

Marijuana was in vast amounts (that which had not burned up in the attack)

7 laptop computers (whose content were being downloaded as we read the list.

10 million in US currency

30 million in counterfeit US currency, all nice and neat packaged, still bearing the seal of the PLA printing facility in Shanghai.

"The Chinese?" PLA meant People's Liberation Army, the Chinese Army.

"It appears Caesar was not quite as naive as we thought, He was covering all his bases. He probably had an agreement with the Chinese to flood the Southwest with the funny money. Considering how much product he had to sell, working the fake money into the economy wouldn't have been that hard. Sooner or later local economies suffer and there's so much funny money, people hold on to what they know is real.....Marquis is right in saying no telling how much more of this stuff has been destroyed by the firefight."

As we all pondered the ramifications of our discoveries, a simple fact hung in the air. We'd not just stopped a major cartel seeking to establish itself, but something very much bigger.

"Colonel we've got bogies inbound from the west, three Chinooks." A corporeal interrupted our thoughts.

"Have they identified themselves?"

"Only IFF, they're friendly, if they're telling the truth."

"Target time?"

"Two minutes."

"Do we have assets airborne?'

"Scorpions 3 and 5, sir."

"Get me a visual and get it quick." The Colonel keyed his radio.

"This is Scorpion Leader to Scorpion swarm... We have inbound from the west, three CH-47s.....as of now we don't know who they are or their intentions... Be on your toes.. Scorpion Leader out."

"Not ours?" quizzed Gen. Spivey.

"If they are, they arrived damn late and didn't follow protocol."

"Colonel, Scorpion 3 has a visual. The birds have no identifying numbers or lettering."

"Have they threatened 3 or 5?"

"No sir, and they will not answer our calls."

The Colonel let out a sigh.

"Damn strange. I want those birds covered like fire ants on a picnic. Scorpion Leader to group. Go weapons active, but hold your fire. I want eyes on everything and everyone that gets out of the choppers, and don't let them near any wreckage."

"Sir, the choppers have split into three parts. One is headed for the river area, one toward the mounts and one toward us."

The unmarked CH-47 rotated and landed just south of town and twenty black fatigued clad men exited. Some started to examine the remains of the night before and were met by TNG forces and rudely turned away.

Juan keyed his radio,"Get Dominique out here and get the Governor and State's Attorney General on line."

A group of ten figures came into the square. Nine tried to look at wreckage, and were once again rudely denied. One man came up to us. He had Captain's bars and a name tag saying "Smith", no other identifying badges or insignia. With his sculptured physique, blond hair and blue eyes, and perfect smile, he looked like someone out of central casting. He also had the attitude to match. It faltered slightly when he saw General Spivey.

"Colonel,....General, Sheriff, I'm Captain Smith and here are my orders."

The Colonel looked at the orders and cursed, handed them to the General who shook his head, and then gave them to Juan. Juan just him a very angry look.

"Our attorney will look this over." Juan passed it to Dominique.

"There will be no need to check it. As you see, the Department of Homeland Security has taken over all this." Pretty boy waved his hand over all the area. "You will also supply us with the additional manpower to move all evidence including everything you have collected....Too bad you couldn't remove the bodies....By the way what's with the silver crosses?

At that point Col. Travis lost it."What!? No good day, how you doing. No you sure kicked butt last night. No glad you guys won. No sorry for the losses. No hope you had a good meal after the battle.....I bet everyone on those freakin' choppers has a name tag that says 'Smith.'...Sheriff, tell 'Capt. Smith' about those silver crosses."

"Captain, those silver crosses you so casually ask about are townspeople. My people, yes many are illegals, but they came here to evade the cartels, and when the cartels came, they didn't run. Those crosses were to help us not to shoot them, but they became targets for the cartel."

Captain Smith just shrugged his shoulders, "Not my problem, besides no great loss. Now, Colonel..."

I had been sitting there listen to this pompous arrogant ass, totally angered by his attitude, and the fact the government was trying to cover up what happened. But when he said those wonderful courageous townspeople were basically nothing more than trash, my anger turned to rage. A strength from where I don't know roared through me, I stood up and slammed my right fist into pretty boy's jaw. The Captain went backward and blood and teeth went flying. With my energy gone I fell back into the chair. Pretty boy was on the ground for a moment and then he got up still spiting out blood and teeth. He was seething and reaching for his sidearm.

"Stand down Captain," ordered the Colonel. The Captain removed his hand from the holster.

"Sheriff, I demand you arrest this man at once for assaulting a federal officer."

Juan was stifling a laugh. "For what reason Captain? I didn't see anything. Did you see anything General?"

Jim hadn't said a word until then. "Nope, Sheriff, I didn't see anything. Did you Colonel?"

"No General, all I saw was some arrogant bastard trip over his high heels and bust up his pretty face...Nope I didn't see a thing, but I will say this. Captain, you and your men have fifteen minutes to collect what you can, and then your butts better be back on your birds."

The Captain, through his smashed face, registered shock. Juan's phone buzzed and he took it.

"General, I must protest in the most vigorous terms that the Colonel is in violation of a federal order and must be relieved of his duties, plus I have been assaulted by a civilian who must be arrested. We must be allowed to continue, and Professor Reynolds will be restrained and come with us."

The fact that this was the first time my name had come up specifically wasn't lost on any of us. Juan whispered something in Jim's ear.

Jim spoke in a soft and even tone. "Captain, you seem to have a inflated since of importance. As highest ranking officer in the field, until relieved by a superior officer or the Secretary of the Army or the President, you're the one on shaky ground..Now you have twelve minutes to collect what you need and leave...By the way the Sheriff tells me the the Attorney General of the State of Texas has asked for and gotten an immediate stay of your orders. A judge from the Fifth Circuit, who happen to be in state was more than happy to grant it...You now have ten minutes to leave the area."

"I don't believe it." stammered the Captain.

Dominique walked by us and and handed a sheet to the Captain.

"This is the stay of your orders as issued by a judge of the Fifth Circuit, and duly delivered by representative of the Judge Advocate General's office. Now move your butt."

The Captain had to comply but was not happy. He looked at me and said, "You'll get yours."

Juan, who should have been smiling, was suddenly in deep thought.

"I think we should head back inside and discuss some things, and Jack you look like you need to lie down."

We all headed into the City Hall. Jim was assisting me because my punch of pretty boy had taken what little energy I had.

"Jack, you need to keep a reign on your anger. Yes, the captain deserved it and you were the only one who could get away with it. Take my advice. When this is all over take a sabbatical and work through what you've seen. You can't, though it's easier said than done, make it personal. And all this will be with you until your last day on earth. Welcome to what many veterans go through."

I knew Jim was right, but now I had even more admiration and respect for what my student veterans had faced. One inside, we settled in a conference room. Someone found me a lounge chair and Devon had another IV hooked up to me. Pancho Villa had come back out and settled himself in my lap. The raid by Homeland was disturbing to say the least. They had literally stolen the truck driver's body from the hospital all those days ago, and, as we found out, had tried to move our wounded. That action was met by a gauntlet of DPS officers, flanked by San Antonio Police Department. Frustrated Homeland officials left the hospital, but stationed a watcher outside. Juan broke the silence.

"You noticed when pretty boy demanded all forensic evidence he included Jack in that. That is a very broad interpretation of evidence. Now I can understand him wanting us to arrest Jack, but all that falls under my jurisdiction. Any thoughts, gentlemen and lady, on why Jack is being singled out?"

Everyone cast a glance my way. "Hey don't ask me. All I am is a college professor and minister. There's nothing that important about me."

'High profile scapegoat." spoke Dominique. She turned to me. "As of now Jack, I am your attorney. I'll take a leave of absence from the JAG's office to represent you. For some reason your high profile as a professor and a civilian makes you the best target. They can say this wouldn't have happened if you hadn't been here. Remember the 'video' excuse used to explain the Benghazi, Libya terrorist attack? The government arrested the film-maker without probable cause just to cover their butts. Unfortunately you're the new irritant in a embarrassing situation for the US government." She looked around the table. "Gentlemen, we've got to find a safe place for our 'person of interest'"

"I think I can assist with that." came a familiar voice from the door. It was David Matthews of the Texas Rangers. I've come to take Jack into custody...protective custody. Orders from the Governor himself."

About that time Guardsman stuck his head in and announced, "Colonel, we've got more bogies inbound from the east....Two helos and they identified themselves as FBI...and they're requesting we clear the impound lot as an LZ."

"Damn it, I'm not running DFW airport here. Is the impound lot clear?"

"Yes sir."

"How long until arrival?

"Seven minutes sir."

"Ask...no, demand, what is their business.....Major Lewis (Dominique)."

"Yes sir."

"Since you're our legal beagle in this thing, you make the call and request of them their intentions, and corporal tell them the impound lot is occupied and they need to land east of town."

"But sir, the lot is clear..."

"Corporal, you heard my orders." The corporal disappeared and the Colonel keyed his own comms. "Scorpion Leader to Scorpion One. Captain, can you put my chopper in the impound lot in three minutes? If you do I'll buy the steak dinner."

We could already hear the Blackhawk spooling up before an answer.

"I'll have it there in two and a half. I want mine big and done medium."

"Copy Scorpion One, Scorpion Leader out."

Dominique stuck her head back in. "FBI says they have an arrest warrant for one Jackson C. Reynolds Ph.D on the charge of killing an international, our favorite druglord."

I was dumbfounded. All of us had killed a number of people. But I had not killed Caesar.

Ranger Matthews spoke, "Professor Reynolds, we need to leave. If they get here and serve that warrant our hands become tied. We've got to get you to Austin."

"Agreed." said Juan. "We'll delay the FBI as long as we can, but you need to go....now!"

"But what about my stuff at the ranch?" Things were moving too fast for me.

"It's okay, Professor. I've already been by and gotten everything...Please sir?" Ranger Matthews was sounding more urgent.

"Okay, okay, I'll go. Colonel, I want to thank you for the body guards last night. I didn't need it, but Sargeants Thomas and Michaels never left my side."

The Colonel looked perplexed. "Professor you've been through a lot in the last twenty-four hours, but I didn't know where you went until this morning, and to my knowledge I have no Sargeants named Thomas and Micheals."

Jim just sat back and gave me a very thoughtful look, and then pointed toward the door. "Get!"

CHAPTER 26

The Chevy Suburban was parked just behind City Hall, loaded to the roof. I stopped and glanced at everything when Marquis came up to me.
"We've got all 'your stuff' for you." The wonderful deputy who had become my friend, took my right hand. "You take care of yourself, you're one of us now. If you ever need anything, Boss, just call." Marquis gave me his card and gently assisted me into the front seat. We all knew "my stuff," while it did include my things from the ranch and City Hall, was also all the evidence they could possibly pack into the Suburban. When David started up the SUV, we heard chopper blades tooling up. As we cleared town we realized we were not alone.
"It appears the Colonel is not letting us travel alone."
To each side about sixty yards out were two AH-6s, and flying above and slightly behind us a Blackhawk DAP. I should have been impressed by our entourage, but I wasn't. I was depressed and needing to talk to Ellen, and my phone's battery was dead. "David, can I use your phone? I really need to call my wife and let her know I'm okay." He made no move to give me his phone.

"Jack, why don't you wait until we've got you settled. You know the Governor is keeping her apprised of the situation."

He was deflecting and I knew it.

"What has happened?...What are you not telling me?"

The Ranger was weighing his answer carefully.

"Jack, all I'm saying is you're exhausted and hurting, you know how incoherent you feel... Your responses might worry her even more, and seriously, how do explain getting shot four times?" He did have a point.

"Ranger, be honest with me. Is my wife okay?"

"Jack, as far as I know, she's doing fine."

I knew he was still hiding something, but I wasn't about to get any more in formation. For the rest of the trip we were silent. I pondered how I had gone from a respected tenured professor at a major Texas university, with his own grants and research, to an enemy of the state.

When we got to the airfield, it was still a very active place. Beside fuel bladders for the Guard helicopters, there were several DPS vehicles and choppers, plus a Beech Air King 350 with one with one prop rotating. After we stopped I slowly extricated myself from the SUV. A group of DPS officers and Guardsmen immediately began removing "my stuff" and placing it on board the Beech. The Governor met me as I hobbled toward the plane. He was surprised to say the least.

"My God, Jack! They told me you were injured, but not this bad. Let's get you inside."

I wanted to do some quick retort to the Governor, but I was hurting too bad. Concern was written all over his face. A quick glance before entering the aircraft revealed out TNG escorts were still hovering nearby. In their own way, they were reassuring. The interior of the Air King was plush, and the seat I landed in was the best thing I'd felt in a couple of days.

"Jack, this Dr. Michael McKnight, my personal physician. He'll be the man in charge of your health for the near future."

Dr. McKnight shook my hand and then stuck a needle in my arm.

"Sorry for the rude welcome, but I could see your pain meds were wearing off. Now buckle up...Oops, sorry. Let me assist you."

It's hard to buckle you seat belt when one arm is in a sling. The Governor was already buckled in.

"Jerry, let's get this thing going."

The pilot looked back at us. "Governor, we've got a problem and can't go anywhere."

"Mechanical?"

"No sir, but you better come see this."

The Governor was out of his seat and looking out the windshield.

"What the hell?"

"We've already tried to radio him..No response."

By that time I was able get a peak past the Governor. There about two-thirds the way down the runway sat an armed observation helo, and it wasn't one of ours.

"When did he arrive?" Demanded the Governor.

"About thirty seconds ago. He came in low and fast. I don't think the TNG guys saw him before he positioned himself."

"Get me the Colonel!"

"No need to. The Blackhawk is in communication and is getting instructions."

"Put it on the PA, Jerry."

The first voice we heard was the Colonel's.

"Scorpion 7, go to attack plan Delta. Give that bastard a

five count and then make mincemeat of him. Place yourself between him and the Governor's plane."

"Copy that."

The big bird rotated and placed herself between us and the intruder. The two AH-6s positioned themselves ninety degrees on opposite sides of the intruder.

"Unidentified helo, you are not responding to our calls. Therefore we must assume your intentions are hostile. You have until the count of five to vacate or we will open fire. One."

The Blackhawk started down the runway slowly.

"Two....three...Weapons lock....four..."

As the Blackhawk increased it's speed, the pilot started to say "five." The small helo scooted off at high speed to the northwest.

"Scorpions 4 and 5, follow him and don't lose him. Find out where that bogey came from."

"Copy." Our little birds were off for the chase.

With our blocker out of the way the Blackhawk moved to the side and we taxied to takeoff position.

"Jerry, get us home as fast and low as safety permits, and don't go to the primary airfield. Head to the secondary location. Tell my office I want a medivac copter waiting to take us to Home Base."

"Copy, Governor. Everybody hang on."

We were pressed into our seats as the Air King's turboprops screamed and we shot down the runway climbing into the air. Once we gained altitude and nobody seemed to be chasing us, we all began to breathe again.

"Governor," I asked. "What if things had gone south back there? We still wouldn't have been able to take off."

The Governor just smiled. "Well, for one I'm glad it didn't, and two, Col. Travis had already dispatched other Blackhawks to carry us and our cargo back to

Austin....But I'd give a year in office to know who that was and who sent them." He then looked me straight in the eyes. "When you kick over a hornet's nest, you kick over a big one."

"I've been told that." was my only response.

The flight to Austin was less than an hour, and where I would end up was among a number of questions I had. But I really needed to call my wife.

"Governor, I'd really like to call my wife. I need to let her know I'm okay. Well, a little worse for wear...But surely this plane has a phone."

The Governor had been looking out the window. He turned to face me and I read the message.

"What's happened?!"

"Jack, let me say you have a warrior for a bride...Currently she's resting comfortably at Fort Worth's Harris Southwest, not far from your house."

"What the hell happened?!" He held up both hands to try and clam me down. "Don't tell me to calm me down! Would you if it was your wife?"

"You're right...Now please try to relax and I'll give to whole story."

The Governor then related the story of the attack on our home. We'd known Caesar had connections with the MS-13 gang, and that was reinforced in the blatant threat given prior to the fight. The Governor's office and DPS had been in constant contact with the Fort Worth Police Department. The nice thing was that FWPD had a substation less than a mile from our house. FWPD had planned carefully, expecting any incursion to be in force and heavily armed. The Gang Unit had picked up vibes that MS-13 was in town, but not until the State contacted FWPD they knew the intended target. When San Miguel went hot FWPD put their plan into effect. Marked cars blocked our street's access points and waited. About

11:30 pm an older model Chevy Caprice turned onto one of the cross streets. Its lights were off and it moved slowly. When they saw only one marked unit they gunned the car and one member popped up through a hole where a sunroof had been. He pulled out an AK-47 and prepared to fire.

At that very moment, a FWPD tactical vehicle raced up from the back and rammed the Caprice. The shooter's gun went flying off into the dark. Then multiple police tactical units came in and the firefight was on. It was brief. All the MS-13 members were killed, with no injuries to the police. Meanwhile, a second MS-13 team had entered our backyard from the street behind us. FWPD and Ranger Moore had expected a two pronged attack and were ready. Ranger Moore had put Ellen in our central bathroom's bathtub and wrapped her with body armor. This MS-13 team had body armor so the firefight lasted longer and was more intense. Moore and FWPD had killed five of the intruders, but one was very elusive. He was getting close to the bedroom window when Moore had to change clips. He immediately tagged her with two shoots, one in the vest, but the other was a through and through and broke her collar bone. She wasn't dead, but incapacitated

The guy cleared the bushes and was preparing to finish off the Ranger when he heard a loud yell or scream. The next thing he knew was a multi-pointed axe planted in his nose and sternum. The blow didn't kill him but stunned him enough to allow a Fort Worth Tactical officer to put two rounds in his forehead. He fell backwards out the window, with the blade still firmly stuck in him.

The Governor showed me a picture on his phone.

"What the hell is that thing?"

"Are you saying my wife did that?" I was astounded.

"Like I said, she's a warrior, but what is that thing?"
"It's a Batleth." I responded.
"A bat what?"
"A Batleth. A Klingon battle axe. You know from Star Trek."

He still looked bewildered.
"Never mind, what happened?"
"Apparently she heard Ranger Moore go down, and whatever protective warrior instinct kicked in. She grabbed this thing, let out some kind of yell, and slammed it into the guy. She saved my Ranger. I and Texas will be forever thankful to her."
"But you said she's in the hospital."
"Only for observation. Once the all clear was given, the shock caught up with her. She started shaking and trembling, so we thought it best to remove her to a secure and peaceful location. She was worried about Ranger Moore. I'm sorry to say the house took a bit of a beating."

The Governor than sat back, but I knew there was more on his mind.
"What about Tabitha and the boys?'
"I wish I could say it was all positive in Houston, but I can't."

Ester and his sister had grown up in one of the more affluent sections of Houston. Milton and his wife of forty years Frankie, had done well for themselves. Milton was a very respected member of the business community, and Frankie had a Master's in Social Work and had been a fireball in the minority community. It didn't matter which minority, if she could help she was there. That was until she came down with a rare pulmonary disease that robbed her of her energy. So at sixty, Milton Long sold his assets and retired to take care of his beloved wife. When ask about Lenny coming to their residence with the anticipation of getting help with his PTSD, the Long's just thought of it as expanding their family. And so it was that not only was the Long family in harm's was, so was Lenny.

Again, like Fort Worth, Houston Police Department had done excellent planning, including a heightened presence in the Long's neighborhood. HPD felt they had a good plan, increased patrols in the area and tactical units moved to a substation just a few minutes from the Long residence. But Milton Long was no wall flower. His son, Ester, had gotten his football build from his dad. Milton also had a gun collection that any Texan would envy. His most treasured piece was a Mossberg 930 Tactical. Anyone who attacked his house would make the acquaintance of 'Babe", his favorite shotgun.

All seemed well until a city council member took offense of the "increase militarized" police presence, as she called it. In a strict breach of protocol and security the Chief took her aside and advised her of the potential threat. She would hear none of it, and declared that if they didn't "tone down" their presence she would push for budget reallocation, meaning 'cuts.' Very reluctantly the Chief ordered a pull back of resources, increasing response time. It was a move that would prove deadly.

The attack, as in Fort Worth, was two-pronged. But instead of a direct assault they used stealth. Two gang members crept up from behind as the gang's car caused a distraction. The senior officer had just keyed his radio when the two gang members riddled the car with their AK's. The officers never had a chance, but the open mike heard it all and HPD rolled with vengeance. In the Long household, they heard the automatic weapons. The Texas Ranger placed Tabitha and Frankie in bathtubs wrapped in body armor, and Milton got "Babe." Milton told Lenny to take cover, having been told by Ester of Lenny's response when a gun went off, but something happened. Lenny, who at San Miguel, cowered like a frightened rabbit, suddenly became the master soldier he used to be. His mind worked faster than ever. At the sound of the guns and the gang's car accelerating, he shoved Milton to the floor and ordered the Ranger to the back of the house. An RPG round hit the corner of the house and not the window it was aimed at. The big brick house took the hit, but shrapnel flew everywhere. Milton took hits in both legs, breaking one. The Ranger at the back of the house had two Sig Saur .45s and an M-4 but he was up against multiple intruders with automatic weapons. The Ranger took out two before he took a hit to the body armor, stunned. Lenny was on the move. He grabbed "Babe", winked at Milton and ran out the backdoor. There were seven resounding blasts from the backyard and then silence.

    HPD made the run to the Long residence in three minutes. The driver of their Striker tactical vehicle rammed the gang's car going full speed. The MS-13 team didn't stand a chance. HPD unleashed hell on the gang members. Later it was noted by the medical examiner during the autopsy, that the bodies were so full of bullets she gave up determining the kill shot. By the time the Tactical teams made the backyard all they found was the hobbled Texas Ranger, tears in his eyes, keeping guard over Lenny. Lenny had personally taken out the remaining gang members, but was hit five times himself. Yet Lenny had the most peaceful expression on his face. It was as if in those final minutes, something he'd lost was returned.

    Inside the Long house, aside from Milton's wounds, Frankie had gone into cardiac arrest. Tabitha tried to rally and help but was overcome by shock. The entire family was flown to one of Houston finest critical care hospitals.

HPD was not just mad, but damn mad. Two of their own were butchered needlessly, all because of a councilperson's arrogance. It was only professional strength that kept them from dragging her to the location to see the results of her actions. It would come out later that the councilperson had been receiving payments from Caesar to "grease the skids" and allow the cartel to operate in Houston. She would resign, denying all culpability.

CHAPTER 27

The Governor sat in silence. Part of me ached for the Long's but thanked God he brought Lenny back to us if just for this time. Yet I needed to ask one more question.

"What about the boys in Pasadena?" the Governor turned his head and quietly chuckled.

"If only the Long's night had gone as the boys."

Tabitha and Juan's boys were staying with Mei's parents in the Texas coastal city of Pasedena. Mei's father Tony Nguyen was a former officer in the South Vietnamese Army. After escaping with his new wife from Saigon in 1975, they settled in Pasadena, Texas, which had a growing Vietnamese population. He'd bought an old shrimp boat and turned it in to a million dollar enterprise. He was to Pasadena what Milton was to Houston. Tony was especially honored, if not humbled, that his grandsons loved to work on the boats. So for the boys to be sheltered there was an easy call. But another reason was the Vietnamese community looked out for their own. Numerous friends and employees descended on the Nguyen home, guns in hand. If the MS-13 gang got past the police, there would be a very unwelcome reception waiting. By sunrise on Sunday morning no action had occurred. Even Pasadena PD and Texas

Rangers were baffled, until an anonymous call came in about a two car fire three miles from the Nguyen's residence. What police found was pretty gruesome, but answered all their questions.

There was no doubt PDP had found the remains of the MS-13 hit squad. A sign in Vietnamese was found on the burned out vehicles. In a very rare show of unity the the local gangs sent their own message.

"Our people, our town, you die."

Even the PDP Gang Unit was appreciative of this intervention. When I asked the Governor if the state would try to find the gang members and bring charges, he looked at me and said. "Why?" I agreed.

We'd almost reached Austin when an awkward topic came up.

"Governor, I believe you had someone on your staff that was in the cartel's pocket."

His shoulders sagged a little and still looking out the window he replied, "I know."

He turned to face me and I saw anger and hurt.

"It was my Special Counsel."

I was shocked. That was Juan's law school buddy.

"For months we'd been having only spotty success with Operation Border Star. Intel would come in, and our teams would deploy, only to arrive there too late, or nothing would be there at all. If we did arrive late, it would only be by a few minutes. It was a constant pattern that kept repeating itself...We tightened down lines of access and communication, but it continued. So when San Miguel became active we hoped our leak would not endanger anyone. We were wrong... We knew it had to be an inner circle person when Caesar started to describe in detail where all your families were. Only a handful knew that information. Of that inner circle, six of us had known each other for years, and some of us had served together in the military. That left only one person. We caught him in the Capital Parking garage. He immediately lawyered-up, and shut up. My guess is once we get our forensic people on it, we'll find a pretty good money trail, if not more. Looks like we're about to land."

We emerged from the King Air under a beautiful Texas sky, not a cloud from horizon to horizon. "Severe clear" was what a north Texas meteorologist called it. For the first time in two weeks I felt totally apart from San Miguel. I took in a deep breath and promptly collapsed on the tarmac.

I didn't completely pass out as my mind was alert to what was happening. Dr. McKnight slapped a BP cup on my arm and started listening to my chest. It was a drop in blood pressure...again. I remembered there were two choppers waiting for us when we landed. One was a medical helo and the other was a DPS copter. While I was being cared for our cargo was transferred to the DPS helo to take to a crime lab.

I was placed on a stretcher and another injection went in my right arm. It was starting to hurt as much as the left arm by now. The turbines whirled on one copter, and for a moment I thought "Wait I'm not on board." It was the DPS bird. While being placed on the medical bird I over heard a few brief conversations.

"University Medical, Governor?"

"Yep. Dr. McKnight will want to find the source of the BP drop..."

"We got company, and they're coming fast." yelled a DPS officer.

"Damn it, how did the Feds find us this quick.....No! Take him straight to the Radisson. APD will have the street blocked off so you can land. Get moving, I'll meet you there after I have a discussion with our Federal associates....Officer, once their SUVs are in the gate, close it and block it."

I felt the chopper tool up and lift off. Dr. Mcknight was shining a light in my eyes. I started to say something, but the doctor placed a light hand on my chest.

"Rest Jack, you're safe now."

I closed my eyes and dreamless sleep took over....I vaguely remember movement and various noises, but for the most part I was in a cocoon.

How long I slept I don't know, but when I awoke I was confused. Where I had expected a hospital room....this was not it. I was in a king size bed covered by a sheet and light blanket, and all my clothes were gone. Also gone was the grit and dirt and sweat residue I had carried since the battle. Someone had given me a bath. Then there was this cute woman sitting a few feet away. It was then I realized I was attached to another I.V. I was getting tired of those. My left arm ached and my body was still saying nasty things to me. It was then I realized not only were my clothes gone but so was my wedding band. My stirring caught my lovely attendant's attention.

"Hello Dr. Reynolds, I'm Dr. McKnight's P.A. (physician's assistant). How do you feel?"

My first thought was about a scene from Mel Brook's movie "Blazing Saddles," when Gene Wilder woke up to to see Sheriff Bart.

"Puzzled" I looked around. "Where am I, where are my clothes, and where is my wedding ring?"

The P.A. Pulled out a phone.

"Doctor, he's awake and lucid. Okay." She put down the phone.

"Dr. Reynolds, you're in a suite at the Radisson Hotel in downtown Austin. Your clothes are being cleaned, and other clothing is in the dresser. We removed your wedding ring because your arm was wanting to swell, as a safety precaution we removed the ring so we wouldn't have to cut it off. It's on the nightstand next to you along with your watch and phone.

I felt embarrassed. "Did you say 'we'? Now I would like to know who part of that we is."

She laughed. "I'm Camille, please call me Cam. No need to be embarrassed. It was thought best to keep the circle of people with access to you small. You're in pretty good shape for a man of sixty."

"Thank you, I think." I didn't know whether to appreciative or more embarrassed.

"I think I'm beginning to understand why your students like you. But let's get down to the issues. Your body has taken some serious punishment. We, like Dr. Akers, are surprised your heart didn't stop from the concussion of the rounds. Your clavicle is cracked, but it's your internal bruising that has us most concerned...Your external injuriesare healing and should be good in a couple of weeks, with some residual soreness. On a scale of ten what is your pain level?"

"Five to six. I'm feeling more stiff than anything. Is there any way you could get me a hospital gown or some underwear and shorts. I want to try and get up, but...well...you know."

Cam laughed. "Let me check your vitals again, and we'll see about getting you into something that fits loose. I will definitely say your wife has a keeper."

"Why was I not taken to a hospital?"

"Maybe I can answer that." Came a voice at the door of the suite. "Is our patient presentable?"

"Yes he is, Governor. We're trying get him something loose to wear." "I've got some stuff with me....Camille, could you give us some time?"

Camille rose, "His vitals are good." She left, and the Governor came in.

"Here, the doctor told me for the next few days you'd be wearing loose stuff. Nothing better than sweats." The Governor placed a bag by the bed. In were sweats, Texas A & M sweats.

"A & M? Seriously?...But thank you. Please bring me in the loop, and when can I call Ellen?"

The Governor pulled up a chair and sat down. As I got dressed he filled me in.

"We were going to fly you to the hospital when the Federal authorities came charging in. The Radisson was going to be for family, but we knew what might happen at the hospital, so we changed plans and here we are. We have a complete blockade for you, so nobody federal or press gets near you. If I were you, I wouldn't use your cell. Call Ellen on the room phone. My guess is your phone is jammed with calls from friends and press. We're flying Ellen down on Wednesday (it was Sunday), and you'll be reunited. We've briefed her on your injuries and long term prognosis. You might not want to watch any news. Depending on who you watch, you and the San Miguel crew are either heroes or despicable vigilantes. The State of Texas tends to see you as the former.

Now let's just say the crap has hit the fan big time. That 'official' document has got Washington in a fit. The Administration is flat denying anything, but our handwriting people have validated the authenticity of the signatures. Suddenly all the signers are unavailable or out of the country. Right now, we're playing whack a mole on who does their press conference first, the Administration or us. Last night the White House Press Secretary did a preliminary briefing for the 'inside the beltway' media crowd, and while it was scripted....You know the usual BS about gun control, people taking the law into their own hands, better immigration policy, states usurping federal law....it didn't go well. One reporter, I believe from Fox News, asked if the President had even seen the document and video. The reply was classic spin; anybody can forge a document, and videos can be scripted and don't carry much weight. Someone blurted out 'you mean like Libya?' That definitely frustrated the Press Secretary. The Fox reporter pressed the question. The Press Secretary blew him off and went to an AP reporter, apparently hoping for friendlier questioning. The AP reporter demanded the Press Secretary answer the Fox reporter. The Press Secretary left in a huff. It was fun to watch."

"What about the warrant for my arrest?"

"That was addressed briefly, but more in the sense of us (Texas) protecting, or in their terms 'withholding,' you from federal authorities. They're determined to push the warrant." My heart sank. "But I'm going ahead to give a press conference this evening at 6 pm. I believe with the evidence we have uncovered, we'll give a sound argument that the warrant is without merit. Jack, we're still finding more stuff in that debris field."

The Governor looked at his watch. "I've got to run and prep for tonight. I'll check on you after the presser." I was left to my thoughts. Getting into the sweats was painful and I finally had to ask Cam to assist me with the shirt. By mid afternoon I finally called Ellen.

"Hello?"

"Hey honey, it's me."

"Jack, it's so great to to hear you. I almost didn't answer when I didn't recognize the number...." She was tearing up. "They told me you were hurt...how bad?"

"Well my warrior princess, I should be asking about you. You put up one hell of a fight. What ever made you think about using the Batleth. I'm so proud of you."

There was sobbing on the other end of the line.

"Everything was happening so fast. Liz, Ranger Moore had me covered with the...the "

"Body armor."

"Yes, that stuff...Jack it was horrible, the gunfire, all the noise...I just wanted it over...and then I heard her get hit and collapse..(she started talking more slowly) I didn't know if I was going to live or die, but I sure wasn't going to let a dear friend get hurt. I knew nothing about shooting her gun, so I just grabbed what I thought I could use. I just did what I did."

I could tell she was tired just reliving it in telling me.

"Now Ellen, to think you were upset at me for buying it."

There was a little chuckle on the the other end of the line.

"Yea, I'll take back that one." She started crying again. But the house, the cars, the yard, they're so damaged. I know insurance won't cover it all."

That's my wife. She lives through an attack by a crime gang, nearly kills one to help save a friend, but she's more worried about getting our home and cars repaired. I also realized we'd both need some counseling to work through all we'd been through.

"Everything will be taken care of." I reassured her, but even I was wondering how it would be taken care of. "We take one day at a time, and one step at a time."

"But what about you? They told me you were hurt...."

How do I tell her? I finally just decided to tell her all, she'd know if I was withholding anything.

"It was a hard battle, Ellen. I got shot in the arm. What they call a 'through and through.' It's coming around pretty good. I did get hit three times in my vest" I heard her start sobbing again. "I've got a huge bruise covering half of my upper body, so you'll have to hug me lightly for a couple of months, but I'm alive and you can thank Juan for that. He double vested me. It would have been worse if he hadn't. That's why they've got me under medical observation."

There was a moment of silence

"I'll thank Juan at some point, maybe just before I kill him for letting you get hurt. No, that's just my worry talking. I'm glad he took care of you. But you said it was bad. All I've gotten is spotty news reports. I've just quit Facebook altogether. Many were supportive, but so much anger at you and Juan's department. I gave up."

"Probably a good idea. Rosie and Ester were wounded pretty bad." Now it was my turn to struggle. "We lost Chico. I lost a student, Misha."

"Oh my, Misha? How? Why? I know you'll tell me the whole story. I do regret not seeing him. What about Juan and the others?"..

"Wounded, shaken rattled, and just flat exhausted. Tabitha's family got hit hard like you did, but interference kept Houston PD from getting to them quickly. Her father suffered a broken leg, and her mother had to be hospitalized for heart attack. Keep them in your prayers. And one of my students died defending the Longs" I started choking up. "As you can guess, there's more, but I'll share as you want it. Now do what your doctors say. I know Bill and the church will be checking on you. I'll see you Wednesday. Love ya."

"Love you too." The line went dead.

I laid on the bed, no real comfortable position, but after talking to Ellen, it began to hit me how our lives had changed forever. After finally getting some sleep I decided to start writing about the experience I had been through.

CHAPTER 28

I took a break from writing, still trying to grasp all that had occurred. It was overwhelming. Turning on the TV had become an experience. Fox News called the incident a victory of the American spirit. MSNBC said I should be tried and shot. What s CNN said, I won't mention. The Governor had been right. The documents we'd found were making the rounds and the administration was trying to refocus the light on me and not the signatories. I changed to a local channel and saw protests on my own campus. I had been reluctant to check my email. It was beyond full, but one stood out—my department chair.

"Call." Immediately!"

She answered on the second ring.

"Jack, what the hell happened on the border? The news is saying you killed a foreign national. Other news is talking about an invasion and scandal. What's happening?"

I explained the best I could, reassuring her that I hadn't killed the person in question. But when I explained that I was in protective custody and didn't know when I'd get out, what was bad got worse.

"Jack, to be honest, I don't know if I can hold your position."

I was stunned.

"You don't know what the day has been like. The Department of Mexican-American Studies is demanding your ouster. The President is under pressure to fire you. The Dean is trying to reason with everyone to wait until the full story is in. There are calls for a boycott of our department, if not defunding."

"Deidre, I'm sorry. I asked for none of this. I'm innocent of all charges, but…but you do what's best for the department."

Tears burned my eyes. That campus had been my home for over 20 years.

"Jack, I'll try to hold things here. I've known you long enough to know you did what you had to do. I'll let the department in on things and we'll go from there. But if the President says to fire you, I can't stop that. Take care and know we're worried for you."

Deidre hung up. I was lost. I pulled out my devotional and saw the verse for the day: Psalm 46:10. "Be still and know that I am God." I was still wiping the tears from my eyes when there was a knock at my suite door.

"Come in." I said it, even though I didn't want any visitors.

The Governor walked in with a smile on his face.

"Good news. The forensics results came back and showed your gun was not the one that killed Caesar, as if we didn't already know that, and as if I had any doubt." He paused and sat down. "For someone who was just proven innocent, you seem pretty glum."

I poured out what had just transpired.

Thinking for a moment, he leaned forward. "I'm a politician, and I know how public opinion can change in an instant. We, and I mean the State of Texas, have got your back. Since I'm Governor of this great state, I have a little pull with state universities." He patted me on the good shoulder as he got up. "You don't worry about your job... Now get some rest. If you need anything, just tell the Ranger at the door." He turned to leave.

"Governor? I talked to my wife."

His face became a little more serious. "Ellen is a tough lady. Most people would probably fall apart after MS-13 put a ton of bullets into their house. I looked into her art. She does do wonderful work."

"Thanks." I replied. "She developed some of the medium herself."

"Like I said, she's tough. Your pastor's been over several times Unfortunately, she's under siege by the media. We've got a guard outside her room around the clock, backed up by Fort Worth P.D."

"What about moving her to a hotel after the hospital" I asked.

"We'll take care of her... Do you know of anything that might assist us in doing that?"

Finally a smile crossed my face. "She needs to be able to do her art, and we have a friend who's a massage therapist. I'm sure Ellen could use a massage. If you could arrange it? Get her one and I'll pay for it, and one for Ranger Moore. She deserves it. When she is able."

The Governor laughed. "We'll set it up, and don't worry about the tab. If I get word back that this therapist is as good as you imply, I may visit her myself. Get some rest."

Getting some rest was easier said than done. Television was out of the question, so with a some pain meds, I went back to compiling my account of San

Miguel. It was amazing what had happened in roughly two weeks. Even then I knew it wasn't truly over. Somewhere around six I ordered dinner and, not keeping to medical guidelines, red sangria. I found a network covering the Governor's press conference and sat back.

"Ladies and gentlemen, I want to welcome you, and to hopefully answer many of the questions as to the major action that took place in San Miguel, Texas this last Friday night. Now I need to remind you that some of the information you will receive is preliminary. We, and I mean Department of Public Safety and the Texas Rangers, are still combing through all that's left of the massive incursion by the Santos Diablo cartel. Which from here on I refer to as the cartel.

Let me state from the top, none, and I repeat none, of this would have occurred had the leader of the cartel, one Caesar Cortez, not believed he had in his possession a legitimate document titled 'The 16 X 16 Protocol.' He believed this gave him full rights to an area of ten square miles of the sovereign state of Texas. Ladies and gentlemen we don't give up any part of Texas without a fight. This document, which you have you have copies of in the folders found on your chairs, has been verified by our hand writing analysts as bearing the signatures of many members of the current Administration. Now the Administration is denying anything about this document, but it is interesting that none of the parties whose signatures we see are available for comment or questions. I have authorized our two Senators, through their offices, and committees to find out why this even exists....Let me say there is one signature missing, the President of the United States, and that is crucial. It was that absence, and a few other points, that tipped the legal counsel to the Sheriff's department of Vizaro County that the document carried no legal weight. Even with that established, the cartel decided to seize the area anyway. What resulted was what shall be referred to as the battle for San Miguel.

    Let me address one more matter before getting into the mechanics of what happened. It has been told to you by the Administration, and certain parts of the media, that we are sheltering a wanted man, Dr. Jackson Reynolds. Yes, we moved Dr. Reynolds from San Miguel to here even while he FBI was seeking to land and present the warrant for his arrest. We moved him for two reasons. One was medical. Dr. Reynolds was seriously wounded in hand to hand combat with one Hezbollah terrorist and was able to shoot another before being shot four times himself. Secondly, there was something not right about the swiftness and the directness of the arrest warrant. As we got more details about the parts of this warrant we found our suspicions to be correct. The warrant stated specifically that Dr. Reynolds killed Caesar Cortez with a 9mm Beretta. I have right here in this evidence bag that particular weapon, which I personally gave to Dr. Reynolds for his safety. Our forensic people have determined the gun has not been fired for at least ninety-six hours. Cortez was killed Friday night. If that doesn't prove to you Dr. Reynolds didn't do it maybe this will...Jake, bring that slide up."

    There was an audible gasped from some in the room and others turned their eyes away, as a very graphic photo of the dead druglord appeared.

"You will note ladies and gentlemen that the damage done to Mr. Cortez could not have possibly been inflicted by a 9mm. The one big hole and the totally obliterated head were done by a fifty caliber sniper rifle. Dr. Reynolds could not have possibly been the one who took out a psychopathic killer...No, someone in Washington wants a good decent man to take the fall for a major Administration screw-up! That is why we have advised out Attorney General to grant Dr. Reynolds as much legal defense as is necessary."

The Governor was handed a slip of paper. He read it and his shoulders sagged. He took a deep breath and then addressed the reporters.

"It has come to my attention that cost of this incident has risen by one more life. As many of you know, the Salvadorian gang MS-13, in cooperation with cartel, mounted attacks on family members of those in San Miguel. The one that occurred in Houston at the home of Milton and Frankie Long was devastating. These are the parents of Tabitha Cordova, wife of Sheriff Juan Cordova, and Ester Long, Deputy and brother-in-law to Sheriff Cordova. Ester was severely wounded and currently remains in serious condition in a San Antonio hospital. Their mother Frankie Long has passed from cardio condition that was extremely aggravated by the attack."

The Governor shook his head.

"A lot of good people died because our government made a deal with the devil. I'm not just mad.I'm damn mad, and I and the state of Texas demands accountability and answers! We will not stop our investigation until we have reasons and answers"

It was at that point I turned the TV off and pulled out my sangria. I knew the answers I, we, the Governor, and the State sought would never be fully coming. Nothing would replace the lives that were taken. To all those involved, whose lives were forever altered, nothing would be the same again. Yet we had stopped something that could and would have been much worse.

It was about 8:30 pm when the someone knocked at the door, and let themselves in. It was the Governor.

"Did you watch the news conference?"

"Yes sir."

"Jack, do we need to get Dr. McKnight? I thought you'd be more positive...What are you drinking. I know the good doctor did not prescribe it."

"It's red sangria, and there's one for you in the fridge."

He retrieved the drink and sat down.

"Nice Now talk to me."

"What political gain do you expect to get from this?" I looked straight at him. "Everyone knows you have greater aspirations than being Governor. Don't get me wrong, you're good at your job, and I believe you're, to quote yourself 'damn mad' at what happened. But you know as well as I, part of this overall situation was to make you and the state look bad. Now, your political worth has shot through the roof. Will that have an effect on seeking answers for all that's happened?"

The words just hung in the air for a minute as the Governor took a sip of the sangria.

"Good stuff. Man, you don't pull punches, do you? You're too intelligent a man for BS. Yes, my advisers said the political capital from this is immense. But you also know how much I love this state. Politics can be as illusive as the answers you and I seek, and fleeting as the lives that have been lost. I promise you as a friend, and I hope we have become friends, I'll see this through. Is that acceptable?"

"Yes sir." And we clicked our glasses. "It is good sangria."

The Governor got up to leave. "Oh, by the way, I told your wonderful wife I'd look at buying a piece of her art. Well, make that two pieces. My wife saw a piece she has to have, and I keep my promises. When you're well enough, we will be having you and the wife over to the mansion for that barbecue."

The room phone rang, and since I couldn't move fast, the Governor answered it. After a moment he handed it to me.

"Is it Ellen?" I was concerned.

"Jack just take the damn phone."

"Yes."

It was Deidre, department chair. "Jack, my gosh, the Governor. Well, I know you have friends in high places. The Chancellor called the university president and me, and said in no uncertain terms, you are to retain your position, all grants are to remain in place, and you scoundrel, you're to get a raise. Many of us watched the press conference, and we're just glad you're alive. Take as much time as you need before coming back. I'll be in touch. The Governor no less." And with that she hung up.

"You happier now?" Said the Governor with a Cheesier Cat grin.

I chuckled and hurt, "Yes sir I am. Thank you, Governor."

"No problem." He headed for the door, but pulled up. "You know if the political winds do blow a certain way, I may be calling on you for advice."

I was shaking my head emphatically,"No, no, no, don't you dare. The last person that ask me for advice got me where I am today."

The Governor left the room in full hearty laughter.

EPILOGUE

I have been a reporter for a Dallas-Fort Worth news outlet for twenty years. I've covered Mexico, the border, immigration, cartels, and law enforcement, but nothing prepared me for the scene in San Miguel. I have been friends with Dr. Reynolds for a number of years and it was his intervention with the Governor that allowed me to be one of the first reporters into the town after the battle. The picturesque town so vividly portrayed by Ellen Reynolds photographic series "San Miguel: Before the Battle", currently on display in the State Capital Rotunda, was nothing but destruction. I truly believed that, despite the Sheriff, his department, and all those that gave their lives and won the battle, they had lost the war. The town was going to die. I was wrong.

I sit here in Sunne's Cafe nearly a year later and can't believe what I see. It is a town reborn, a rebirth that no one could see coming. It would take too long to go through everything that has occurred, but I will try to give the highlights. First of all, I must say thank you to Sheriff Cordova and his department for their full cooperation on answering my many questions.

Rosie, the loyal motherly deputy who was wounded, has recovered and is back at her desk in City Hall. Her cheerful personality personifies the new San Miguel. She does tear up at the thoughts of that night and the precious lives lost, but the tears subside as she looks with pride on what has happened since to her town.

The big deputy, Ester Long, who was severely wounded during the battle, is nearly fully recovered. He has so much recovered that he and his doctor wife, Mai, are now expecting their first child, a boy. While Chico is gone, the deputy is far from forgotten. Jack was right in saying Chico and Sarah were a couple. Sarah, the brave sniper that not only blew away the sadistic drug lord but delayed the Russian Hind long enough for the Texas National Guard to attack, is now a deputy herself. Not just a deputy, but a new mother also. She and Marquis became good friends and now are engaged to be married. They are wanting Jack to officiate the ceremony.

I walked down to the little church that had played such a great role in the story. Aside from some freshening up, it was as Jack portrayed it. Maria welcomed me as if we were old friends, but to her there are no strangers. We talked at length about her role (which she downplayed) during and after the event. As she had given Selena shelter prior to the fight, she continued to take care of her. Selena had not been killed by the very deep knife wound, but it had nicked her spine causing paralysis which lasted for several weeks.

Maria was at her bedside in San Antonio all during her stay. For many she became the resident saint at the hospital, with other patient's families having her pray for their sick and dying relatives. Now she cares for Salena, who remembered nothing of her years with Caesar, but has reverted to an innocent child-like mentality. Yet Caesar still haunts her from Hell. He'd left with AIDs and it is only a matter of time before she will die from it.

I left the church feeling uplifted and walked to the impound lot behind City Hall. It was no longer a staging area for battle, but back to its usual role. There were more vehicles as the Sheriff's department has had to expand with the extreme growth of the town. Yet there is one prominent reminder of that night, The Thing. Yes, it's battered and shredded from the Hind's cannon and heavy machine gun fire, and its mini-gun has been removed, hopefully to never fire again. It will become a monument, a memorial to all who lost their lives that night. Sargeant Penny Jones, who refused to leave her post in the turret firing that mini-gun until ordered, nearly had her name added to the list. She exited the Thing at the last possible moment before it was battered, but in the process received serious wounds and to this day is still recovering.

It was a night of heroes and heartbreak. Many will say one of the biggest loses was also one of the strangest stories to come out of San Miguel, Misha Antonov. The Russian mercenary and former student of Jack's was invaluable bringing down the cartel. He and his partner Dimitri literally destroyed Caesar's base of operation, but that was not all. Those memory sticks he sent to Ellen for safe keeping were actually access files to five of the mercenaries' overseas bank accounts, all except for Dimetri. He went back to Russia and became an Russian Orthodox priest. The contents of the five accounts were given to the the town, fifty-five million dollars. That was the seed money for San Miguel's resurrection.

There were other reasons for Sam Miguel's revival. The American public was fascinated by this 21st century battle of the Alamo. Within weeks, the curious started to arrive. The entire length of San Miguel Road was a crime scene, and evidence removal was a logistical nightmare. But the public still came. There never was an accurate accounting of how many cartel members died. Numbers ran close to twelve hundred, and that was probably on the low side. Bodies were continually being found down river for days afterward. People wanted to see this and realize it really happened. Now these months later, hotels and truck stops surrounded the I-10 exit for San Miguel. The gravel road was now paved all the way to town.

Texas is a state filled with history, and the battle of San Miguel only added to the mystique. It also didn't hurt that with the cartel danger gone, gas and oil producers come back. Wells now dot the landscape and the property rights and leases went to the town. More precisely, the land rights belonged to Sheriff Juan Cordova, and had belonged to his family for five generations. His royalties were helping fund the resurrection of his beloved town. But the effect of the battle was not limited to Texas.

The ramifications of the battle and the false treaty sent shock waves through Washington. Denials and finger-pointing were rampant Calls for investigations and special committees were met with calls of partisan politics. The Vice President left the country for an extended "visit" to allies. The Secretary of State decided to retire due to "health and family considerations." A rift was opened between the White House and the FBI due to the administration's duplicity, and it continues to haunt the President. But in all the chaos the bottom line was forgotten. The sovereignty of the United States was violated and American citizens lost their lives.

Jack and Ellen are doing well, but are more reclusive now. They have moved to another location in North

Texas, and there is a near constant law-enforcement presence near their secluded residence. Jack is planning retirement from his professorship, but is still doing research on several projects. Ellen is an artist in demand. Her work is now on the "must have" list for many. Public appearances are widely spaced, but her status as a warrior brings as much notoriety as her art. She has plans for a new series on San Miguel, chronicling the town's rebirth. I look forward to it's unveiling.

    As I finish this much too long summary of Jack's account and the aftermath, I need to go to one more location. North of town lies the cemetery, and it's the history of San Miguel. Many graves, some dating from the late 1800's, have only very worn crosses. The names are known only to God. Others from later years have headstones, many with Latino names. But there are a number of new headstones. The battle brought an influx nobody wanted, yet they are a part of the town forever. Their sacrifice is never to be forgotten. There is one that stands out among all the others, the final resting place of Misha Antonov. It is a four foot tall black obelisk with two flags crossed, Texas and Russian.

Aside from the usual inscriptions there is something that meant greatly to the Russian, a Bible verse.

**Come to me, all you who are weary
and burdened, and I will give you rest.**

Matthew 28: 11

Jason Alfredo Gonzalez

ACKNOWLEDGEMENTS

A project such as this is never done in a vacuum. From initial concept, through writing, typing, proofreading, and final edit, many people have been involved, and I wish to express my gratitude to as many of these people as I can remember.

My wife, Elva, did the intial typing/editingof the manuscript, then stepped in again during the final edit. I can't thank her enough. Love you.

To my former students who listened to my ideas and gave me their reactions, thank you. Your input was more than helpful. I especially want to thank those students who were veterans. Their comments helped me immensely.

To my colleagues at UTA who encouraged me to keep going: Your encouragement was so needed. Thank you.

My friends from the James Patterson Master Class have encouraged me and cheered me on, especially Monica Luisi. Thanks so much.

To those who have read my early drafts and given feedback, thank you. Your time and effort is very much appreciated.

I am honored to have as valued friends three best-selling authors who have inspired and encouraged me in this endeavor: Mark Davis, who wrote the foreword of this book, Alfredo Corchado, whose writings and reporting for the Dallas Morning News covering

Mexico and the border are clear and inbiased, and Taylor Anderson, author of the "Destroyermen" series. Thanks for your friendship, help, and inspiration. Along with them, two other reporters, who are friends have inspired me: Jason Whitely and Sandra Gonzalez.

    As well, there are sources I cannot name, who talked with me about tactics and strategy used in the book, and gave me insight into what law enforcement faces on the border. Their input was invaluable. Thank you. You know who you are.

Made in the USA
Lexington, KY
15 November 2017